*To those just finding themselves.*
*You're not alone, we're always changing.*
*Evolution means you're alive.*

WITCHES OF MOONDALE: BOOK THREE

# Home is Where the Where Hex is

## Lou Wilham

Midnight Tide
PUBLISHING

# Chapter 1

R us jerked awake.

Her left foot was *freezing* where it hung over the edge of the bed, the blanket not covering it. She must have kicked the covers off in the middle of the night. But that wasn't what woke her.

Something was holding on to her, the grip cold, insubstantial, but tight around her ankle.

Something not alive.

A spirit.

When reaching across the bed for Az turned up cool, empty sheets, Rus shimmied closer to the nightstand, careful not to dislodge the shade's grip as she bent her head over the edge of the bed to peek down beneath it. The face peering back at her was young, with wide eyes staring unblinking and glassy. Likely a little older than Aihuan when they died, but not by much.

"Hel—" Rus croaked, stopped, cleared her throat, and tried again. "Hello there, little one. Would you mind letting go of my foot?"

They looked at her for a moment, head tilted, then released her ankle with a muffled "Sorry."

"It's all right." Rus shot them a smile and slid from the bed to kneel on the floor next to it. "Why don't you come out here, and we'll have a chat?"

They frowned, their upturned nose crinkling in thought. "Why?"

"I just want to know why you're here." Rus scooted back to give them room as they slid out from underneath the bed, joints popping and jerking in a way that was not at all human. Objectively terrifying, if Rus didn't know that spirits tended to forget how living things moved. "Can you tell me your name?"

"Isabel."

"That's a nice name." Where had Aihuan found this one? The school? The graveyard? The coffee shop? They needed to have a discussion—*again*—about bringing spirits home. Thankfully this one wasn't some nastier being masquerading as a child, but it was only a matter of time before Aihuan came across one of those. It was a miracle she hadn't thus far. "Do you know what happened to you, Isabel?"

"I was sick." Isabel shrugged, not meeting Rus's eyes.

They looked around her attic bedroom instead. Taking in the pile of clothes in the corner that Az was consistently on her about, the mess that was her workspace, and the wilting plant Az was trying to revive on the windowsill. Az hadn't moved in, but she'd made herself at home there just the same. Mixed her dirty laundry in with Rus's. Piled her books on one nightstand. Added one of Indigo's crocheted blankets to the end of the bed. It made the space homier. And Rus had hardly noticed until that very moment, seeing it through someone else's eyes, that it had happened, so subtle was Az's infiltration into her personal space. *Infiltration* maybe wasn't the right word, but Rus digressed.

"I waited."

"You waited for what?"

"For my mama to come," Isabel said, meeting Rus's gaze finally. "But she never did. And then I laid down."

Tears lodged in Rus's throat, making it hard to find her voice again, but find it she did. Because someone needed to help Isabel move on. To see their mama again. "How long have you been stuck here?"

Isabel shrugged again.

Rus didn't know why she'd bothered asking. Time moved differently for spirits. But it was a point of pride to gather as much information as she reasonably could before she helped a spirit move on. To document it at least for herself so she could find patterns in the kinds of spirits that stayed and the ones that didn't. So far not much had come of the data, but one day, maybe it would.

"Huaner said you could help me find my mama. That's why she brought me."

*Of course she did.* It would be annoying if it weren't so painfully sweet. Aihuan believed her auntie Rus could help every spirit and didn't see any reason why she shouldn't. It wasn't like it hurt Rus to do it—she just didn't want Aihuan bringing every stray shade into the safety of their home, thereby making all Rus's carefully constructed wards virtually useless.

"You can, can't you?"

"I'll do my best." Already Rus's magic flittered around her fingers like mist, glowing and green, reaching out to answer its witch's call. But even if she didn't say it, she knew that Isabel's mama might already be gone. She may have reincarnated, hoping to find her child again somehow. Rus couldn't leave Isabel to languish though. They needed to be given the opportunity to find peace, whatever that looked like for them. And they couldn't do that on this plane.

"What do I need to do?" Isabel asked, their voice small

as they shrank back into themselves, away from Rus's extended hand and the magic that had settled into the scars on her bare arm.

"Just take my hand, and the magic will do the rest."

"Will it hurt?"

"No. It won't hurt at all." She didn't know that, not for certain. But many a spirit had returned from the After to aid her when she needed it, and not one of them had ever complained. Add that to the fact that they never screamed when she sent them over. She'd have to ask next time a spirit visited her to help out. It'd be good to have an answer once and for all. Then she'd have something to tell the spirits who asked. She hoped they felt warm when they crossed. Safe. Loved.

Isabel stared at Rus's hand for a long moment, their fingers twitching where they rested against their thigh, warring with their indecision. Unsure. Rus couldn't blame them for that. She didn't have any answers about the After. She didn't know what it was like there. She didn't know how it felt to get there. She didn't know how spirits adjusted. Nothing. All she knew was that's where the dead belonged, not on the plane of the living where they would either fade or slowly lose their grip on themselves and what was real, making them destructive.

"This is what Huaner meant when she said I could help you," Rus pressed. She didn't know what time it was, but she could hear Fernando and the kids downstairs eating breakfast. She needed to get down there and help get the girls ready for school or she'd never hear the end of it.

When Isabel didn't move, Rus let out a soft sigh. "Would you like to say goodbye to Huaner first?"

Isabel nodded, the bob of their head making their hair

fall into their face. They looked like that scary little girl from *The Ring* like that.

"I'll go get her. But then we need to get you moving along, all right?"

Another nod and Rus stood, her knees creaking as she went. The back stairs groaned to announce her presence in the kitchen as she came into view of the round table where her little family sat. Well. Most of her little family. Az was in class already. "Huaner?"

"Hmm?" Aihuan asked, raising her head from where she'd been shoveling waffles into her mouth.

"Can you come upstairs with me for a minute?" Rus was careful not to let on that there was a spirit in the house. Meiling was still afraid of them and had grown comfortable in the knowledge that they couldn't cross the threshold of 157 Mourning Moore unless invited in.

Aihuan looked at Rus for a moment, then her eyes widened and she nodded, wiggling down from her chair. When they made it to the landing on the second floor, she looked up at Rus and asked, "Are you mad?"

"I'm not mad." Rus's shoulders drooped on a deep exhale. It was hard to be mad at Aihuan when she was technically doing the right thing, and when she looked adorable doing it. Big brown eyes, and curly hair wild around her face. She probably hadn't brushed it. Another task to add to Rus's ever lengthening list for the morning. "But I do recall asking you to please not bring them into the house. Remember?"

"But it was cold out last night." Aihuan's bottom lip poked out, her eyes going even bigger somehow. Goddess above and below, Rus was a fucking sap for the puppy eyes, and everyone seemed to know it. "And Issy is afraid of the bugs."

"Huaner, we agreed they could wait on the back porch, but not in the house." Rus let her tone dip into something more authoritative. This was a rule, firm and set in stone. She could not budge on this. Lest Aihuan bring something dangerous into their home on accident. "Understood?"

"Yes, Auntie Rus." Aihuan huffed.

"That's my little monster." Rus smiled and pushed the door open to her bedroom where Isabel waited. The spirit lit up when they saw Aihuan, their face forming a bright smile the likes of which Rus had never seen on a ghost before, and they moved forward to hug Aihuan tightly.

"You're going then?" Aihuan asked, but she sounded happy about it. No sadness or regret tainted her voice. No hint that she'd miss her new friend. "Auntie Rus is going to help you cross over?"

"She is. I just . . ." Isabel looked at Rus for a moment then ducked their head shyly. "I wanted to say goodbye."

"This isn't goodbye," Aihuan said with a smile full of wisdom far beyond her years. Rus wondered where the fuck she'd learned that. Az probably. Elwoods were like that, chock-full of wisdom and bursting at the seams with their goodness. Az especially. "It's just see you later."

"How much later?"

"Who knows! But if you want to come back and visit, you just have to call out to Auntie Rus." Aihuan turned to look up at Rus, her expression earnest. "Right, Auntie Rus?"

"Right." Rus nodded, offering what she hoped was a confident smile. "Just call for Icarus Ashthorne, and you can come back to visit."

"But even if not"—Aihuan shrugged—"I'll see you again someday."

And wow, okay, Aihuan being that all right talking about her own future death was weird. Rus needed to cut this short before these two sent her into an existential crisis. She didn't have time in her schedule for one of those today.

"All righty, let's get this show on the road. You've got school." Rus swiped at her face, hoping neither child would notice how the corners of her eyes burned with tears. But if the looks on their faces were anything to go by, they had. She reached out her hand, her bright green magic reaching with her, and took hold of Isabel's shoulder.

There was a moment where Isabel looked up at her and smiled, then the spirit was gone. Sent to the After, to hopefully be with their mother. Maybe she'd been right, maybe it didn't hurt them after all. Quiet settled around Rus and Aihuan, and they both breathed a little deeper before Aihuan looked up at Rus and asked, "Can I have some chocolate chips on my waffles?"

"Uncle Nando said no, didn't he?" Rus laughed softly, brushing her fingers through Aihuan's hair and getting caught in the tangles.

"Yes." Aihuan huffed.

"I'll make you a deal. You let me brush your hair, and you can have exactly ten mini chocolate chips on your waffles. How's that sound?"

"Mm!" Aihuan dipped her head in agreement, and they headed back to the kitchen where Fernando and Meiling waited.

"Az was gone early this morning," Rus said, hoping to head off any conversation about what had just happened upstairs as she made her way to the pantry to grab Aihuan her chocolate chips. When Fernando raised an eyebrow in question as she dumped exactly ten onto Aihuan's plate, Rus shook her head.

That seemed to be enough of an answer for him, but the little white mouse on his shoulder—his familiar, Calida, or

Cal for short—moved onto her back paws, pressing her tiny face in toward his ear to murmur to him. When she was done, Fernando smiled and nodded before returning his attention to Rus. "I thought you said Az wasn't moving in?"

"She's not. She just spent the night last night." Heat crawled up Rus's neck at the mention of Az spending the night. It wasn't like they had *done* anything. Not yet, anyway. There was time. And still lots to talk about and sort out between them. But she hadn't thought *that* was where the conversation would head when she'd brought it up. In retrospect, maybe she should have. Still, it was a good way to head off the discussion about the spirit who'd been hiding under her bed when she woke up.

If only it didn't make Rus so unsettled. An emotion she couldn't source. Yet.

"Last night. And the night before that."

"And the night before that," Meiling added unhelpfully.

"And the night before that!" Aihuan agreed, shoving a big bite of waffle into her mouth.

"Are you three going to get to a point anytime soon?" Rus groused. She'd poured herself a cup of coffee, unable to force down the smile that came from seeing Az's mint-green mug on the drying rack next to the sink. Damn it.

"Why don't you just ask her to move in already? Make it official," Fernando pressed, hiding his coy smile behind a mug that looked more milk than coffee. He was being a jerk and he knew it, bringing this up in front of the girls. Thankfully, they didn't seem to mind one way or the other. They liked having Az around, but they weren't going to try forcing her hand.

"It's a process." Rus turned to look out the window, the dreary late spring mist creating a fog through which she could only just see the house next door. The last owners had moved out a couple weeks ago. Nesta—one of Rus's friends and the one who'd sold her their current home, 157 Mourning Moore—was the realtor on the sign, but they'd asked Rus to take a look at it before they really put their effort into selling it. They needed to know if the last owners left anything behind, like unsettled spirits. She'd have to check on that this afternoon, after the rush at Necromancer's had calmed down. It would be easy money, as far as Rus could tell. She almost felt guilty accepting the commission. But Aihuan was growing like a cemetery weed, and she and Meiling would need summer clothes soon. "I don't want to rush things."

Not rushing things had been entirely her idea, not Az's, because Rus knew they couldn't go back to how things were, and she wasn't sure how they'd work now. Or if they'd work at all. Maybe they wouldn't. Maybe once all the drama and the danger died down, Az would see what a fuckup Rus still was and leave her like she should have all those years ago.

Either way, Rus couldn't risk it with the girls involved.

Meiling snorted loud enough that it sounded like it might have hurt. When Rus turned to look at her, she was smiling, sarcastic and cutting. Fucking teenagers, man. "You'll be married by next year."

*Oh.* Oh, Rus hadn't thought about it but . . . but she did *want* that. Shit, how had her thirteen-year-old known she'd wanted that, and Rus hadn't known it herself?

"Next year? I'm calling November," Fernando joined in. "We've got a pool running."

"Oh, a Samhain wedding!" Meiling brightened. "Auntie Rus, a Samhain wedding!"

"What pool?" Aihuan, who was the only one *not* a traitor in this fucking house, asked. "Can we go swimming in it?"

"It's not that kind of pool, Huaner." Meiling rolled her eyes. "It means they're betting."

"You know telling me about the pool kind of skews the results, doesn't it?" Rus sneered at Fernando, who held up a hand and rocked it back and forth. She scoffed, clicking her tongue, and pushed it from her mind. Because giving it too much thought, looking at it too closely, would only intensify the ache in her chest. The reminder that maybe that was a thing she wanted. A thing she *shouldn't* want. A thing she shouldn't *let* herself want. She wasn't right for Az. Never would be. It—

"It doesn't matter," Rus sniped, her sour thoughts turning her tone to something less playful. "A'ling, the bus is here!"

Meiling grunted, dropped her dishes in the sink, and headed for the door. "Bye, Huaner!"

"Bye, jiejie!" Aihuan stuffed another bite into her mouth that was more chocolate chip than waffle, and the door creaked open to let Meiling run down the walk for the bus.

"And you, little monster, agreed to let me brush your hair, remember?"

"Fiiiiiine."

"What about me?" Fernando asked, his eyes dancing with good humor. Little shit.

"I'm not talking to you until I've finished my coffee." Rus held her mug up as if she were cheers-ing Fernando and took a big gulp from it. "Till then, nothing out of you."

Fernando raised his hands in surrender, but the grin on his face said this conversation was far from over. Because nothing about returning to Moondale was ever going to be easy.

# Chapter 2

"Class dismissed," Professor Higgins called, her eyes flicking about the students, most of whom had started packing up ten minutes before the class was supposed to end.

Not Azure. She refused to close her notebook until the very last word was spoken. Until she had absorbed every list bit of the lesson. Too much of her life had been spent not doing what she wanted. She would not show these hallowed halls the disrespect of rushing out of class.

Hallowed.

The halls of Moondale University were hallowed.

And in these hallowed halls, Azure Elwood was going to learn something new. About herself. About her magic. About how to be the woman Rus needed beside her as they started their coven together. The woman she'd always wanted to be. Because the woman who helped Rus start a coven had to be someone *special*, someone powerful, someone who lived up to everything Rus had always believed of her. Azure hadn't been that woman months ago before Rus returned to Moondale, living the life that people expected of her, putting her own happiness, her own fulfillment, on the back burner in favor of doing what she thought her family wanted of her.

And like that expectation, Azure shouldered her messenger bag, letting the strap cut into her skin as she gave the professor a respectful dip of her head on the way out the door.

"Good work today, Azure," Professor Higgins said, a smile crinkling the corners of her eyes.

"Thank you."

It had been months since Azure had left her old self behind, the one who put her whole life on hold for a legacy she didn't want. Fall turning to winter turning to spring. Blooms opening. Trees turning green. And Azure finally felt, for perhaps the first time in the eleven years since Rus left, like herself. Like the person she was always meant to be.

It was exhilarating.

It was terrifying.

As she stepped out into the hall, inhaling the scent of floor cleaner and body odor lingering from other students, she realized it was making her happier than she thought she'd ever been.

Her phone buzzed with a notification almost as soon as she took it off do not disturb, and she couldn't help the smile that lit her face at the text from Rus.

RU: *We're doing pizza for dinner, is that good*

*If not, too bad*

*See you when you get home*

Or maybe the swell of happiness had more to do with the fact that after classes at the end of the day, when she drove down the mountain toward Moondale, she would be headed straight for 157 Mourning Moore, a place that was quickly becoming *home*, even if she hadn't officially moved in.

*It's only a matter of time.*

The nights she spent across the street at her aunts' were fewer and further between these days, but Azure wasn't willing to jinx it. To speak the words out loud for fear the universe might punish her for getting ahead of herself. She'd wait. They'd take things slow, as Rus wanted, for now. Until Rus asked her to move in. Then . . . Well, then she may very well ask Rus to marry her on the spot. But that was a thought for later.

"Miss Elwood, a word," Dean Cochburn said from where she was lurking outside of the classroom Azure had just exited. That would be a worrisome turn of events if Azure weren't so sure she'd done absolutely nothing wrong. Her grades were fine, she didn't have any overdue books, and she hadn't damaged university property. She was, by all accounts, the model non-traditional student. So why did Dean Cochburn want to speak with her?

Scratch that, it *was* worrisome.

"Of course." Azure dipped her head and tried to swallow the fear that threatened to grip her by the throat. Why was it that no matter if someone knew they hadn't done anything wrong, they always felt guilty upon entering the office of a school official? Maybe it was just Azure. Maybe she simply had a guilty conscience. There was really no way to tell; she had no one to compare notes with other than Rus. And Rus would definitely have done something that warranted being called to the dean's office.

What made the whole experience stranger was that Dean Cochburn wasn't much older than Azure herself. A couple of years, a couple more gray hairs, but still young by witch standards. How had she gotten the position then?

And yet, Azure found herself slouching in on herself like an errant child called to the principal's office for writing in Sharpie on the bathroom wall.

"You're not in trouble." Dean Cochburn smiled, walking around her desk to settle into the chair on the other side and motioning for Azure to take one of the leather tufted ones. "I just wanted to have a discussion about your . . ." Dean Cochburn hummed, seeming to try to think of what word she wanted to use for a moment before she settled on, "partner."

"What has Rus done?" Azure asked, sitting up straighter, all traces of her own guilt or shame at being called to the dean's office gone in the face of standing up for Rus.

"Nothing. Nothing." Dean Cochburn shook her head, her lips quirking up at the corners, as if she approved of Azure's protective instinct. "At least nothing bad, anyway. Some of my colleagues have recently used her Ghost Tracer app? The one meant to track fluctuations in negative and positive energy?"

Delight zinged up Azure's spine, making her light up with a smile of her own. "Yes, Rus worked very hard on that."

"I'm sure she did." Dean Cochburn nodded. "It's quite the marvel."

"It is," Azure agreed, practically glowing under the praise to Rus. It was hard not to. Rus so rarely got the recognition she deserved. Even after creating something like the Ghost Tracer, something that had seemed impossible, the Board of Magic still refused to recognize her unique genius. Instead, they seemed to take her creating it for them as their due and focused on the necromancy. *Always* the fucking necromancy. As if it was the whole of Rus, the sum of her parts, not merely one piece in an ever-expanding puzzle that Azure thought she may never fit together in its entirety. Because Rus was always growing. Always changing. A marvel. Dean Cochburn had used the right word.

It bothered Azure more than she'd ever be able to put

into words. It was also why she needed to step it up. Why she needed to get to a place in her spellcrafting and talisman work where she was just as beneficial to their coven as Rus was. To really put the other covens and clans who had thus far stagnated to shame. To prove to the board that the Coven of the Forgotten would not be relegated to the shadows, would not be cast aside simply because their leader was a necromancer. That they would innovate.

"But I imagine you didn't call me here just to hear me brag about Rus's accomplishments." Something she'd willingly do for hours, honestly, but Azure had learned quickly that few people cared for it.

"Not as such, no." Dean Cochburn chuckled softly. "What I wanted to ask you was if Icarus would have any interest in guest lecturing? I think our students could really benefit from her expertise in magical technology. There's so much out there that the professors here aren't covering."

*Because the current crop of professors have been here since my aunts went to Moondale U*, Azure didn't say. But from the look on Dean Cochburn's face, she knew that to be the truth.

All deans for the university had to be approved by the Moondale Board of Magic, and for whatever reason they usually didn't last long in the position. Either deciding to retire, taking a sabbatical, or just straight up quitting some few months after taking the post. Azure had never paid much attention to it before, but she was paying attention now. Couple that with the fact that Dean Cochburn was likely the youngest dean Moondale U had ever seen? Changes were coming, and Azure was glad of them. Gladder still that she'd be there to witness them.

"So what do you think? Is that something she'd be interested in?" Dean Cochburn pressed after Azure must have been quiet for too long. Mired in her own thoughts.

"I'll discuss it with her. Currently, she has a lot of other commitments between her daughters, her business, and the work required to start a coven. So it might have to wait till at least fall semester, if at all." Azure *wanted* Rus to do this. She would push for this, even if Rus tried to wriggle out of it. Because Rus thrived when she was teaching someone something new, and Azure loved to see the look in Rus's eyes as she lit up from the inside. But she wasn't willing to promise it to the dean of her university until she'd gotten Rus to agree.

"Oh. To that end." Dean Cochburn smiled wider, leaning more against the desk to close the space between them as if she were about to tell Azure some great secret. "I might have a couple of covenless witches working here at Moondale U that she could . . ."

"Run into?" Because Rus was weirdly against direct recruitment, which was going to drive Azure off her bloody broomstick. But if she could put Rus in a room with a witch who was covenless and get them talking . . . Well, Azure had little doubt that Rus could convince anyone to join their coven once she got going. She just needed to get out of her own way. Azure could facilitate that, easily.

"Yes. Run into." Dean Cochburn nodded, seeming to understand where Azure was going with this. "One of our lab techs, in particular, I think would be perfect. You met him, I believe. Hunter Delacroix? My girlfriend said he drove out to Moondale a couple weeks back to talk to Rus about the Ghost Tracer."

"I remember." He had seemed nice enough to Azure. His aura was weak, but that didn't mean anything given that he was covenless, and witches without covens generally were on the weaker side—Rus being the exception. "You said he's a lab tech here?"

"Yes. And were Rus to give a guest lecture, I'm sure he'd attend. Very likely with questions in hand." The smile on Dean Cochburn's face felt distinctly conspiratorial, and Azure found herself mirroring it.

"I'll see what I can do." Which was the truth. "But in the meantime, I would like to meet Hunter myself. Just to vet him a bit before he meets with Rus about coven initiation."

Azure trusted Dean Cochburn's judgment as far as Hunter being a good, responsible witch was concerned, but there was more to joining a coven than that. She needed to know if he'd be a good fit with them. He had seemed pleasant when he'd met with Rus weeks ago about the Ghost Tracer, but he'd wanted something from them then. And Azure hadn't seen him for more than a few minutes before she was shooed along so he and Rus could talk logistics. Then there was the matter that Rus had some concerns about his use of the Ghost Tracer to hunt vampires. As far as Azure knew, nothing untoward had come of that, but it paid to be diligent.

"Of course." Dean Cochburn grabbed a sticky note from a drawer on her desk and began scribbling something on it. "This is the lab where he works. It's in one of the older science buildings. I've tried to get him out of there. We have state of the art facilities he could be using, but he insists."

"Any particular reason?"

When Dean Cochburn looked up from what she was writing, her face was split into a wide grin, her eyes laughing. "Something about acoustics. I'm sure if you ask, he'd be more than happy to tell you all about it."

"I see." The piece of paper had a building and lab

number on it, although Azure was beginning to think perhaps Hunter was the only one using that particular building. "I have time in between now and my next class. He should be in, correct?"

"He should. If he's not there, he'll be at the dorm address on the back. He's been staying there with one of our professors since . . ." Dean Cochburn frowned, the happiness fading from her gaze. "Well, he lost his wife some months back, and it's been hard for him to adjust. He moved in with Professor Marcelino and his Venator class and seems quite comfortable for the time being."

A witch living under the same roof as a group of vampire hunting Venator. No wonder he wanted the Ghost Tracer to hunt down vampires. A piece of the puzzle that was Hunter Delacroix slotted into place. It didn't make him any less eccentric seeming, but she felt she understood him a bit better. "Is there anything else I should know?"

"About Hunter? No." Dean Cochburn shook her head, a crease forming in her brow. "But there is something about —" She cut herself off, her fingers flexing against the wood of her desk.

When she didn't continue, Azure asked, "About what?"

Dean Cochburn's bright blue eyes flicked over Azure's shoulder for a moment, her lips moving in a silent spell. The walls surrounding them shimmered faintly, and Azure's ears popped. A silencing ward. Protection from listening ears. "The Board of Magic."

"We are very aware that much of the board hopes we'll fail." It was hard not to be aware of that fact when every meeting Azure attended, all the elders apart from Nixie and Aunt Carmine snubbed their noses at her. She'd been asked why she was attending at least three times during each session and had rapidly taken to staring at the person until they shut the fuck up. It worked with most of them. Except Brant Ironwood, the prick. But when it came to Ironwood, Nixie was more than happy to talk over him until he stopped, and that helped.

"It's not just that." Dean Cochburn had gone eerily still, her gaze focused so intensely on Azure that it made Azure shift uncomfortably in her seat. "I think—" She stopped herself again, shaking her head, as if something was holding her back. As if she feared whatever words she meant to say might be a mistake. She continued, "If I were you, I'd not let on that you've been in talks with anyone at all until you've got things pinned down. Do you know what I mean?"

Azure didn't, but she could see the wisdom behind the advice anyway. If no one knew she and Rus were meeting with anyone, then no one could try to talk the potential members out of joining the Coven of the Forgotten, or try to poach them. Not that that was likely to happen. If Hunter Delacroix hadn't been lured to one of the other covens in Moondale by now, he wasn't going to be. "Yes, I think I understand. Thank you, Dean Cochburn."

Dean Cochburn nodded and the magic fell away, leaving Azure with the faint sensation of her ears ringing. "And please, call me Vanessa."

"Thank you, Vanessa."

"You're welcome, Azure."

THE BUILDING VANESSA sent Azure to was small, holding only five lab spaces, and looked more like it was the sub-basement to a building much larger than itself, except the upper floors had never been added. It sat squat and dingy among the taller, more modern buildings on campus. But there was a presence to it, an energy, that made Azure understand why Hunter Delacroix had chosen it as his space. It wasn't as meddling as 157 Mourning Moore—it was hard for any building outside of Moondale to take on that kind of sentience—but it was close.

As if Hunter Delacroix had steeped the place in his hopes, dreams, and magic for years and years.

As if the one-story brick building was taking on a life of its own.

Maybe it would, in time. If he lived as long as witches tended to and continued his research under its roof. Azure wondered, as she headed down the hall lit by yellowed bulbs, if the building would resent her for what she was about to do. But then, she supposed, it was a good thing it wasn't in Moondale after all. The university was located outside of the city and ward limits to make it viable ground for other witchlings to learn magic, and she'd hate to have a building after her.

Lab 5 was behind a solid metal door, where all the others to that point had been wood, and a sign hanging from it read "Delacroix Labs" in blocky lettering.

Azure knocked, and when no answer came, she pushed through.

A wall of sound hit her like a truck. Azure nearly stumbled down the uneven steps into the lab, suddenly understanding Vanessa's mention of acoustics. Inhaling deeply to calm the way her heart pounded against her ribcage—a fight or flight response she couldn't quite source—she twitched her hand, and the volume on the stereo in the corner lowered.

Hunter looked up from where he'd been hunched over the black-topped lab tables to blink at her from behind a pair of goggles that made his eyes look enormous. "Can I help you?"

"Yes, I believe you can. I'm—"

"Oh! You're Icarus Ashthorne's partner! What did she say your name was?" He frowned as if trying to remember.

"Azure Elwood."

"Right!" Hunter grinned widely and pushed the goggles up into his mass of curly dark hair before replacing them with a pair of glasses that he pulled from where they'd been hanging from his collar. He stood and came toward her, hand extended as if to shake, then paused. "Wait. Did you say Elwood?"

"I did." She tried not to laugh, but it was difficult when Hunter blinked at her, bewildered for a moment before continuing.

"As in, the Jade Waters Elwoods?"

"Those would be them, yes. My aunt Carmine is the Jade Waters elder."

"Huh." Hunter crossed his arms, rocking back on his heels. "And you're dating a necromancer?"

"I am."

"Huh," he said again, looking suddenly impressed, a smile crawling across his brown face. Azure liked him already. "Neat. So what can I do for you, Miss Elwood?"

"Just Azure."

"Azure," he repeated, the light gleaming off the piercing in his lip as he smiled. "Cool."

"Indeed." Goddess, he and Rus were going to get along like a murder of crows, weren't they? He already had the look of a member of the Forgotten. Add to it the weirdly bubbly personality, and he'd fit right in with Fernando and Rus. It was going to be fantastic. "I came by to see how the Ghost Tracer was working. And Vanessa said you might have some other projects I'd find interesting."

She hadn't, but it was as good an excuse as any. And what Hunter spent his time on in this lab, what he was passionate about, would give Azure a far better gauge of the kind of witch she was dealing with than anything else.

"Vanessa?" Hunter blinked, his nose curling, then he realized and laughed. "Oh! Nessy. Yeah, sure, come on into my lair and let me show you around."

Goddess. He was going to be perfect for the Coven of the Forgotten, wasn't he? She couldn't have found someone better if she'd placed a wanted ad in *Witch Daily*. Now. She just had to get him and Rus talking.

# Chapter 3

It was a beautiful day. A chill, late spring rain settled in like mist outside of Necromancer's, dampening the sounds of the street, cooling the heated sidewalk, and making the world appear to glimmer. At least to Rus. She loved days like this, even when the damp and the wet sunk into her joints, making her knees ache. Even when Fernando pulled her cane out from where it was tucked behind the hall tree in the foyer and poked her with it until she took it with her. Thank the Goddess for cushioned matts or she'd probably have collapsed hours ago.

"You could go sit down, take a break. I've got this," Fernando said from where he stood behind the steamer. His hair was getting long these days, straggling on the ends. She'd have to suggest he let her trim it soon. Although after last time . . . Maybe she'd ask Az to do it instead. She had a steadier hand and was less likely to be possessed by some asshole spirit who would try to shave half her friend's head. Why spirits did shit like that, Rus didn't know. But it was good enough reason to let Az hold the clippers instead.

"Nah. I'm okay." Rus shook her head, standing up straight again where she'd been leaning against the counter behind the register. Maybe she should have put her brace on this morning—that likely would have helped. But Az was already gone when Rus woke, so she wasn't there to guilt

Rus via looks alone into putting it on. "I'll just take a hot bath when I get home. That should loosen things up a bit."

Fernando eyed her for a moment, clearly skeptical, then shook his head and muttered, "Azure is going to kill me" under his breath before he turned back to making his own drink.

It was just before lunchtime, so things were slow for the moment. They'd pick up soon though, and Rus didn't want to have to pull herself out of one of the deep booth seats when that happened. A body in motion stayed in motion, and all that.

"What Az doesn't know won't hurt you," Rus sing-songed as she snagged the ceramic mug from his hands and took a sip. With a soft hiss at the burn of too-hot chai scalding her tongue, she shook her head. "It needs more nutmeg."

"*You* need more nutmeg."

"What does that even mean?"

"I don't know. But Azure never complains when I make her chai," Fernando said, sulking.

"Verbally." Rus laughed to herself. "But you haven't learned to read her facial expressions the way I have. It hasn't got enough nutmeg."

"If you know her so well, why don't you just marry her already?" Fernando blurted. His back was to her, but his neck turned red. He'd pulled his hair up into a small pony-tail at the base of his head to keep it out of his face while he worked. He clearly hadn't meant to say it, even though he'd been razzing her about that very thing only a few hours prior, which kind of made the whole thing funnier.

"Maybe I will," Rus said, not giving him any reprieve from the embarrassment of saying exactly the wrong thing at the mostly wrong time. All the while, her heart tripped along in her chest, her nerves humming with something that she was beginning to realize she *really* wanted. She hadn't allowed herself to think too hard about it that morning, to look it in the face, but . . . Now she *knew*. She knew very well. She wanted to marry Azure Elwood. And soon. Maybe Fernando was right, maybe they wouldn't make it to November. Not if Rus couldn't wrangle her selfish impulses.

"Do you think she'll have me as her wifey?" Rus asked, trying to hide the way her skin grew over warm, and her stomach twisted at the thought. Could she let herself have that? Could she want that? Would Az allow it? Would the board? Would the world in general? She wasn't good enough for Az. Not in the least, but—

Fernando scoffed, and Rus turned back to the front of the store, her throat going dry.

"Do we think who would have you as their wifey?" Violet Elwood asked, one perfectly plucked brow raised in question—or condescension, Rus was never really sure with her.

As far as she knew, Az and Violet hadn't made up since their fight a couple of months back when Az decided to leave Jade Waters and quite literally walked out on Elwood Sibling Bonding Night. There had been no Elwood Family Dinners since then. And Indigo had made some indication once or twice that he'd taken sides in the feud between Violet and Az. Rus didn't love that she'd come between the sisters, even if Az assured her that hadn't been the case. She knew there were other reasons for Az leaving Jade Waters. That she'd also done it for herself, not just for Rus and the girls. But it still felt a little like Rus had made Az choose between her and the Elwoods, and that had never been her intention. In fact, that's why she'd left Moondale to begin with, to avoid making Az choose between Rus and her family. And yet, here they were. Eleven years later, like nothing had changed. Fuck.

"No one," Rus said, and hoped to the Goddess that Violet wouldn't push the issue. It was always hit or miss with her. Some days she could be as antisocial and taciturn as Az, and others she was likely to poke until someone screamed at her like Indigo did sometimes. Taryn, Violet's wife, shifted beside her whether in support or chiding, Rus wasn't sure, but Violet heard the silent communication and lowered her raised brow. "What can I get you two?"

"Earl Grey for Violet." Taryn stepped forward to rest her hands on the counter and look at the menu over Rus's head, effectively putting her much too close to Rus's bubble. Her gray eyes narrowed in concentration while they all waited for her to decide what she wanted. "And I'll have a coffee with room for cream. Both medium size. To go."

"Got it." Rus nodded and typed in their order on the screen in front of her. "So how is the centennial prep going? Az keeps bringing home—" She cut herself off and cleared her throat, her eyes looking anywhere but at Violet Elwood. Fuck. She really needed to learn when to keep her mouth shut, didn't she? *Home?* Not that it was any secret that Az had been staying with her, but she didn't particularly want to rub it in Violet's face. "Anyway. I just keep hearing a lot about it."

"Early stages still. Early stages." Taryn flapped her wrist and pulled Violet in closer. Linking them by their elbows almost forcefully. Rus wasn't sure how she could tell, but something shifted in Violet's expression, or her posture. She seemed to make herself smaller. "But we're very excited about everything, aren't we, Violet?"

"Yes. It's going to be really great." Violet nodded.

"And you? How is the hunt for new coven members coming?" Taryn's gaze narrowed again, keen and cutting, and every hair on Rus's body stood on end. She didn't think she liked being on the receiving end of such an expression from Taryn Elwood. There was something about Taryn that felt . . . calculating. It settled uneasily against Rus's nerves, setting off alarms in the back of her mind. "I haven't heard anything about you finding anyone."

"We have some prospects." Which was complete bullshit. But the feeling of being pinned down, of the lights above prickling at the back of her neck, made Rus unable to tell the truth. Because Taryn would take that information with her and report it back. To who? Rus didn't know. But she didn't want Taryn to know that thus far Rus had fuck all by way of possible coven members. Goddess, what was taking Fernando so long with those drinks? "You know how it is."

"Yes. Of course. Of course." Taryn smiled, sharp and sly, then turned to accept their cups from Fernando. "Thank you, dear. And it was nice seeing you, Rus. We really ought to go out for coffee sometime, to catch up."

"Right. I'll text you." She wouldn't. They both knew she wouldn't. Because Taryn didn't really want to go out for coffee and catch up. That was just a thing people said to the people they'd gone to school with. To be polite or some bullshit.

"That's a nasty one, she is," a soft voice said near Rus's ear. When she glanced at the spot from the corner of her eyes, she saw a spirit floating there, wispy like smoke. They hesitated for a moment, as if wondering if Rus had heard them, then trailed behind Taryn and Violet.

"Tell me about it," Rus muttered to herself once they were gone.

She and Taryn hadn't run in the same circles back in the day, but she hadn't exactly liked what she'd seen of the other woman. There was a lot of backstabbing going on in high school that Taryn hadn't really grown out of like most girls did. And when they did wind up in a class together, or bumped into each other in the halls, Taryn had made a point to avoid Rus. By then, the necromancy had started becoming an issue, so Rus couldn't really blame her. It wasn't until after Rus left that Taryn really started making a name for herself, it seemed. Marrying an Elwood. Getting in good with many of the Board of Magic elders. Like a switch had flipped. But then . . . that happened with some people. They reached a certain age and just said fuck it.

"What was that?" Fernando asked, setting a fresh mug of chai in front of Rus for her to try.

"Taryn and Violet have a shade attached to them. Well . . ." Rus tilted her head, watching the couple load into their car through the front window. A fine mist settled around them, thicker than the rain falling, and drifting up from the ground instead of down. Rus couldn't tell how many there were, they overlapped so much, but there were — "More than one."

"Are you going to offer to exorcise them?"

"No." There was no sense in doing extra work she wasn't being paid for. And the spirits weren't hurting anything. Yet. Plus, exorcising that many at once would cost her a lot in terms of energy reserves. A lot she didn't currently have to spare. "But I'm going to keep an eye on it." Rus took the mug and sipped it, blanching. "Nando. How much cinnamon did you *put* in this?"

Fernando shrugged, took the mug, and went back to the steamer, humming along the way. Then the bell over the door rang, and Sunila Elwood stumbled in, pixie cut hair windswept.

"Well, if it isn't my favorite necromancer!" Sunila Elwood looked nothing like an Elwood—at least not any Elwood Rus had ever met. She was a petite woman, which wasn't uncommon for the family, but what *was* uncommon was the sheer messiness and chaotic energy she exuded. If Rus had ever studied auras, she fully believed Sunila's would be a riot of colors that all clashed against each other but somehow went together perfectly. Rather like her outfit, which was a button-up covered in different blocks of color, and a pair of high-waisted bellbottom jeans. Rus wondered idly if Carmine had seen this outfit if Sunila would still be running Elwood & Co.

"Aren't I like . . . the *only* necromancer you know?" Rus asked, tilting her head, but it was hard to fight the smile that wanted to take over her face. Sunila was a ball of energy so bright, it was infectious. She was everything an Elwood wasn't. Undisciplined. Bubbly. And ridiculous by turns. Making her seem even less one of them than Indigo, and yet, she was Elwood by blood, not marriage. Funny.

"Potato. Potato." Sunila flapped her wrist and bounced slightly as she stopped in front of the counter.

"You just said potato twice." Fernando shouldered his way in beside Rus, bumping her lightly with his hip. "The exact same way."

"Did I?" Sunila's grin widened, her brown eyes lighting up in good humor as her dark brows lifted to wrinkle her forehead. Seriously though, how the fuck was she an Elwood? "Well, handsome, why don't you go grab me a vanilla latte with an extra shot?"

Fernando spun on his heels, and Rus caught the hint of pink on his cheeks as he made his way back to the steamer.

"An extra shot?" she asked, returning her gaze to Sunila. "As if you need the caffeine."

"Oh, Rus, darling, you have no idea." Sunila flopped across the counter, reaching her hands over to the opposite edge and gazing up at Rus as if she were devastated. "It's so boring over there. I don't know how Azure stood it all these years, if I'm being perfectly frank. I mean sure, these last few months she had you to gaze longingly at through the window. But otherwise?" Sunila sucked on her teeth in obvious distaste. "What. A. *Drag*."

"I'd like to say I feel bad for you but . . ." Rus shrugged.

Sunila let out an affronted noise and stood straight, her hands on her hips, but once Fernando returned with her drink she was all smiles again. "So, I saw my cousin and Taryn come in here a bit ago. What'd *they* want?"

Rus twitched her brow upward in question. It was curious how few of the Elwoods seemed to like Taryn, given the match had been board sanctioned.

"I think Taryn was fishing for info about the coven." Rus tapped her fingers against the counter, her nervous energy needing to go somewhere. She didn't know who Taryn was reporting to, but she knew it was someone. And given Taryn's track record, there was little doubt in Rus's mind that whatever information she garnered would benefit her and few others. "I told her we had a couple candidates."

"Which was a lie." Sunila sipped from her drink thoughtfully.

"Well, obviously. I don't think she believed me anyway."

"No, she probably didn't." With a wrinkled nose, Sunila frowned. "She can spot a lie from a mile away. It's freaky as fuck."

"Hard agree," Fernando said. When Rus turned to raise

a brow at him, he just lifted his shoulders. "She wigs me out."

"I think she wigs everyone out." Sunila chuckled. "It's like there's no fucking life behind her eyes or something." She waved her hand in front of her face as if to show what she meant. But it was hard to imagine Sunila without any life behind her eyes.

"I thought you were supposed to be polite to your in-laws. Isn't that like . . . Elwood law?" Rus tilted her head, a smile twitching at her lips.

Sunila choked on the next sip of her drink and glared at Rus for laughing. With another cough, and a little beating against her chest, Sunila said, "That's a good one. Anyway, back into the breach! I'll see y'all later!"

Sunila gave them a lazy salute then she was gone.

Rus bumped Fernando with her shoulder. "You good?"

"Yeah. 'M fine," Fernando grumbled and ducked his head, likely to hide the heat in his cheeks before he returned to the steamer. "I'll get your afternoon buzz ready."

"No decaf this time! I can tell the difference."

"Sure. Sure."

# Chapter 4

There was a soft murmur about 157 Mourning Moore this evening. It was . . . nice. Normal. Rus felt strangely like she'd stepped back into her childhood, the small orphanage home full of quiet voices and the running feet of children. She wondered how many of Meiling's friends had lied to their parents about where they were going tonight. If they'd told their moms and dads, and so on and so forth, that they were at someone else's house. Not the necromancers. Not the house surrounded by a graveyard.

Guilt crept along her spine, making Rus hunch in further on herself. Still. At least her reputation hadn't kept the girls from making friends.

Yet.

Meiling was at an age where her classmates thought communicating with the dead was cool for some unknown reason. Likely because they were rebelling against their parents. Which wasn't a good reason to get into necromancy, but hey, who was Rus to judge? Going against a system that already didn't care for her because she was a medium was exactly what had turned her to her specialty. That and the fact that some asshole had killed her familiar.

Either way, it was good to see Meiling making friends. Finding a home for herself—

"Is that a Ouija board?" Rus frowned, moving onto her toes so she could peek through Meiling's cracked bedroom door without creaking the floorboards. The bit of laminated cardboard in question lay between the three girls, looking as innocuous as could be even though it could bring their whole fucking house down around their ears.

Fuck.

She thought she'd taught Meiling better than that. And besides, wasn't Meiling *afraid* of spirits? Peer pressure. Had to be. Rus may have missed a time in her life where her knees didn't ache when it rained, but she sure as shit *didn't* miss peer pressure.

"A'ling," Rus called. The door to Meiling's room creaked open further of its own accord, 157 Mourning Moore joining in on the scolding. With an outstretched hand, Rus called the planchette to her palm, where it settled gently. "What have we discussed?"

Meiling looked for a moment like a deer caught in the headlights. Like a child who'd gotten their arm stuck in the cookie jar. Then she sighed loudly, as if put upon—an act, because without the other two teenagers looking at her, Meiling mouthed the word *thank you*—and said out loud, "No spirit boards."

"No spirit boards," Rus agreed with a nod. She hoped Meiling realized it was an acknowledgment to the thanks. She knew what it was to be pigeonholed into a situation she didn't want to be in. Goaded and bullied, even by her own friends, into something that made her uncomfortable. It was a part of growing up. But that didn't mean Rus couldn't make it easier on Meiling. At least, while she was there. "And why is that, A'ling?"

She hoped the other kids heard this and took it to heart. Hoped they recognized the danger they were putting themselves in by fucking with things they didn't understand and couldn't control. She doubted it. People, even witches, who couldn't see the dead didn't usually fully grasp what the shades and spirits that lived alongside them were capable of. That was part of the problem. Part of the reason why finding people to join the Coven of the Forgotten was going to be an uphill battle. Folk—just like humans—feared what they did not understand. And as much as Rus had tried to educate Moondale, that too was an uphill battle.

"It's like sending out a mass text to a bunch of randos with your social security number." Meiling rolled her eyes, but Rus knew there was real fear there. How couldn't there be? The other two kids were at risk fucking with forces they didn't understand, sure, but the one who was in real danger here was Meiling, who was a medium. Who hadn't learned, yet, how to expel a spirit once she'd invited it in. Maybe Rus needed to get to those lessons finally.

"Exactly." Rus's fingers tightened around the planchette until the edges cut into her palm.

Meiling needed her to play the strict parent now, and she was going to. She didn't like it, but it was necessary, and maybe it would put a bit of fear into these two, whose parents clearly hadn't done a good enough job warning them off from fucking with forces they didn't understand.

"Get that thing out of my house before I call your parents and tell them what you're up to." She waited a moment, watching the wide-eyed teenagers, and when none of them moved she growled darkly, the lights flickering with her irritation. The whispers of spirits rose up around her along with the green mist of her magic that loomed across the floor like gas. "*Now!*"

They scrambled to comply. Scooping up the board and putting it back in the cardboard box it'd come in. A store-bought one then. Even worse for the lack of protective magics woven into its makeup. The planchette joined the board with a *thunk,* and Rus stepped out of the way to let the three of them shuffle past her on their way to the stairs.

The front door creaked shut behind them, and Rus headed for her own room in the attic. Out of earshot, she tilted her head toward the ceiling and grinned. "The lights were a nice touch."

The house groaned around her as if in agreement.

"Oh 157, we're going to do great things, you and I." Rus chuckled to herself as she headed for the wardrobe against the wall to start digging out her gear for the evening. A creak on the stairs from the second floor to the attic was the only warning before Az joined her.

"I just watched three teenagers run in slippers across the lawn to throw what appeared to be a board game into the trash," Az said by way of greeting. It sounded like she was swallowing back a smile. "What did you do to them?"

Dragging a small duffle bag from the bottom of the wardrobe to check it, Rus dropped onto her butt and grinned up at Az, wide and happy. "Not much. Just a little flex to convince them that I'm *way* scarier than any imagined frights they might get out of a Mattel-made spirit board. How was class?"

"Good." Az slipped out of her jacket on her way across the room, and bent to press a kiss to Rus's lips, lingering for a long moment as if she wanted to push things further. To see how much Rus would let her get away with. But then she pulled back, her mouth curled up at the corners, and moved to Rus's desk. "I spoke to Vanessa Cochburn. Do you need warding talismans tonight?"

"The dean of Moondale University? And yeah, bring the talismans. Then I won't have to salt the entrances." Rus shook herself, trying to get her brain to focus again. It was always hard with Az in the room. Especially when they were talking about two things at once, and Az looked so fucking pretty in her white mid-length skirt and flowy pale-blue velvet blouse. She looked so *soft*. Rus had the unreasonable desire to rub her face on Az's stomach, to feel that velvet against her cheek. It wasn't fair.

"Yes, the dean of Moondale U." Az grabbed a handful of the crinkly papers she'd been working on over the last few days. They were an experiment, a modification on Az's traditional warding talismans that should, once stuck to the entrance of a building, make all exits impenetrable to spirits. They hadn't tested them yet, but now was the perfect time, in Rus's opinion. Whatever was in 155 Mourning Moore probably wasn't malignant enough to hurt them—it'd just be annoying, if there was anything at all. So they could afford to play fast and loose.

"What did the dean want?"

"She wants you to guest lecture." Az went to grab the container of salt from the desk, frowning at finding it empty. "We should still use the salt."

"Then we won't know if the talismans work, Az." Rus sighed, leaning back so she could watch Az.

She'd moved toward the bed and was shimmying out of her skirt and tights, giving Rus a full view of the black boy shorts underneath that she'd stolen from Rus's drawer that morning. How was it fair that they looked even better on Az? Curving gently around her ass and full thighs where they seemed to make Rus look flatter. Rus shook herself and turned back to her bag to give Az some privacy while she changed. Not that she hadn't seen it all, but . . . It had been years. Goddess above and below, Az was going to be the death of her.

"We won't know if they work if the spirit doesn't try to leave either. I'd rather be safe than sorry." Az would always rather be safe than sorry. It was cute, almost, how worried she was for Rus's safety. And because Az was going to be there too, putting herself in the line of fire if things went wrong, Rus would cede to her caution. Because if there was one thing she couldn't—wouldn't—risk, it was Az.

"Ugh. You're no fun." Rus huffed and rolled to her feet to head for the pantry for the salt. She should probably start leaving an extra container in her kit. But they'd run out downstairs last week, and she had yet to get to the grocery store to pick up another one, meaning her exorcism kit was doing double duty. Which was kind of par for the course being the guardian of two growing girls, and the town's only of-age medium. While she was there, she grabbed some other herbs they might need, in case things got hairy, and stuffed her pestle and mortar in along with everything else. Az was right—it was better to be safe than sorry. Especially as Nesta hadn't even been inside the place yet, so they had no idea what they were walking into.

"I SAW your sister and her wife today," Rus said conversationally as they entered the house. Azure wasn't sure if Rus was trying to ease Azure's nerves or her own. Not that Azure was really nervous. This was Moondale, after all. Nothing that bad could fester here. Not without being noticed. Or maybe it was just to avoid talking about the other thing, the guest lecturing thing. Goddess, if Rus Ashthorne was one thing through and through, it was exasperatingly stubborn.

155 Mourning Moore had been empty only a couple of weeks, and from what she understood the family who'd

lived there prior hadn't run screaming into the night. They'd simply decided they needed to downsize and bought a place closer to the center of town. They were an older couple, so it made sense. But still, Azure could see why Nesta would be concerned. Even houses that were inhabited for a long period of time could attract things to them. At least, from what Azure had seen of Rus's work thus far.

"How are they?" Azure cared. She did, really. She wanted her sister to be happy, healthy, and whole. Just because they were fighting didn't mean she wished ill upon her. It simply meant that she didn't want to talk to Violet herself. Not until Violet fucking apologized for being a bitch about Azure leaving Jade Waters. There was no excuse for her behavior, and just because they were family didn't mean Azure had to put up with it. Period.

"They seemed well enough." Rus crouched to line the front threshold in salt while Azure stuck one of her talismans to the door using a bit of magic. "Taryn asked how the coven building was going."

"Of course she did." Azure didn't trust Taryn as far as she could throw her—never had, even before she'd married Violet. There had always been something about the woman that screamed that she'd do anything for a little bit of power. Then they'd graduated from high school and Taryn had been matched with Violet. It didn't make a whole lot of sense, given that Taryn came from a family with no influence in Moondale. It felt like a trick. And Moondale herself seemed to do everything to oppose the match. To prove how wrong they were for each other. But Violet was infatuated with the idea of familial duty and wouldn't listen.

"I'm going to check upstairs. You sit tight, this shouldn't

take long." Rus moved to press a kiss to Azure's cheek, leaving behind a warm tingle.

"Are you wearing your amulet?"

Rus pulled it from beneath her shirt in answer and winked before trotting up the front steps. Azure waited approximately five seconds before following her as quietly as she could. Because she wanted to watch the way the otherworldly green light of Rus's magic twisted and turned around her slowly, lighting her up like some beautiful dark creature. Because she wanted to be there if someone needed to pull Rus out.

She settled quietly in front of Rus in the master bedroom, her legs crossed in a careful lotus pose to mirror Rus's own, and waited, listening to the faint whispers, watching the way Rus's eyes shifted beneath her lids. It took more effort, Rus said, to cross over into limbo when she was wearing the pendant Azure made for her, but it was safer this way. She was less likely to bring something back with her unknowingly. And Azure wasn't willing to risk another possession like the one with Kaytee. So she insisted, and she came along, and she waited.

When Rus finally surfaced, it was with a gasp, like coming up for air after being under water for too long. "Okay so," Rus said, swallowing hard, "first thing's first, we need to make some tweaks to the pendant."

"It makes it too hard to slip into limbo?"

"It makes it too hard to *move* once there." Rus turned her neck from one side to the other and arched her spine as if stretching out sore muscles. "I think the protection on it is too heavy."

"I can lighten it." Azure nodded. Rus's sister in all but name—they'd grown up in the same orphanage before Phyre was adopted by the Ironwood family—was extraordinarily talented and had helped to forge the first pendant. But Azure already had some ideas on how to do that. Not to make the protection any less, obviously, but to make it feel lighter. To make Rus's magic shoulder less of the load. She might have to incorporate some of her own magical essence into the metal when Phyre made the next one. That should take on some of the burden. It would require recharging, and some blood, but that was a small price to pay for Rus's safety. And they both knew that if a tool made what Rus did too difficult, she wouldn't use it, danger be damned. "Was there anything left behind by the previous owners?"

"No spirits. Just some residual emotions. I don't even think this house is sentient like 157 is."

"The previous owners lived here a long time. They were humans." Not that that meant anything. Even humans could put some of themselves into their homes the way folk did. But the feeling Azure got from this house was rather calm and settled. As if it had spent the last few decades relaxing with the couple that lived there. Living a life of relative tranquility.

"I almost feel bad taking the commission off Nesta for no work." Rus stood, wiping her hands on her jeans. "But we can always use the extra cash."

"Speaking of extra cash," Azure said. "You never did answer me about the guest lecturing."

Rus sighed and rubbed at her forehead as if chasing away a headache. "Because I don't know how feasible it is right now, Az. With the girls, and the business, and then my house cleanings. When do I have time?"

"If you really want to do it, we'll figure it out." Azure could tell that Rus did. That even if she was trying not to think about it, to push it off, it was something she would enjoy. It would make her happy. Rus deserved to be happy.

She'd spent so much time since returning to Moondale, and even before then, fighting to survive. Azure wanted to give her things to enjoy now that she was settled. "Maureen and Carmine would be happy to help out with the girls. So would Indigo and Cagney." Rus's best friend Cagney would of course be happy to help, but she didn't mention Greer, Cagney and Nesta's boyfriend, and Rus's self-proclaimed nemesis, because she knew what kind of shit *that* would stir. "You have family here in Moondale. You don't have to do it all by yourself anymore."

Rus hummed, her footsteps thudding softly against the steps where she walked in front of Azure toward the front door again. She was taking her time, working through the problem. Azure recognized the silence between them as that. This was not a *no*. This was a *let me think about it*.

"If you did this," Azure pressed—sometimes Rus needed a little pressure, a nudge in the right direction—"it would be a good way to find more members for the coven. Not recruit directly, but see who might fit."

"I'm not pulling in kids." Rus stopped on the bottom step and whirled to glare at Azure.

"I'm not suggesting you do. Guest lectures aren't just attended by students, they're also attended by professors and faculty. There are some witches working at Moondale University who live in Ironport, and since there is only one coven in Ironport . . ."

Rus narrowed her eyes. "You're telling me Ironport has a bunch of covenless witches."

"Some. Not a bunch. But some. Besides," Azure continued, and hedged her bets, "don't you want to make sure that the new crop of Moondale witches aren't complete magical luddites?"

"You're playing dirty now, darling." Rus laughed and

leaned toward where Azure had stopped on the stair above her, making them of a height. "I want you to remember," she murmured, her breath ghosting over Azure's lips, "when I become a cranky old professor, that you asked for this."

"You'll be adorable in elbow pads." Azure grinned widely, grabbed Rus by the waist, and pulled her into a kiss so deep it made Azure's toes curl in her boots. Rus let out a happy mumble, her fingers curling around Azure's jacket collar to hold her close, their bodies plastered together in the empty house on the corner of Mourning Moore and Grimwood Lane, and Azure thought perhaps life couldn't get any better than this.

# Chapter 5

Azure Elwood would rather be at home.

That went without saying, really. It was midnight on a Friday, who wouldn't *rather* be curled up in their bed with their significant other? No one. So perhaps it was more appropriate to say that Azure Elwood would rather be *anywhere else* other than the squat Board of Magic building that looked more like a one room schoolhouse than a magical town hall.

Working retail.

Fighting Black Friday shoppers at the mall.

The grocery store.

All places she considered the worst kinds of hell, and she'd rather be at any of them than sitting in the peeling metal chair at the peeling laminate table stuffed too full with people who all thought they were the smartest person in the room.

They weren't.

*She* was obviously the smartest person in the room, and that was only because Rus wasn't there. Which made this whole thing worse. Rus wasn't there. She was at home, likely hunched over the desk in the bump out in her room, fiddling with one of her many inventions. Watching Rus work for hours while she muttered to herself sounded far more enjoyable to Azure than sitting here. She was biased, of course, but that didn't change the facts.

Alas, this was the price Azure paid to have that. To have Rus at home in 157 Mourning Moore, and not out in the world somewhere getting into Goddess knew what trouble, danger threatening her little family. This was the price Azure paid for their safety. For a *home* with Rus in it.

It was worth it.

Nixie Virnan caught Azure's gaze from across the table and winked, a sign that Nixie was about to do something very annoying.

Correction. It was only *just* worth it.

"Now that everyone is settled," Nixie said, her smile polite and icy all at the same time. Azure wondered if Nixie could teach her how to do that. It seemed an invaluable skill. "Let's begin by welcoming the future elders you all have chosen to sit in on these meetings."

Future elders. As if any of the current elders were likely to give up their seats, Nixie included. Still, each elder had been tasked with bringing a young protégé of sorts to the first of the centennial planning meetings. Azure didn't really see what this would solve, other than to have someone there willing to get coffee and agree with everything their elder said. But no one had asked her opinion on the matter. Shame, really.

How Taryn wound up there, Azure wasn't sure. Likely because Aunt Carmine hadn't wanted to bring Sunila or Indigo, who would be looked down on as too young by the others since they hadn't graduated from college yet or been inducted into Jade Waters officially besides. Or maybe she was trying to smooth over some of the ruffled feathers she'd caused by siding with Azure on the whole leaving-Jade-Waters thing.

It didn't matter.

What did matter was that they were sitting next to

Azure, and Taryn's perfume was fucking unbearable. It smelled of grave flowers.

Goddess, Azure just wanted to go the fuck home.

Aunt Carmine didn't look much better than Azure felt. She was pinching the bridge of her nose as if she had a headache, and dark circles ringed her eyes. Azure would have to pull her aside after the meeting and ask her if she was feeling all right. She hadn't been to the house in the last few days. Maybe Aunt Carmine was sick. Or maybe Aunt Maureen was. Azure made a mental note to go by and check in on everyone.

Finding the balance between two homes was proving more difficult than Azure had anticipated. She hadn't been invited to move into 157 Mourning Moore, so technically she was still living with her aunts and brother. But she spent most of her time across the street with Rus and her family. Most of her clothes were there, and even Lizzie, her familiar, had found a spot for herself in Aihuan's room. Which was unbearably adorable, but she wasn't going to let on that she thought so to Lizzie, lest she stop.

Still, if something were wrong at home, Indigo would have told her. Wouldn't he? She'd check in. She'd stop Aunt Carmine as soon as the meeting was over and ask her what was going on.

"Now," Nixie was saying when Azure tuned back in to her speech, "we have much to do and not a whole lot of time to do it. I know October seems far away, but in reality it's not much more than a handful of months. It'll be here before we know it. So let's try not to quibble about things, and just focus on getting them done. Yes?"

Everyone present murmured in agreement, and Nixie's smile widened, showing off the top row of her pointed teeth. A clear threat that if people didn't stick to the plan, she would make their lives difficult. Arguably, Azure didn't actually know much about Nixie Virnan, but she knew she wasn't someone to be trifled with, even though she looked like a frail old lady when she wasn't smiling like that.

"Wonderful. Now, there are a number of events we need planned, but first and foremost is the centennial ceremony at the Heart of Moondale. That will likely take the most preparation and magic to put together."

It was also the cornerstone of the whole celebration. The most important thing the folk of Moondale would do for the past hundred years as well as the next hundred. How it was handled would shape their town for centuries to come, and the magic that flowed through it. That ceremony was not to be taken lightly. Should not be done by someone who—

"I think Carmine and I can handle that," Taryn offered, her smile wide and guileless. "The Heart of Moondale has always been looked after by the Jade Waters coven, so it only makes sense that we would handle it now. And I'm more than qualified to—"

"Carmine?" Nixie asked, cutting Taryn off. "What do you have to say about this?"

"I agree that this is something the *Elwoods* should handle." Aunt Carmine said their surname with a weight Azure had never heard before, as if she perhaps didn't consider Taryn to be one of them. "That being said, I'll take care of it. Taryn's talents would be better used elsewhere." Carmine sat up straighter, though Azure could tell from the tightening of her mouth that it pained her to do so. She had never much cared for being put on the spot, and it was clear this made her uncomfortable. Especially with the way Taryn's posture had gone rigid, her fingers flickering with irritated magic, sparking like poppers in the summer heat.

Azure curled her fingers tighter around the fabric of her skirt, crinkling it, but didn't say anything. It wasn't her place to. Not anymore. She'd forfeited that right months ago when she'd had Aunt Carmine strike her name from the Jade Waters coven list and signed her name to the Coven of the Forgotten instead. Even if she was still an Elwood by blood.

"Agreed," Clianthe Greer said, before Taryn could even hope to object.

"The ceremony is too important to leave it to someone so young," Gilroy Herne added. The druid elder of the Grove of Elderwood had just come out of hibernation and seemed to think he needed to make up for the time he'd lost while he'd slept through the late fall and winter months. Azure kind of hoped the planning for the centennial kept him too distracted to look her and Rus's way. He would have Things to say, no doubt, about a necromancer starting her own clan in Moondale. And he and Brant Ironwood had always been too close for Azure's comfort.

"Then if we're all in agreement, we can schedule a separate meeting to discuss that next week." Nixie waited a moment for any objections, and when none came, she nodded and scratched something onto the pad of paper before her. "But since you're so eager to get started, Mrs. Elwood, I think you might be perfect for planning the town festival."

"The festival?" Taryn asked, her tone carefully neutral. Azure was sure that if Taryn let whatever was going through her mind play across her face, her expression would have been wrinkled in disgust. "The one for the normies?"

"It'll be a huge undertaking," Clianthe Greer offered. "I think all of our assistants should work on it."

"Agreed." Enfys Snowthorn sat forward. The elder

from the Clan of Crescentia was an older man with a long white beard and a wizened face. If Azure were to compare him to anyone, it would be the normies' Santa Claus, only not quite so jolly. Which was kind of amusing. Humans would likely think a cupid *would* be jolly, but Enfys was just as grouchy as the next porch-sitting curmudgeon.

Taryn wasn't buying it. She gripped her pen so hard, it was shaking in her hand. "I think I would be far more valuable if I were to put my talents toward the planning at the Heart. Surely all the other assistants can handle the planning for the *festival*." She said the word *festival* as if it was something beneath her, unworthy of her attention. Not that she could really do anything to change their minds. Once the elders decided on something like this, that was it. There was no avenue for appeals for this kind of thing. And besides, they were right. Taryn was an event planner—she'd have the festival sorted out easily.

"We need the festival to be as successful as possible," one of the potentials spoke up, their voice soft. Azure didn't recognize them. She thought she knew everyone in Moondale. But the young person sitting to the right of Nixie was as unfamiliar as any tourist who came into Azure's shop. They had wide dark eyes, boasting no pupil, and a tuft of short curly hair cut close at the sides and long on the top of their head. Azure reflected for a moment that she'd never actually seen any of the Ladies of Nimue outside of Nixie at these meetings, and she frowned. If she was going to be the elder for the Coven of the Forgotten, she'd have to brush up on Moondale society.

"And why's that?" Taryn turned on them, her face twisted in distaste, a rictus that Azure thought she'd never seen before. Taryn usually hid her spite much better than that. "We don't need the tourist revenue, we always—"

"The extra foot traffic brought in by the centennial festival will help charge the lei lines," Azure said before she'd even realized she was going to speak. For some reason, she'd thought this was common knowledge. A thing every child of Moondale understood. But maybe it was only taught to her because of her lineage, because she was the one who was meant to take the elder seat when Aunt Carmine retired. Maybe it wasn't widely known at all. Maybe it was a privilege to have been taught these things from an early age. "The lei lines being adequately charged is crucial to the ceremony surrounding the Heart of Moondale. If they aren't, the ceremony could drain the folk trying to conduct it."

"Correct." Nixie grinned, showing off both rows of her pointed teeth. "We need all the excited energy everyone will produce from a well-planned festival to help the ceremony along."

And then Azure said something she never thought she'd say in her entire life, because she was not the type to volunteer for group projects, and she disliked Taryn in particular. "I'll help Taryn head up the group in charge of the festival."

"Perfect." Nixie's grin turned sharper, as if that had been her plan all along and Azure had walked right into it. Fuck.

But when Azure looked about the table, she found Brant looking absolutely pissed with this turn of events, which maybe made it worth it. "So it'll just be the Elwoods in charge of the festival?"

"And why should Azure Elwood be in charge? She's not even a member of an official coven," Gilroy pressed.

"Because she volunteered. I don't see any of your protégés jumping up to volunteer." Nixie shrugged, not looking up from the piece of paper where she was jotting some notes. "Or would you prefer she help her aunt plan the ceremony at the Heart of Moondale? I'm sure she'd be happy to help with that as well. And she's more than qualified."

Azure nodded. She wasn't really sure what she was agreeing to, but she had a feeling Nixie was playing a game with the other elders, as if she'd read them as easily as books and was putting them in their place.

There was no more descent against her and Taryn working together to head up the festival committee, and Nixie finally lifted her head from her notes. "Wonderful. Let's continue."

NIXIE DIDN'T GIVE Azure time to catch her aunt before Taryn hustled them both out the door. She reached across the table and tapped on Azure's notebook to get her attention, then jerked her head toward the offices at the back of the room. With everyone else focused on getting their shit and getting home as soon as possible, it didn't seem like anyone even noticed when Azure followed Nixie to her office. They placed an anti-listening charm on the door.

"How is the search for coven members coming along?" Nixie moved around her desk to drop into the chair behind it, letting out a huff of breath as if she'd been holding herself upright for far too long and only now felt comfortable enough to slouch.

"I've been in contact with one prospect. And I've mostly talked Rus into guest lecturing at Moondale University. The dean thinks putting Rus in front of some of the covenless from

Ironport will get them interested in the Forgotten." It wasn't the best news, nor was it exactly a sign of progress. But it was a step in the right direction. She just hoped they didn't run out of time before Rus was able to charm some witches their way.

Nixie scrubbed at her face with both hands, letting out another long sigh. "You need to speed it up."

"Why?" Azure's stomach dropped to her feet.

"Gilroy Herne has been very chummy with Brant Ironwood, in case you missed it."

"I hadn't." It was honestly hard to miss with how they'd shown up together, sat together, and spent the minutes leading up to the meeting murmuring softly to one another low enough that Azure hadn't caught a single word. But she'd caught plenty of glances. She'd known Brant wasn't happy with the turn of events a few months back, even though that turn of events meant Rus was going to be producing more technological marvels for the clans of Moondale. That didn't seem to matter in the face of who created those advancements. Foolish. Closed-minded. Prick. "They're not exactly trying to hide it."

"No. They wouldn't. They're confident that they can turn the opinion of the board." Nixie leaned back in her chair, looking up at the ceiling. She suddenly looked very tired. Like she really was over five hundred years old just like everyone thought. "They plan to appeal the decision in the next month or so. They want you and Rus out before the centennial is even close."

"We were supposed to have until October." Azure choked out the words past a dry throat. *Month or so.* They had a *month* to get new members. Could Rus even get a lesson plan together that quickly? Not to mention she didn't know what the summer session schedule at Moondale

University looked like. "What about the Ghost Tracer? It's still only in beta."

"They think they can get someone else to finish it for them."

"But it's Rus's—"

"She made it for the board. Even if there was no paperwork or money exchanged, the magical word is law here, and she agreed to make it for them. So it belongs to them."

"Those—that's just—how can they—" Too many words. There were too many words. All of them crowding for space on her tongue as Azure's magic lashed around her like a raging sea, her blood boiling. "What can I do?"

"For one thing"—Nixie dropped her head to meet Azure's gaze with a gleam in her eye—"get the two members the covens said you needed, and then some if you can. But at the bare minimum, two by the end of the month." It sounded easy when Nixie said it that way, but they both knew it wasn't going to be. "Also, get yourself a coven house. It can't be either of your residences, it has to be someplace else. That'll give you more of a foothold in Moondale, which will be difficult for them to nullify."

"We did the ceremony at the Heart—"

"Yes, I know. And Moondale accepted you, but the coven's name on a title? It shows you're serious. It gives us something legal and tangible."

"Okay." Azure swallowed, the sound loud in the quiet room. "Okay, we can do that. I'll talk to Nesta about finding us someplace. Anything else?"

"Have Rus patent anything she has. The digital grimoire. The Witchling Tracker. Any other bits and bobs she has lying around. She needs those filed through the official channels in Moondale. Then the board can't steal them, and it's a paper trail of the Forgotten's efforts to contribute to the community."

"That should be simple enough." Well, the filing should be simple. Finding all of Rus's inventions and trying to translate them into something that would make sense on paper might be harder. But Azure was sure she could enlist Fernando and Meiling to help with that. Maybe even Hunter . . . if they got him to join sooner rather than later.

"Right. The hard part"—Nixie leaned forward further, bracing her elbows on her desk—"will be finding out who's behind all this. Gilroy and Brant have nothing to gain from pushing you and Rus out, other than the fact that they don't like Rus. But there are plenty of people they don't like. They have a running feud with Dhiren—the djinni elder of the Circle of the Emerald Forge—and have never once tried to have him run out of the town."

Goddess above and below, Azure had a fucking headache. "Why *is* someone trying to push us out?"

"No idea." Super helpful, that's what that was. Present Azure with obvious treachery and offer her no reason behind it. "All I can think is that having a medium in town would put a damper on their plans for the centennial."

Azure raised her brows. "You have a suspicion who it is."

Nixie smiled, all sharp teeth and sinister lines.

"And you're not going to tell me."

"Where would be the fun in that?"

# Chapter 6

The ache in Rus's neck woke her around three a.m. The sharp pain caused from falling asleep at her desk. Again. She'd posted herself there after Az left for the Board of Magic meeting, to while away the time until Az returned. Because she knew she wouldn't sleep—a strange side effect of sharing a bed for the last few weeks. She'd spent eleven years sleeping alone, even when she'd been with Kaytee. Eleven years starfishing across the bed, taking up as much room as possible. And even before that, she hadn't slept with Az often while they were still young. But after that first night, after Az curled around her in the middle of the bed, and Rus curled right back like yin and yang, it was hard to sleep without her.

Rus shook the thought aside, stretching her neck from one side to the other, cracking the vertebrae along her spine. She should probably see someone about that.

"Add it to the list," Rus murmured with a laugh.

The chair scraped against the floor as she turned to check if Az had made it to bed yet. But the covers were still pulled up perfectly against the pillows, just as they'd been after Az made the bed in the morning. Because she did things like that—made their bed. Rus was the type of person to throw the covers back onto the bed where she'd kicked them off and call it good. But Az literally folded the quilt down, placed the pillows, and folded it back up over them. Like in a fucking hotel or something. It was adorable.

So either the meeting wasn't over yet, or Az had decided to sleep at her aunts' instead of coming home.

Home.

When had 157 Mourning Moore become not just Rus's home, but Az's as well? When had she started calling it "their" bed?

Fuck. She was too sober for that emotional rabbit hole. And it was too early in the fucking morning for it anyway. Scrubbing at her face, Rus grabbed the hoodie from the back of her chair, tugged it on, and headed down the stairs. She'd make herself some coffee and stay up. No sense in trying to go back to sleep now when the girls would be up in a few hours—a clear indication they weren't hers biologically. Morning people, the both of them. She could get some more work done anyway. Lesson planning was for the fucking birds. But she'd been hit with inspiration after Az tried to talk her into guest lecturing, and she'd learned a long time ago to use that when she had it. Even if she wasn't really sure if she was going to do it yet.

It was a good idea. An opportunity to share what she'd learned out in the world with a whole new generation of Moondale witches. To make her hometown better for having been there. She knew that, arguably. But there was a voice in the back of her head that reminded her that this was the same town that had basically run her out. That had scoffed at her inventions eleven years ago. That even now didn't seem to understand the wider scope of what was possible when one mixed magic with technology.

It wasn't just the fear of further ridicule making her hesitate, it was also the hurt. The thought that why *should* she offer them help when they'd never offered her any?

Why *should* she make this place better when it had been happy enough to spit her out like something gone sour?

But then there was the argument of the students of Moondale U not being the people who had done that to her. Being too young to have been there for all of that. And—well, she was going round and round in circles over it, honestly.

Why did life have to be so—

The light in the kitchen was on, casting itself in a square against the wall at the bottom of the steps.

"Nando? What the fuck are you doing—" Rus stopped on the last stair, her bare toes flexing against the edge of it when Az came into view. Az's long plum-colored hair was down loose around her shoulders, windblown. The clothes she'd changed into for the meeting were rumpled, and she had a pair of reading glasses perched in between her fingers, precariously close to falling to the floor. She'd fallen asleep sitting up, her big brown eyes closed in restless sleep, her back arched forward to lean against the table. That was going to ache later.

"Oh, honey," Rus sighed and scuffed across the kitchen to shake Az awake gently.

Az grumbled, her eyes blinking heavily, nose scrunching when she turned her head to glare sleepily at Rus. Fucking adorable. "What?"

"Come up to bed." Rus hushed a grumble from Az, her fingers carding through Az's long hair, brushing it back from her face.

"I need to finish going over this centennial festival outline Nixie gave me. I'm not letting fucking *Taryn* set up the schedule of events." Az's voice was raspy from sleep, and she leaned into Rus's touch like a cat. Couple that with the fact that she'd used the word "fucking" out loud, and she must really be tired.

"There will be time in the morning. I'll even help." Rus took Az's hand, wrestling the glasses from her to set them on the table, then began to stack the papers together again. "But you need to come up to bed, or you won't be doing fuck all tomorrow."

"Don't wanna." Az pouted and reached for Rus's waist, pulling her in close so Az could bury her nose in the fabric on Rus's stomach, letting out a soft noise of contentment. And okay, so, that was a thing. A thing Rus didn't know she was into, but a tingle ran all along her skin, and suddenly she *wanted.* It burned through her in a way it never had before, not with anyone else. There had been hints of desire with Kaytee. Traces of it while watching good-looking actresses in movies. But none of that even held a candle to the feeling that curled her toes at that exact moment. Like a lightning strike. It was just Az. It had always been Az.

"Well," Rus said, swallowing roughly around a tongue so dry it stuck to the roof of her mouth. What the fuck did a person even do with this feeling? How did other people— people who weren't so clearly fucking asexual—walk around feeling like this all the fucking time? How did they *function?* "I didn't say you had to sleep."

Az pulled her face away from where she had been nosing around Rus's hoodie, her chin resting on Rus's belly so she could look up at her with wide brown eyes narrowed by sleep and hazed over by lust. "I don't have to?"

"No." Heat crept up Rus's neck settling into her cheeks and ears. "You could finish what we started when we were working on the house cleansing."

A soft hum rumbled up Az's throat and she closed her eyes, leaning more heavily into the hand Rus slid down her neck, her thumb brushing Az's jaw. Goddess, she was lovely like this. Soft, and calm. She could be beautiful as a blade and twice as sharp, but like this . . . Not many people got to see Azure Elwood like this. "I thought we were taking things slow."

"Is almost three months not slow enough for you?" Rus joked to hide how much she wanted this. How much *need* buzzed along her skin right beside the ever-present nerves. If they took this next step, what would that mean for them? How would things change? And what if—what if Rus wasn't good at it anymore? What if Az saw Rus without her clothes on, littered in scars, and was disgusted by the sight?

Az raised one brow on her mahogany-brown face, her eyes dancing with mischief and judgment all in one, and Goddess above and below, Rus felt so deeply for this woman. So very deeply. How had she ever thought anyone else could compare? "We go at your pace. If you say stop, we stop."

Warmth curled up cozy and soft in Rus's chest like a contented cat. "Come on. Before the girls wake up and we can't get any privacy for hours."

That got Az moving. The chair nearly toppled in her rush to stand. She threaded her fingers through Rus's and pulled her up the stairs, 157 Mourning Moore hiding their ascent so as not to wake the rest of the house in their hurry.

Rus was giggling by the time Az spun her around and pressed her back into their bedroom door, all aches forgotten when Az's hips ground hard against her own. Rus reached for Az's jaw again, hooking her thumbs under to tilt Az's face back, giving her better access to her mouth. The first kiss was soft, quick, testing, Az still letting Rus set the pace. But Rus wasn't going to let that stand, not when heat pooled under her skin, her toes curling against the hardwood floors. She bit at Az's lower lip, sucking it between her teeth, and Az sighed, melting further into her.

Slipping one hand from Az's jaw, Rus reached for her shirt and tugged, trying to get it up over Az's head without once letting go. The fabric resisted, unstretchy and unforgiving as it was, and Rus grunted in irritation. "Fucking fancy-ass clothes. Can't you just wear elastic like the rest of us peasants?"

"You like that I don't dress like the peasants," Az teased, her tongue licking into Rus's mouth, meeting no resistance, swallowing her up. Goddess, Rus hoped the house made this room soundproof. She didn't want the girls hearing, and there were still Meiling's friends. Fuck. Meiling had friends over. Maybe this was a—

Az's skirt hit the floor, leaving her in a pair of pale-blue briefs. The soft velvet blouse followed soon after, exposing a matching pale-blue bra. Then her free hand was at the waistband of Rus's sweatpants, and she stilled as if she'd seen something, read something in Rus's body language. Maybe she had. Rus's skin felt too hot, tight, but there was an increasing churning in her belly. Anxiety over baring herself the way Az would want. Az pulled back to meet Rus's gaze with her own. The distance left Rus feeling cold all over, but the look pinned her in place. "Is it still yes?"

"Wh-what?" Rus stumbled forward, seeking Az's warmth and sending them both reeling toward the bed. 157 may or may not have helped by tilting the floor so that Az fell over the footboard, and Rus followed right after her, feet still on the floor, laughing breathlessly, self-consciousness momentarily forgotten in the silliness. "This fucking house, I swear. What the fuck was Nesta thinking?"

"Can we not talk about Nesta while I'm trying to get my

hand down your pants?" Az groaned, flopping her head back against the bedding.

"Right. So . . . what was the question?" Rus mumbled against Az's throat, finding a spot to worry beneath her ear that had Az's hips rising to grind against her. This had to be the most awkward position to have sex in, ever. "We need to get up on the bed. Leaning over it is killing my back."

"Imagine how I feel." Az grabbed Rus by her waist, and with a bit of magic, they both floated just above the bed, up toward the headboard, and flopped down onto it in a tangle of limbs.

"Weird flex, but I'll allow it."

"Answer the fucking question, Icarus," Az rasped, giving Rus's hip a pinch. "Do you still want this? We can stop if this is too fast for you."

Rus pulled back, pushing up onto her elbows so she could look down at Az. Her hair was sprawled around her on the pillows, her cheeks flushed, and a dark mark was forming on her neck from Rus's teeth.

Instead of answering Az's query, which seemed fucking obvious as Rus wasn't pulling away, just slowing down, just giving herself time to not overthink, Rus said, "I don't do regrets. There never seemed to be any use for them. But if I hadn't come back to Moondale . . ." She sucked in a breath, the humid air between them and the fierce look Az gave her catching in her throat, and she had her answer before she'd even voiced the question. "You'd have haunted me, wouldn't you?"

"To your grave," Az said, but it sounded like a vow. And she seemed to take Rus's words for what they were—a resounding *yes*—because she grabbed Rus by her ass, shoved her leg between Rus's, and rolled them so Rus was on her back below Az, hidden in the curtain of her hair, hips pressed into the bed.

"I should—I should warn you." Rus took a deep breath, trying to quell the fluttering of her heart. Goddess, when was the last time someone had seen her naked? Not since before the scars on her chest from where she'd fought the demon fox that inevitably killed Kaytee. Not since before the scars on her stomach where she'd been attacked by spirits failing to save Aihuan and Meiling's parents. Not since before the scars all up and down her arms from every time she'd used her magic. Scars. Scars. Scars. Her body was a patchwork of her biggest mistakes, her missteps. And she—she wasn't sure she wanted Az to see them. To find her wanting because of them.

"I've got a few—" She swallowed, her throat gone dry, and licked her lips. Why was this so hard? It was just Az. But no. There was no *just* about Az. It was true what Az had said—she'd have haunted Rus to her grave. "I've got a few more scars than last time you saw me naked."

Az blinked at her for a moment, as if she was confused by what Rus was saying. "I know."

"You—you *know?*" Rus choked on the word, wanting to shy away from the intensity in Az's gaze. The way her warm brown eyes had Rus pinned beneath her more surely than any hold on her body could have. Did Az know what she did to Rus? Well, there was no way she didn't, likely.

"Yes. I know." Az sounded the words out, spaced them carefully as if doing so would keep Rus from shying away, from skittering back into herself like a terrified animal. "I noticed them when you were wearing that tank top, working out in the yard the other day." She smiled a little, the corners of her lips tipping up almost in a smirk. "It didn't cover near as much skin as you thought it did."

"Oh. Well." Rus blew out a raspberry, all the fight leaving her, all the anxiety rushing out. It felt . . . it felt *good*. To have Az teasing her that way. To have her looking at Rus with fondness, and joy. Goddess, she was lost on Az, wasn't she? How had she ever thought she could stay away? "Then by all means!"

"Good." Az's smirk crawled up her face, growing into something more sly. "Now get out of that fucking hoodie before I do something drastic."

"Like what?" Rus grabbed the hem of the sweatshirt and started pulling it up over her head without further prompting.

"Do you really want to find out?" Az growled against the bit of skin on Rus's stomach she'd been pressing her face against in the kitchen. Nipping a slow path up from Rus's belly button to the sports bra she'd been wearing all day, heedless of the scars that lay there. "That too."

"Maybe I do." Rus grabbed the hem of the bra too and started to work it off, getting it stuck around her shoulders. "Help."

Az snorted a soft laugh and moved back on her knees to help extricate Rus from the constricting piece of clothing. Maybe it should have spoiled the mood. Maybe it should have made the fire in Rus's belly go out. But it simmered right along, and Rus liked the way Az laughed with her. Liked how easy this felt. Goddess, why had she waited so long?

Then every other thought flew from her head as Az set back to work, biting hard at Rus's collarbone, over where one of her scars was, leaving a mark of her own. She followed the path of mottled flesh with teeth and tongue alike. Remapping Rus's body once scarred by her own lack of self-worth and Kaytee's abuse, one mark at a time.

By the time she'd slid Rus's sweatpants and underwear from her hips, Rus had leaned her head back against the pillow, her eyes shut and a sigh of contentment on her lips. The fire in her belly still there, still warm, but not as urgent as it had once been. Not satiated, but content.

Rus hummed, rasping and breathy when Az reached for a pillow to prop up her hips, giving Az better access. The first swipe of Az's tongue against her folds caught Rus off guard, and she jerked, wriggling at the new sensation. It really had been a long time since someone had touched her, hadn't it?

Shame curled in her gut. Too hot. Almost melting away the need.

But Az lifted her head to meet Rus's open eyes. A question. True to her word, still. They could stop whenever Rus wanted to. They would only go as fast as Rus wanted them to. And that was enough to have Rus nodding slowly, to have the embarrassment dissolving to nothing. Az reached for her hand where it was fisted in the bedding, and threaded Rus's fingers into her hair, then she leaned back in, her tongue brushing against Rus's clit, the tip of one finger sliding against her entrance. Tracing her wetness.

Rus's toes curled, her hips lifting a little off the pillow when the next warm press of Az's tongue made her entire body tingle. A gasp ripped from her throat as Az pressed her finger inside, taking her time so as not to hurt Rus. Tender. Caring. Goddess, Rus *loved* this woman.

Something pinched her clit—teeth maybe—and Rus lost what composure she had. Her hand fisted hard in Az's hair, giving it a sharp tug that made Az moan, and Az's finger slipped past the knuckle into Rus's entrance, a second joining it as it slipped out. And then Rus's hips were rolling right along with the rhythm Az set, grinding against Az's mouth. Her breaths coming in sharp bursts as she tugged on Az's hair, trying to tell Az what she wanted with that alone. It didn't do anything to speed Az along, to make her do that again, but it did draw sounds from Az that rolled off her tongue and vibrated up through Rus's core.

Az brought her to the edge, to the point where every fiber of Rus's being was humming, singing to the tune of Az's movements, then she pulled her mouth away and began a slow, torturous trail of kisses and bites along the marks on Rus's skin again. All the while her fingers stayed pressed deep into Rus's core, letting Rus grind down against her palm, but not providing any other stimulation.

"Az. C'mon, don't be like that," Rus begged. Fluttering her lids open barely to eye Az through her lashes.

A flush ran warm and dark along Az's skin. Her lips shone in the soft lamplight as she smiled at Rus and shushed her gently before returning to rebranding Rus her own. Beautiful. Goddess. She was ethereal. Something else entirely. Not of this world.

And just as she crashed her lips against Rus's, magic flooded through Rus, running like the roll of the tides from her core along every nerve ending in her fucking body, lighting them up, setting them aflame, but not burning them. Like the first brush of warmth after too long out in the cold.

The gentle scrape of Az's still underwear-clad mound rolling against her thigh was almost an afterthought, a faraway thing she hardly noticed. But she lifted her leg, pushing back against Az, drawing a soft, grateful hiss from Az for her efforts that made Rus all the warmer.

Rus choked on a gasp, her mouth falling open, letting Az lick into her, working her slow and steady, winding her up, and up, and up.

Then Rus finally came, gasping against Az's lips, her fingers so tight in Az's hair that she was sure she was ripping out strands by the root, the other hand clawed tight around Az's shoulder.

It was less an earth-shattering dive off a cliff, and more a slow descent with a parachute. Floaty and soft.

She reached for Az, pulling her up to settle her weight on Rus's body, pressing her into the mattress, even as Az refused to release her, held her fingers inside to give Rus something to grind slow and languid against. Her own fingers moving to slip between Az's legs, brushing over her wetness, her clit, working her slow and steady even while Rus floated, half aware, half conscious, her eyes closed. Listening to the sounds Az made while Rus brought her to completion, and she came with a soft, happy sigh.

It took them a while to catch their breaths, the sweat cooling between them, but when they had, Rus nosed along Az's neck and mumbled the first words that came to her mind. "I think you ought to move in. Like . . . officially."

"Is that what you want?"

Rus shrugged. It *was* what she wanted, but she could hardly breathe life into the words, because once she did then it could be taken from her like so many other things. And maybe it was too fast. Maybe she was asking too much. Maybe she shouldn't allow herself this. Maybe it would ruin Az further. Maybe it was selfish. Goddess, fuck her orgasm-addled brain. So instead, she asked, "It's what you want, isn't it?"

Az hummed her agreement against Rus's temple. Relief washed through her, with shame nipping at its heels. What did she have to be relieved about? Wasn't she just thinking how this might hurt Az more than help her?

"Once we've got everything with the coven settled, I'll

start packing. We don't have time for it now," Az said, her voice louder than the panic going on inside Rus's head. At least for the moment. But how long could Rus focus on Az instead of her own frantic thoughts? Rus wasn't sure.

"Okay." Rus pressed a kiss to Az's throat. "How'd the meeting go?"

"I don't want to talk about it now. I just want to sleep," Az grumbled, snuggling in closer to Rus's chest, her leg thrown over Rus's hips. "Grab the blanket from the foot of the bed, I'm too tired to pull down the covers."

"Yeah. Just . . . don't tell Indie we slept under it naked." Rus chuckled, lifting a hand to curl her finger toward the crocheted blanket so it unfolded and came to rest over them.

Az snorted a laugh. "Shut up and go to sleep."

"Yes, ma'am." Rus pressed a kiss to Az's head and let herself drift.

She could worry about the implications of all . . . *this,* later.

# Chapter 7

Something was bothering Rus about this whole thing.

Just as she promised, Rus sat down with Az a few hours later, after showering and getting dressed, to work on the schedule of events for the centennial. She knew it was important—the order in which things happened. She hadn't been brought up to take over a clan the way that Az had, but Rus had been there for enough of those lessons—they'd been inseparable, best friends, for a time when they were children—to know that the order of things would affect the flow of energy to the lei lines. Too much energy all at once would overwhelm them, have them running over like a river during rainy season. Too little and a dam could form, stemming the flow to the Heart of Moondale.

That wasn't what was bothering her though.

It was the fact that Taryn had inserted herself into these discussions somehow. Rus had known Taryn was a power-hungry social climber from the moment Taryn and Violet were matched. It was obvious, although maybe not to anyone else. But Rus had been hungry all her life, looking for what scraps of affection and recognition she could get. She had an orphan's hunger. And she could see that same hunger in Taryn's eyes when no one else was looking.

Not that there was anything wrong with being hungry. It just made absolutely no sense when it came to Taryn.

Taryn wasn't an orphan. She had a mother and a father.

A coven. The Circle of the Silver Flame, Brant Ironwood's coven, in fact.

No. Her family wasn't as well known or respected as the founding families like the Elwoods and the Greers. Nor had they found a foothold in the community the way the Ironwoods had some years back.

But she'd never lacked affection or recognition. Taryn's parents were respected, liked even. And Taryn herself had friends. She was a healer by nature, and people loved her for that. Unlike Rus, whose innate ability was to talk to the dead, which always made people squeamish. There was no reason for that hunger in Taryn's eyes. For the way she seemed unable to quench that thirst no matter how many people came to her party or said happy birthday to her in the hall. Rus had lived her life on the fringes. Taryn hadn't. She hadn't been head cheerleader or anything, but she also hadn't been *alone* like Rus had been when she went back to the orphanage at night after classes.

So it wasn't the hunger itself but the way the hunger manifested, in Rus's mind. Taryn wasn't just seeking a place for herself—there was more to it than that. Rus didn't have proof, not yet. It was just a vague feeling she'd gotten from Taryn and her actions.

And then there was the question of why now? Why was Taryn inserting herself so heavily *now*? Carmine Elwood was in good health and had many years as the elder of Jade Waters ahead of her. Another thirty, at least, but given how long witches lived, perhaps another fifty or so. Yes, Az was out of the way, but that meant the seat should fall to the next Elwood in line. Indigo would be old enough by the time Carmine was ready to retire. Taryn didn't stand a chance.

So what was her end game?

Add to all that Nixie Virnan's warnings that Az had relayed and . . . well.

Rus was missing something. And if she'd learned anything from her travels, it was that when she was missing something, sometimes the spirits were the best people to ask.

"I'm gonna swing by the house next door, make sure we cleared it like we thought," Rus said, brushing a kiss to Az's temple. "You can hold down the fort here with the girls?"

Az looked up from the paperwork she was filling out. It was their criteria for a coven house so Nesta could find them a place that best aligned with their coven's goals and energies. Az pushed her glasses further up her nose, and her brown eyes flicked from Rus to look around the kitchen. The house was quiet. Meiling was out with her friends, Fernando was at Necromancer's, and Aihuan was napping with Lizzie—Az's familiar who had made a permanent home for herself in Rus's youngest daughter's room. The perfect time for Rus to slip out and host a séance without anyone trying to stick their nose into what she was after.

"I believe so," Az answered after a moment. "Is there something I can help you with?"

"No. I've got it. I just like to check at different times of the day to make sure everything is settled. It shouldn't take me long. Half an hour at most. I'll be back before Huaner is up for lunch." That wasn't technically a lie—she did like to vary the times when she checked a house. Midnight was best, 3 a.m. was decent, but during the day usually yielded nothing. Still, whoever would be moving into the house would be there all the time. She needed to know what could happen in the middle of the day just the same as she did the middle of the night.

Az frowned at her, brows creased, as if she could see

that Rus was holding something back. She likely could. Rus was always painfully transparent to Az. "What's going through your head right now?"

Rus sighed, her shoulders sagging. Hadn't she learned over the last few months that she shouldn't keep things from Az? Hadn't she learned that they were a team? Yes. She had. So she folded like a piece of talisman paper. "I just want to check in with the local spirits. Something about this whole thing"—she gestured to Az's stack of papers about the centennial—"feels off, slightly to the left, and I want to know what it is."

"Do you really think they'll have answers?"

"Maybe." Rus smiled ruefully, brushing her hair back from her face. "Only one way to find out."

"The first rule of necromancy: Spirits lie."

"Sometimes," Rus ceded. "It's a place to start."

Az nodded, tapping her pen against the table as she thought. "I'd like to do my own research as well. There ought to be something in the archives from the last centennial to tell us what to expect."

Rus's heart swelled in her chest, beating hard against her ribs. She hadn't expected Az to join her in her speculations, to see the cracks in Moondale the way that Rus did. And even if she had, Rus hadn't expected Az to support her so much in this. To actively want to help. But she supposed she should have. They were coven after all, weren't they? "That's a good idea. It might be nothing."

"It might be." Az hummed softly, bumping her head lightly against Rus's shoulder until Rus dipped down to press a soft kiss to her lips, a mere ember of the heat from the previous night spreading between them. When Az pulled back, she smiled gently at Rus. "But it's better we know beforehand."

"Agreed." How in the name of the Goddess had they gone from fighting as they had when Rus first returned, to this? *Magic.* She snorted to herself. "I'll be careful."

"Don't go through the veil."

"I won't have to." Rus smiled, pulling away to grab her bag and throw it over her shoulder. "We're right next to a cemetery, the spirits'll come to me."

"Of course. I'd like to set up a meeting with Hunter next week if we can."

"I'll have to look at my schedule."

Az nodded then tilted her head for a moment as if listening to something, her eyes closing a bit. "Take Darcy." Then she returned to her paperwork and let Rus leave without another word.

Darcy was waiting for her at the door, as if he'd answered Az's call. He squawked at Rus in annoyance right into her ear when he perched on her shoulder, and Rus laughed softly, scrubbing at her ear to try to rub away the tickling sensation left behind.

"Well, if you keep doing what she says then she's going to keep thinking she can boss you around." Rus shrugged.

Darcy gurgled, adjusting where he sat, digging his talons into Rus's shoulder harder as if in admonishment.

"Yes, I let her boss me around too. But there's a difference between you and me, old friend." Rus tilted her head to smirk at Darcy. "I like it."

He huffed, unamused, but didn't argue further. Not that there would be any point in it. If Darcy had allowed Az to use his magic once, then a link had formed. A bond. And he wouldn't be able to sever it. Still, it was a familiar's choice to let a witch connect with them that way. It couldn't be forced. There had to be consent. There was also no going back once it was done. Only death could cut the tie. So

Darcy was stuck with Az, just like he was with Rus. Which was honestly . . . kind of nice.

The door to 155 Mourning Moore didn't creak open the way that the one on her own home did. The lack of noise felt distinctly unwelcoming, as if the house itself couldn't be bothered to say hello. Rude.

Darcy did a little hop on her shoulder, adjusting himself so he was closer to her head.

"Yes," Rus agreed. "It does feel different in here during the day."

Which was strange. Houses in general, even the *un*haunted ones, usually gave off the feeling of being haunted only at night. During the day, they were meant to be quiet. But there was something about this one, something unsettled. They had missed something in their last sweep. Something the house was trying to keep hidden. Why?

"Maybe it's just lonely without its owners," Rus said, hoping that was the case. Because she was about to open a line of communication to the dead, an open call, and she didn't particularly want something screaming at her. Spending her Saturday afternoon nursing a migraine was not on her list of things she wanted from her day.

Darcy nipped at her ear in admonishment.

"Fuck off. We have shit to do. If you're going to be a chicken, I'll go back to the house and get Lizzie to help me." Lizzie wouldn't really be any help in this situation. She hadn't opened herself to Rus's magic the way that Darcy had to Az, but he didn't need to know that. It would only make him pissier, in all likelihood.

Darcy grumbled, the sound like when someone had something stuck in their throat that they couldn't get to move, and hopped down from her shoulder. He glided across the narrow foyer into a wide-open front room and perched on the hearth. Rus followed him and smiled.

"Yes, this will do nicely." She pulled the salt from her bag and created a small circle before setting sheets of printer paper at five points around it. Each had a different rune written on it: summoning, protection, communication, light, and something not quite translatable to human language that told the ghosts what she was looking for. She'd done this enough times over the years that she'd learned the language of spirits, the words that would pierce the veil and bring forth who she needed, as well as she had her own native language. Being bilingual in school had really helped. Once a person knew two languages, it was a hop, skip, and a jump to knowing three or four.

She settled into the middle of the circle, her legs crossed in a lotus pose, and hummed a soft tune she'd picked up on her travels. Something longing and lingering, a call. There were other methods of course, but she'd found this one was the quickest.

Time stood still. The light from outside went murky, like a cloud had passed over the sun, and a mist appeared before her. It drifted a moment before settling into the shape of a woman, a witch with long flowing hair and a white gown.

"Child of shadow," the witch said, tilting her head at Rus as if in curiosity. "You sent out a call for answers."

"I did." Rus lifted her chin to meet the witch's eyes. Her whole face was a blur. There were features: a nose, a mouth, two eyes. But they weren't distinct enough that Rus could have picked this woman out of a lineup. It would have been unsettling if Rus weren't used to the clear indication that the ghost hadn't breached the veil, not all the way anyway. She'd come because Rus called, but she refused to leave the relative safety of the After lest the person summoning her meant to capture or dissipate her. Which was fair. One could never be too careful when dealing with unknown entities. "I mean you no harm."

"So says the necromancer."

That was *also* fair, Rus supposed. Necromancers were well known to use spirits, binding them like slaves and powering their own magic using their energy. She knew for a fact that was more of a case of a few bad apples. Not that Rus would shy away from using a malevolent spirit that way, but it was rude for people to *assume*.

"Very well. We'll do things your way." Rus held up her hands in surrender. That meant the spirit likely wouldn't give their name either. There would be no way for Rus to be sure this witch wasn't lying. And there was a high likelihood that if Rus tried to call them again, the witch would simply not answer. Without a name, Rus couldn't force them to.

"What answers do you seek, Child of Shadow?"

*First of all, what is with the child of shadow bullshit?*

They'd have to come back to that. Rus had more important things to ask about. "You were around for one of the centennials in Moondale, right?"

Rus wasn't sure, but she thought the witch might have rolled their eyes. "Yes. Per your request."

"What happened during the celebration?"

"To what are you referencing?"

Rus huffed, shifting her posture on the floor where her back had begun to twinge. "It's only been a hundred years, but no one talks about what the centennial *does* exactly. I know it's when we charge the lei lines to keep the magic in flux for the next hundred years, but there seems to be . . . more? To it? Than that?"

The witch just stared at her.

"For instance," Rus said, licking her lips and adjusting her posture some more, "what would a witch have to gain by inserting themselves into the process?"

"You are asking the wrong questions."

When was she not? It felt like Rus was forever looking in the wrong direction while everything important went over her head. Fuck. "And what's the right question?"

"What *wouldn't* a witch have to gain from inserting themselves into the process? And why is *this* centennial different than all the others?" The witch's spirit flickered, the connection between Rus and the After fading. Weird. That had never happened before. Rus focused her energy, forced the pathway open further, and the witch's face came into view for a second. She looked a lot like Az. An Elwood.

"Okay," Rus said, ignoring the trickle of sweat cooling as it slid down her neck, and the way her head was beginning to spin. This should have been easier to do with Moondale's power at her back, but she was struggling to hold on to the line. As if the veil had grown thicker. It didn't make sense. "Then why *is* this centennial different than the others?"

The witch opened her mouth to answer, but the beginning of what might have been *they*, or *the*, or *though*, or any other word starting with a *th* sound was all she managed before she turned to look at something Rus couldn't see, something in the After. Her shoulders went rigid. The cloud moved from over the sun, the connection dropped, and Rus was left alone with Darcy in the living room.

"Fuck."

Darcy squawked at her.

"No. I don't have the energy to get her back right now. And she probably wouldn't answer the call anyway. Something clearly doesn't want me talking to her." Rus rubbed the sweat from her forehead with her sleeve and stood, shaking out her tingling limbs as she tried to keep herself from stumbling. "We'll just have to hope Az's research yields better results."

Her phone buzzed in her pocket, and she pulled it out to find Nesta's contact on the screen.

"Yeah, what's up?" Rus asked as she moved around the room, cleaning up her mess. The dizziness was fading at least. She could be grateful for that.

"How'd the cleansing go?" There was noise on the other end of the line, like Nesta was in their car and had put her on the Bluetooth connection to the sound system.

"It seemed fine last night, but I went by today and—" Rus stopped, listening to the house creak around her. There was something there. Not a ghost, maybe, but energy. Not left behind by the owners. Something older. "It feels unsettled to me. I don't think you can sell it like this."

"You had one job, Ashthorne," Greer growled from somewhere in the car.

"Yeah well, I'm still doing it, aren't I?" Rus sniped back. "You don't like how I do it, then *you* can fuck around in the spirit world and cleanse Nesta's houses, how about that?"

"All right, enough," Nesta said, cutting the bickering short. "I think you're just feeling the house, Rus. She doesn't like being left empty for long, it makes her anxious."

"The house?" Rus frowned, looking up at the ceiling fan in the front room. "We didn't sense any sentience last night."

"She's shy." Nesta sounded like they were smiling.

"Right. Well, I'll try back a couple times over the next few days, just to make sure it's all clear. In the meantime, you think you can convince that shithead boyfriend of yours to do me a favor?" Not that Rus wanted to beg a favor off Greer, but he was the sheriff.

"No," Greer said at the same time Nesta said, "Sure!"

"What can we do for you?" Nesta asked, ignoring the grumping coming from their boyfriend.

"I want a record of everyone buried in the cemetery on Mourning Moore." Rus moved through the house so she could look out one of the back windows at the view of the graves there. They were farther away than from her own house, the yard larger. And this house wasn't surrounded on two sides the way hers was. But it was still close enough that whatever spirit she spoke to was probably buried there, not somewhere else. "I need to know if there are any Elwoods there."

"Elwoods?" Nesta sounded confused, likely because they were thinking the same thing Rus was. The Elwoods had their own grounds where they laid their dead to rest. There was no reason an Elwood would be buried on Mourning Moore, unless she'd been set adrift by the coven. It was doubly strange because Rus knew for a fact Elwoods tended to reincarnate, not settle in the After. So something had stopped this one from doing that. Maybe because the Elwood family burial rights hadn't been performed on her? If she were cut from the coven, that would make sense . . .

"I'll see what I can find," Greer said.

"Super," Rus muttered, and hung up without another word.

# Chapter 8

By the time Rus returned from the house next door, Azure had finished what she was working on, and Aihuan had woken from her nap. Lunch was a hurried affair as both Azure and Rus planned to put the new knowledge they acquired to good use, and not waste the day devoid of classes and work. Their meal cleared away, Rus turned her attention toward thoughts of what she'd teach at the university when she agreed to do it—not *if*, there was no question of if in Azure's mind, it was merely a matter of when—while Aihuan settled in to color at the kitchen table.

"I'll be back for dinner," Azure promised, putting the last plate from lunch on the drying rack and crossing the kitchen to stand behind Rus. She leaned over Rus's shoulders, her weight pressing into Rus so she could peek at the messy scrawl of Rus's notebook. Something was taking shape there. "Remember, the introductory lecture should be pretty basic." She tapped one neatly manicured nail against the top of Rus's outline. "Maybe start with your protective cell phone case. Indigo found that very interesting."

"Right, and since most of them will be kids, they'll be attached to their phones anyway."

"In theory." Azure hummed her approval and pressed a kiss to the top of Rus's head. It was good to be close to her like this. Good to be comfortable around one another, finally. There was a settledness to Rus today that Azure hadn't been sure she'd ever get to experience. Like maybe Rus was starting to see Moondale as home. It sang through Azure's veins, a melody she didn't want to end. "But also, it's just universal. Everyone has a cell phone these days."

"Not everyone uses social media," Rus pointed out, but she wrote down what Azure said all the same.

"True, but even those who don't pack their phones full of life. Pictures, and videos, and notes, and voicemails. Memories. Connections." She'd heard Rus say the same thing enough times since Rus returned home. It was why she'd finally let Rus bully her into beta testing one of the protective cases. A lighter one than Rus's own. Probably because Rus used her own phone to run tests on things like the Ghost Tracer. Things that could be dangerous if the code got into the wrong hands. And also probably so any spirit who possessed her couldn't use it without her knowledge, which might have been why she kept going through phones. *Clever.* "I plan to ask Aunt Carmine about this Elwood you spoke to while I'm there. Maybe she has some knowledge of what happened."

"Maybe." Rus leaned back into Azure, stretching her back out and sighing as she tilted her head to look at Azure finally. Her brow was creased, unease residing there. A storm was brewing and they both knew it. Azure's potential ancestor had only confirmed their suspicions. A mercy, because otherwise they'd struggle to explain how they knew. And magic folk never seemed to take kindly to the assertion that something was simply gut instinct. Not the way normies tended to, at least. "Do you think Carmine will let you borrow the key to the Jade Waters archive?"

"Yes." That was a lie, Azure didn't actually know that she would. The archive was no longer Azure's birthright. She had given it up along with everything else she'd forfeited by leaving Jade Waters. A decision she didn't regret, as it had given her this—a home with Rus, happiness. But it came with its drawbacks, as all things did. "I'll text you if I'm going to run late."

She stole another kiss and waved to Aihuan before stepping out onto the street of Mourning Moore. This close to the border of Moondale, the street was never overly busy, and Azure was on the front step of her aunts' in short order. She hesitated for a moment, unsure if she should knock or just walk in. Technically, she still lived there. But so many of her things were gone these days that her room was almost barren. It was strange to return to the house where she'd grown up after her decision last night to move in with Rus. Like closing a door on a room still full of friends.

In the end, the house made the decision for her. The front door opened on silent hinges and urged her over the threshold.

"Aunt Carmine," Azure called, hoping someone was home. "Aunt Maureen."

"In here, dear," Aunt Maureen answered from the kitchen at the back of the house where Azure found her and Aunt Carmine sitting at the table, each nursing a cup of tea.

"Am I interrupting something?" They both looked tired. Dark circles ringing their eyes, their shoulders slumped. "Has something happened?"

"Nothing, dear," Aunt Maureen said, a forced smile that didn't reach her eyes plastered on her face. A cut-and-paste from happier, easier times. "Would you like some tea?"

"No thank you." Azure shook her head. "I just came to check in and see how Aunt Carmine was feeling."

Aunt Maureen's eyes flitted to Aunt Carmine's, a question in their depths, but Carmine shook her head.

"Come back to my office," Aunt Carmine said and rose slowly from her chair. "I think you maybe came for a bit more than that."

Guilt made Azure lift her chin and straighten her spine; she refused to be cowed by it. She *had* come for more than that, but her original purpose was to see how Aunt Carmine faired. And this deflection was answer enough. She wasn't well. The question was, how unwell *was* she?

The office door shut behind them as they both settled into chairs on opposite sides of Aunt Carmine's mahogany desk.

"What can I help you with, Azure?" Aunt Carmine asked.

She suddenly looked so small in her overstuffed office chair. Weary and fragile. Azure didn't think she'd ever seen her aunt look that way before. Aunt Carmine had always seemed larger than life. The kind of witch who would stretch the bounds of even a witch's extended lifetime. Powerful. She didn't look that way now. Azure was going to have to corner Aunt Maureen or Indigo to get some answers about this. She knew damn well Aunt Carmine wasn't likely to tell her the whole of it. Never wanting anyone to worry, least of all her children.

"I'd like access to the Jade Waters archives." Azure crossed one leg over the other, resisting the urge to shrink before her aunt as had been her habit growing up. They were equals now, almost, as strange as that felt. Azure was going to be an elder one day soon. "Rus has been in contact with a spirit that she believes is an Elwood who may have been buried in the cemetery across the way."

"And why has she been in contact with an excommunicated Elwood?" Aunt Carmine's eyes narrowed. She didn't deny the fact that such a thing had happened, or that one of the Jade Waters witches was buried in the graveyard right across the street when that shouldn't have been possible, especially for an Elwood. Which made Azure more suspicious. Why was this never spoken of? Not even as a cautionary tale. If anyone would have heard of an Elwood who was excommunicated, it would have been Azure, who many had tried to scare out of loving Rus.

"She was doing some research for me about the centennial." It wasn't a lie, not really. But Azure didn't think it prudent to tell her aunt that she and Rus thought Taryn was up to something and they needed to know why so they could get out ahead of her. It wasn't that she didn't trust her family, but Azure still didn't know why Aunt Carmine had brought Taryn in as her protégé. It didn't fit. And something about that not-fitting stilled the words to explain further on her tongue.

"Only members of Jade Waters are meant to have access to the archives and the coven house." Even still, Aunt Carmine reached into her desk to pull out a ring of keys. "If any of the rest of the coven finds out I've given you this, there will be an uproar."

*That goes without saying.* Not only because she was no longer a member of the coven, but because of how she'd left. Leaving to start her own coven with a witch who many in Moondale considered to be immoral and up to her neck in dark magic had made Azure plenty of enemies. She'd have to go to the coven house late at night and hope no one drove by. Not that anyone should be driving up into the mountains past what most in Moondale would consider bedtime. Maybe she should have Greer drive his patrol car by just in case. But then she'd have to involve him further in this, and they'd done enough of that in the last few months. This wasn't his problem. It was hers and Rus's.

Azure took the keys and tucked them into her pocket. She took a breath, the words on her tongue to press the issue of Aunt Carmine's health, but the expression on her aunt's face stopped them in her throat, and instead she said, "I'll return these in the morning."

"Keep them." Aunt Carmine shook her head. "I don't know how long your research will take, and they were your keys anyway."

It was a serious breach of coven protocol, but Azure wasn't going to look blessed familiar in the mouth. And she recognized this for the show of trust that it was from her aunt, so she ducked her head in deference before she rose.

"Say goodbye to your Aunt Maureen on your way out," Aunt Carmine called. "And shut the door. I have some paperwork I need to do too."

"Thank you," Azure said, knowing it didn't need to be said really, but doing so anyway just before she shut the door. As she spun to head back toward the kitchen, she found Aunt Maureen waiting for her. With a finger held to her lips, Aunt Maureen led Azure down the hall to the mud room at the back of the house and out into the greenhouse in the yard.

Once safely ensconced in the humid, perfumed air, Aunt Maureen seemed to slump further in on herself. She dropped into the rattan egg chair half hidden behind a huge monstera plant and let out a choked-off sob.

"It's bad, isn't it?" Azure asked.

"We're not sure," Aunt Maureen admitted, bracing herself on her elbows and rubbing her face with her hands. "The doctors can't find any cause for her exhaustion. They think it's hormone related, but they've check them all, and her levels are normal. And every day she gets a little more tired, a little weaker. The only thing that seems to help is

Taryn, who's been coming by every few days to try to heal her."

Well, that answered one question. Aunt Carmine felt indebted to Taryn for her help with her health issues, and thus had decided to bring her to the meetings for the Board of Magic. It was foolish, but Azure could see how it had happened. Maybe if she were home more—

"Whatever you're thinking, put that to bed right now," Aunt Maureen said. She'd lifted herself to shake a finger at Azure in reprimand. "This is not on you, Azure. You're allowed to move on with your life. You're allowed to be happy. It's what we both want for you."

"Does Taryn have some idea of what's happening? I know she's not a doctor, but she should have some knowledge from her abilities."

"She thinks it might be stress related. The upcoming centennial is putting a lot of strain on all the elders. As the lei lines become weaker and weaker, so do the elders tied to them. But even that's not certain, it's just a guess." Aunt Maureen leaned back in the chair, letting herself hunch to fit the curved back. She, too, looked very small. When had the mighty women who raised Azure become so frail? And how could she get them back to their former glory?

"Would it help if someone else took her place? At least for the interim?"

"Perhaps, but it has to be an Elwood. Otherwise, it could completely futz up the magic of the centennial."

"Indigo maybe?"

"An Elwood by blood," Aunt Maureen corrected.

Well, fuck.

"I'll speak with Violet." That conversation was going to go absolutely *swimmingly*. But Azure would suck it up and do what she had to if it meant helping her aunts and keeping Aunt Carmine from becoming more ill.

Before she'd even made it to the door of her aunts' house, Azure fired off a text to the group thread that had lain dormant for the last couple of months while Violet and Azure refused to speak to one another.

> Sibling Bonding Night Sunday evening 7 p.m.

It was a white flag of surrender, but Azure was willing to make the sacrifice. One of them had to.

The little dots that meant Violet was typing appeared, disappeared, appeared, disappeared.

**INDIGO**

> Only if Fernando is cooking

The dots appeared and disappeared again. Violet thinking over her answer. Likely typing something, then erasing it, then typing again. Azure held her breath, hardly even looking as she crossed the street.

**VIOLET**

> I'll host.

Azure let out a long, relieved breath. She didn't love the idea of doing it on Violet's home turf, but if that's what Violet needed to feel comfortable, let her have it.

> I'll bring wine.

**INDIGO**

> So that's a no on Nando's cooking then?

**VIOLET**

> I'll make pasta

INDIGO

I don't appreciate being ignored!

Fernando will not be cooking, let it go Indigo.

INDIGO

Fine

VIOLET

See you then.

Azure leaned forward to press her head into the trim around the door to 157 Mourning Moore. Good. This was good. She could make up with Violet and hopefully convince her to take the elder seat in the interim so that Aunt Carmine would have a chance to recover. She could do this. She could. She just wasn't quite sure how, yet.

Aside from begging.

# Chapter 9

The Jade Waters archives were stored in the basement of the Jade Waters coven house. Which was a dusty tomb compared to the warm kitchen where Rus and Azure had been working through Rus's notes on what she'd like to teach—even though she kept asserting that she hadn't decided to take the post. Thankfully, it was just a guest lecture, which meant Rus didn't have to have any actual assignments ready on such short notice. But if she were to take up a teaching position at the university more permanently, she had a good jumping-off point. Or Azure thought so anyway. Not that they'd discussed that, but it seemed the next logical step. And Azure certainly wasn't going to dissuade her.

Azure shook herself. Now was not the time to get ahead of herself and entertain idle daydreams about the soft domesticity of working side by side with Rus at the university. It was a lovely thought, beautiful in its simplicity, but their lives were much more complicated than that right now. Maybe one day . . .

She bit back a curse as Lizzie jumped from where she'd been hiding in the back seat to dig her claws into Azure's legs, her fluffy white tail twitching in disdainful amusement. Bitch.

"Please," Azure said, pained, "for the love of all that is good in this world, explain to me why the fuck you decided to come along?" She didn't even know how the fuck Lizzie had gotten *into* the car in the first place. It was probably better not to ask.

Lizzie chirped from her lap, looking up at Azure with wide blue eyes, innocent as the day is long. Which was such an utter crock of shit, and they both knew it.

"Right. Mice." Azure rolled her eyes and reached for the door again. "Just stay out of the way, and don't let me leave you behind." She didn't give Lizzie the chance to argue as she grabbed her bag from the passenger seat and walked the familiar path to Jade Waters coven house.

It was huge. A mansion more than a house. Painted a pale blue color a few years back when it'd needed a fresh coat. All sweeping eaves and big windows. The kind of home one might expect to see a Vanderbilt gliding down the stairs of. And now, it was a place where Azure didn't belong.

She felt it the moment she put the key in the lock: resistance. A reminder that she'd given this up. That she'd walked away from the power and prestige of Jade Waters. Of Elwood.

*And for what?* she could practically hear her ancestors asking. *For a crow witch and a homeless coven?*

Lizzie pressed her body into Azure's shins firmly enough to shake Azure loose from whatever spell the house had been trying to cast on her to keep her out. When she looked down at her familiar, Lizzie was looking back, big blue eyes wide with knowing.

"Thank you," Azure murmured and pressed into the house, which put up no further resistance.

At least not until she'd turned right at the dual staircases and reached the door that led down into the dank basement. By then, Lizzie had abandoned her to chase the aforementioned mice, and it was just Azure and the spirits of Elwood familiars long passed—the minders.

They trotted along the beam above the door, their tails twitching, eyes narrowed on her in distaste. They said without words, *You do not belong. You are not of this place. Go home, little witch, before we make a meal of you.* All while bearing their feline teeth.

There wasn't any point in arguing with them. They were right after all, she didn't belong here anymore. But that didn't mean she was going to turn tail and run either. Instead, she straightened her spine, closed her eyes, and tried to remember the tune Rus used a couple weeks back to deal with the boggart that had been hanging around the storeroom of Necromancer's. It came to her slowly, and in parts.

The minders hissed, claws swiping out. Blood trickled down her cheek where one of the blows landed. But she kept trying, piecing the melody together until she hummed it, soft and lilting, pressing magic into it that would lull the minders into slowness, stillness. It had completely incapacitated the boggart, freezing it into place so that Rus could bind it, at least until she could calm it down and talk to it. It made the minders drowsy. Their lids growing heavy. Mouths opening to show off pointed teeth as they yawned. And then, all at once it seemed, they decided she wasn't worth the bother and they'd much rather take a nap.

With a deep breath that burned a little from all the magic she'd had to infuse in the music, Azure pulled open the door to the basement and started down toward the archives.

AZURE FROWNED, scrubbing at her nose when it itched from the dust of the book she was poring over, and pulled her phone from her pocket.



She could have. She wanted to. Being apart from Rus when things seemed so uncertain was like missing a part of herself. But Aunt Carmine was already pushing their luck in allowing Azure to be there. If they brought Rus into the equation, there was no doubt it'd get back to the coven and someone would use it as a steppingstone to prove the Elwoods were all tainted. They couldn't afford that. Not so close to the centennial. Not to mention there was the issue of how Azure had gotten past the minders using a bit of necromancy . . .

So Azure was bundled up in one of Rus's softest hoodies, the hood pulled up to cover her head and shade her eyes from the harsh overhead lights of the archive while Rus was at home doing her side of things. Her side of things being going over the list of requirements for a coven house that Azure had written up to hand over to Nesta. She was sure she'd missed something vital to Rus and Meiling's magic, but that was for Rus to add.



Azure hadn't. They'd been nineteen and hiding from

Aunt Maureen, who had been trying to force them to act as waitstaff for some convention or another being held at the coven house. Honestly, Azure couldn't remember the details of the event. What she did remember was nearly burning one of the shelves to the ground when she slammed Rus against it and got on her knees. Hormones, magic, and centuries-old texts did not mix.

How could I forget that. (^_~)

Get back to work, and let me focus.

Fiiiiine. (๏﹏๏✿)

Azure laughed softly, shaking her head as she tucked her phone back into her pocket and returned to the book in her other hand.

The coven list burned her fingertips, threatening to set her ablaze. It knew she didn't belong there, just like everything else in this house. It knew she'd stricken her name from its records, and it wasn't happy about that. Funny how Moondale had been happy enough to make the switch without a single hesitation, but Jade Waters seemed unable to let her go.

Months after casting herself adrift from her birthright, the magic of Jade Waters still called to her, begging her to return. It was the Elwood blood, she knew that. No other Elwood had ever left Jade Waters willingly. Actually, as far as she'd known until this morning, no other Elwood had ever left Jade Waters *period*.

But as her fingers traced page after page of Elwoods—Forest and Clover, Lavender and Lilac, Marigold and Amber—they settled on one other name that had been stricken from the record. One other witch who'd allowed their name to be burned away. Only where her own name had a single strike through it so it was still legible underneath, this name had been scrubbed through so thoroughly that it tore the page in places. Anger.

"What did you do to deserve this?" Azure wondered, running her finger along the name. She couldn't read it through the furious markings. The Elwoods' tradition of naming each generation from a different color family went back much further than Azure had realized. The names around it were in the blue family, so it stood to reason that this witch's name had been a blue name as well. And because it was in the first few pages, this witch had been one of the earliest Elwoods in Moondale. Maybe even a part of the original Circle of Jade Waters.

"But were these your siblings, or your cousins?" Azure wondered, running her fingers over the names Cobalt and Hyacinth Elwood. There was no real way to tell, as the list was not made to show one witch's connection to another, but to the coven as a whole. Still, someone had scribbled years beside the names. Hyacinth, the name just above and obviously the elder of the three, had signed their name to Jade Waters in 1518, over a hundred years before the first human settlers had come to Maryland. Cobalt, the name below, had signed in 1525.

That at least meant she likely needed to look in the records from the 1520s, but Goddess, what she wouldn't give for some indication of the relationship between the three. If they were siblings, and close, Azure couldn't see Cobalt joining Jade Waters after their sibling's name had been burned so violently from the records. That would give her a better grasp on time frame since the following names were clearly from the next generation—yellow names. Buttercup and Marigold Elwood didn't sign their names until 1539 and 1542 respectively. The children of Hyacinth probably.

Fourteen years, maybe, if Azure's guess was right.

Azure rubbed at the space between her eyebrows where an ache had developed. She'd been squinting. Shit.

"All right, fourteen years. Let's start there." Azure rose from her chair, arching her back in a stretch, and moved to the shelves to begin pulling books.

AN HOUR later found sweat trickling down her neck, her chest heaving at the effort it took to hold her breath and move through time. The magic strain was setting in fast. And she was starting to feel lightheaded. She hadn't used her ability to walk through time and see the present so often in such a short spurt for many years. Likely not since she'd been a teenager and was using it to sneak out of the house with Rus. But she had ten pages of notes to show for it, and she'd been through all of her original stack.

So. Progress!

All the records of that witch had been scrubbed away, just like the coven list. Her name burned on every page to the point that it was unreadable. Even her birth records. But it had given Azure something. Cobalt, Hyacinth, and this witch had been siblings. Close enough in age that they should have shared a bond similar to the one Azure shared with her own siblings.

She'd just reached the last page from the year 1521, and that's where she found it.

*It* was a vague mention of the witch in question, not even naming her, but Azure knew it was her because she was denoted as the middle of the Elwood children. "A prophecy. Of course there's a prophecy. There's *always* a prophecy."

Prophecies, by nature, were rare. They'd been more prevalent five hundred years ago, when every parent wanted to ensure their child would be special and powerful, but they'd fallen out of favor over the years as more and more witches believed in forging their own destiny and finding their own path. Making them even *more* rare these days. Perhaps one in a hundred witches had a prophecy given at their birth, if that. Azure and her siblings certainly hadn't had any.

The chair creaked under Azure as she rose to head for the section of the archives where records of prophecy were stored.

"OKAY, but what the fuck does it mean by 'our heart will be open'?" Rus asked, her tone annoyed as she scrubbed at her nose where she was hunched over, her elbows digging into the kitchen table. The annoyance was entirely fair. Azure hated prophecies just as much as Rus. They were always so fucking vague, and never entirely accurate *because* of their vagueness. This one, especially, made very little sense. It was linked directly to the unnamed Elwood. Given on the day of her birth, all while not mentioning her at all. It was strange.

Azure squinted down at it on the kitchen table. Her vision was starting to blur from reading for so long, and from the dust and the late hour. She was going to be worthless tomorrow, but if they figured out what this stupid prophecy was referencing, then it wouldn't matter.

*And on the eve of the 500th year our heart will be open, and while the shadows of our past walk amongst us, all who are closest to our heart and seek its strength may receive it.*

As far as prophecies went, it was short. Most tended to be more than a single sentence. And this one seemed far too important to be so . . . *vague.* Goddess, Azure wished she'd paid more attention when she'd taken that class on deciphering prophecies. She'd been proficient enough in it to get an A, but that was mostly bullshitting her way through it since deciphering prophecies was similar to deciphering poetry. So much of it was up to the interpretation of the reader, or at least it seemed that way.

"I don't know." Fuck, did Azure hate admitting that. Not knowing something made her jaw clench, her teeth grind. Especially something *this* fucking important.

"Shame none of us specialized in prophecy interpretation, huh?" Rus laughed lightly, bumping her shoulder against Azure's. She was trying to make light of the situation, trying to soothe Azure's frazzled nerves. Azure would appreciate it if she didn't feel like the centennial was looming over them in a distinctly threatening manner now. Add this vague-as-fuck prophecy to the list of shit that could go wrong in a few months during the centennial celebration, and the pressure Rus and Azure were under to find more coven members, and they had the perfect storm.

"Why bother when hardly anyone—" Azure stopped herself, her eyes lifting from the words on the page to meet Rus's gaze, a thought striking her. "We don't know anyone who specialized in prophecy interpretation, but we do know someone who did their dissertation in ancient lyrical spells."

Ancient lyrical spells was another area of study that

seemed largely useless, but held some clout. Far more than Azure's current work in original spellwork and talismans. Everyone respected the classics and didn't see any reason to improve upon them. Which was why Azure had received so much pushback when she'd originally wanted to pursue an advanced degree, and specialization, in that field. No one wanted a *modern* Ink Witch. But an *antiquarian* Ink Witch? Well . . . she could be the dean of a prestigious university, even if her skills *weren't* practical.

"We do?" Rus frowned, her nose scrunching as she clearly thought through all their friends.

"Vanessa Cochburn." Azure smiled a little.

Rus groaned, throwing her head back, the chair creaking under her weight. "I haven't accepted her offer yet."

"No time like the present." It would get them one step closer to Azure's idle daydream of tweed and ink-stained fingers too, but that wasn't really the thing to focus on now. "You already have your first couple of lectures planned, don't you?"

"That's just notes. I'd have to actually *write* it. I can't lecture off the cuff."

"Of course not." Azure couldn't hide the laugh in her voice, which Rus didn't miss because she lifted her head to glare at Azure.

"Stop it."

"Stop what?"

"Being so fucking pleased with yourself. You're like a cat licking its paws after killing a bird." Rus huffed, but a smile twitched at her lips. "You know damn well I hadn't actually decided I was going to do it yet. I was just trying to figure out if I even *could*."

"The only way to find out is to try, I find."

"You're impossible, do you know that?" Rus chuckled, flopping sideways so her head could rest on Azure's shoulder where she glared up at Azure through narrowed gray eyes. "Absolutely impossible. Couldn't *you* just ask her?"

"I could, but she's going to ask about you again. And she'd be more likely to help us if we had something to give her in exchange." That wasn't entirely true. Vanessa Cochburn seemed the type willing to help them for no other reason than she'd be interested in looking at the prophecy herself. But if this was the push Rus needed to do something she clearly had a passion for, then Azure was going to give her that push. Ah, the things Azure did for the woman she loved. "Think of it as quid pro quo."

"We're already doing that." Rus huffed. "She's getting me to lecture, and I'm getting access to witches who haven't yet signed themselves over to a coven. Why should she give us anything else?"

"Icarus," Azure murmured, pressing a kiss to Rus's forehead and nudging her gently so she sat up. She reached up, taking a hold of Rus's chin, tender and soft. "The worst thing she can do is refuse to look at it. Plus, wouldn't it be good to have a healthy working relationship with your boss?"

"I wouldn't know. I haven't had a boss since . . ." Rus hummed in thought, then smirked. "Ever."

Azure rolled her eyes. "I have class on Tuesday. Come onto campus with me and talk to Vanessa. At the very least, it'll give you a feel for if you even want to work with her, or be on campus. Plus, you can swing by and see Hunter. I know you've already met him, but I really think he has potential for the coven. And then we don't have to set up an official meet time that works around all our schedules."

"Fine. Fine," Rus grumbled, bumping her forehead against Azure's. "I hate it when you're reasonable."

"That sounds like a you problem."

Rus laughed, long and loud. Likely enough to wake the whole house if it weren't for 157 muffling the sound, providing them with their own bubble of safety, of warmth. It was good to be home after everything Azure had learned. Good to be safely ensconced in 157's welcoming embrace.

# Chapter 10

"So because *you* left the coven, it is now *my* job to clear up your mess?" Violet asked, her wine glass lifted halfway to her lips. There was a casual air to the way she held it that was definitely forced. The paleness of her pursed lips beneath her lipstick and the way the wine sloshed in her glass from a shaking hand were clear signs that she was barely restraining her fury. Which wasn't fair, in Azure's opinion. She had done nothing wrong by leaving the coven to be with the person she loved. It had happened before. People did it all the time.

*But not Elwoods*, a nasty, traitorous voice in her head said. It sounded like Violet. It wasn't wrong, unfortunately. She'd seen the proof of that during her research. Elwoods did not leave Jade Waters. Others left their clans and covens and married into the Jade Waters coven, but not the other way around. Their lineage, which spanned back to before the founding of Moondale, and their heavy ties to the land ensured that was always the best option. It hadn't been where Rus was concerned though. Not that Violet would understand that.

"That is not what I'm saying," Azure said. It was a struggle to keep her voice level, to keep from shouting. All she wanted to do was scream. Scream. And scream. And rail against the rock and the hard place she'd been shoved into. She'd been given no good options when it came to Rus and the Coven of the Forgotten. It was leave Jade Waters or watch Rus's fledgling coven flounder and fail. Watch Rus slip away again. That was not an option. Never was. Even if Violet seemed to think so.

"Then what *are* you saying, Azure?"

In truth, Azure wasn't really sure. She hadn't genuinely expected to lay this problem at Violet's feet and for Violet to jump on the idea that she could be interim elder, thereby giving Aunt Carmine the rest she desperately needed. All the complications that prevented Violet from taking the seat before were still there—that hadn't changed. So what had she expected Violet to do about it? Really? Other than get angry. Nothing, she supposed. But there had been a time in their lives where Violet fixed things for Azure. Where Azure went to her with a problem, and Violet found a solution.

Long ago, she realized. That had been so long ago. Before Rus. Before they lost their parents. She just hadn't noticed, somehow.

"It's temporary," Azure tried to reason, swallowing her pride. She would beg, if she had to. She hoped it wouldn't come to that.

"Couldn't I do it?" Indigo shifted uncomfortably. Guilt crawled into Azure's stomach, making it roil. She hadn't meant to bring him here just to have him sit between her and Violet while they sniped at each other. That wasn't fair to him. And yet, here they were.

"It has to be someone of the same bloodline as Aunt Carmine, otherwise she'd have to cede the seat." Azure shook her head. She'd thought about that. He was young, yes, but it would only be for a couple of months. And he was strong enough that the pull of magic wouldn't be terribly taxing on him. But the rule of blood applied in this instance.

"What about Sunila?" Indigo was trying, Goddess bless him. At least *one* of her siblings was.

"It has to be someone who was born here." Violet didn't even look at Indigo as she answered. She kept her narrowed gaze fixed on Azure.

The number of restrictions on this was ridiculous. Azure didn't understand it, because usually magic didn't give one flying fuck about bloodlines. Moondale usually did whatever she wanted to with her magic, regardless of blood. Tied families together. Let them share power. Bound people who loved each other so they would never have to be without one another, sharing a life in more ways than one. But this? In this, blood mattered. It just didn't make sense. She'd have to do some investigating about that once she had dealt with this particular hurdle. Although she doubted there was anything about it in the Jade Waters archives. Why would there be? An Elwood of the bloodline had always sat in the elder seat.

"Oh." Indigo deflated. "That sucks."

"Well, maybe our sister should have thought about that before she ran off with *Ashthorne*."

Scratch that. Azure *wasn't* going to fucking beg. Not when Violet said Rus's name that way. She wouldn't debase herself for someone who clearly didn't care to see this issue from another side. And why should Violet see it from Azure's perspective? She'd always done exactly what she was told. She'd toed the line like a good little Elwood. The only thing she hadn't done was agree to take the elder seat. And that was because it had always been understood on some level that it would be Azure who succeeded their aunt. Not that Azure knew why. It just was. Maybe because

Violet had become a doctor, done something *useful* with herself.

"What's done is done," Azure said, her tone hard. "So are you going to sit there and watch as the strain of this whole thing makes Aunt Carmine sick just to spite me?"

"Yes, because this is all about *you*, isn't it, Azure?" Violet snarled, baring her teeth. The wine in her glass sloshed as she flapped her wrist at Azure. The sleeve of her shirt slipped farther up her arm, and Azure thought she caught a patch of miscolored skin in the shape of a hand before Violet hastily pulled it back down. Continuing her tirade without so much as a breath. "It has nothing at all to do with the fact that I'm running a medical practice. That I have patients who count on me. That I have a home to take care of. A wife to keep happy—who, by the way, let you come here, and now here you are upsetting me. Whereas you had no obligations outside of running the shop. You could have easily avoided this if only you hadn't been so *selfish*."

There was that word again. Selfish. It didn't have quite the sting to it that it might have had a few months ago before Azure had grown to understand herself better. Before she'd realized that sometimes being selfish was exactly what she needed to be. Rus had shown her that, inadvertently.

Azure took a deep breath and rose from her chair. "Very well," she said, forcing herself not to shout. It wouldn't do any good. And it was exactly what Violet wanted. She wanted to see that she had upset Azure, that she had affected her sister in some way. Azure wasn't going to give her that. She could love her sister, but that didn't mean she had to feed into her toxic tendencies. "If you won't help, then I shall just have to find another way."

Violet wouldn't meet her eyes. Instead, she was staring

at her barely touched plate. She'd had three glasses of wine on a mostly empty stomach, likely gearing herself for the fight that was coming between her and Azure. Azure had to wonder how much of that vitriol had more to do with the wine than how Violet actually felt. They were both in the wrong here to some degree, yes. Even still, that didn't mean she had to sit there and take it. She'd learned *that* from Rus too.

"Thank you for dinner." Azure dipped her head politely and turned on her heel. She gathered her things and was just opening her car door when she heard footsteps behind her.

"Az. Wait up!" Indigo called. He bent at the waist, gripping his knees when he caught up to her, his breath coming in hard pants. It would be comical, would make Azure snort and give him a hard time about regular cardio, but she wasn't in the mood for that right then. "Goddess, when did you learn to speed walk like that?"

"I've always walked that quickly." Azure rolled her eyes. She glanced over Indigo's shoulder to make sure Violet wasn't nearby listening. This was good, she needed to ask Indigo for a favor anyway. "Why don't I drive you home?"

"I—" He stopped, chewing on his bottom lip, and looked over his shoulder at the house. Azure hated herself a bit for the way he'd been forced to choose sides between her and Violet. That shouldn't have happened. It had never been her intention. She'd have to make a better effort to ensure he didn't feel like he had to side with her against Violet. It wasn't fair to ask that of him.

"If you want to go in and say goodbye first, or finish your dinner, I can wait," Azure offered.

"You really don't mind?"

"I have some books in the car. I can work on my

research." It wasn't ideal, but if this was what Azure had to do to make Indigo feel like he didn't have to choose between his sisters, then it was what she would do.

"I know Vi says you're selfish"—Indigo leaned in, the words whisper-soft like a secret—"but you're really the best of us, Az."

Azure released a surprised little laugh and shook her head. "That's nonsense." And they both knew it. If anyone was the best of them, it was Indigo. He was good, and kind, and all he'd ever wanted was for the people around him to be happy. It showed in everything he made. "Enjoy your dinner."

Indigo spun on his heel, gave a halfhearted wave over his shoulder, and headed back to the house.

IT WAS another hour and a half before Indigo and Azure were in the car on the way back to Mourning Moore, but as Azure promised, she waited for him to finish his meal with their sister and busied herself with research.

"I think she blames herself," Indigo said out of nowhere when they'd stopped at the intersection between Mourning Moore and Grimwood Lane.

Azure made a soft noise of confusion.

"For you leaving."

"My leaving has nothing to do with anyone but myself," Azure said. She refused to look away from the road. Indigo's eyes bore into the side of her face, searching, knowing. Like he thought he might find something there that would make this whole thing right again. He wouldn't. "You know that."

"I do."

"I need you to look at something for me, if you don't mind." Azure hoped the change in subject would keep him from poking around at the areas where she was still aching from her fight with Violet. Just because she wasn't going to let Violet dictate her life anymore didn't change the fact that it hurt to be fighting with her sister the way she was. It was hard cutting a person from one's life for one's own good.

"Anything." Because Indigo was a good brother. The best brother. Willing to do whatever he could to help his siblings, to make them happy and safe. Goddess, they didn't deserve him. And he certainly didn't get that selflessness from the Elwood influence. He must have inherited it from his Beecher relations.

She parked out front of 157 Mourning Moore, her gaze flicking to the front windows. The lights were on inside, some animated movie playing on the television in the living room. It looked like home. But where a few weeks ago Azure felt like she was on the outside of it looking in, now it felt like she was simply returning. Like she'd be welcomed in as soon as the door opened. She'd gotten lucky. She was privileged. She recognized that. And she was going to fight with everything she had to fucking *keep* it.

"I found one other Elwood who was stricken from the Jade Waters records. But it seems as if she left on . . . less than favorable terms. I need to know her name." She needed to know more than her name, but a name would be a start to unraveling the mystery of what had happened five hundred years ago.

"And how do you expect me to find that out?" Indigo brushed a hand through his hair, pushing it from his eyes. He didn't sound skeptical or even annoyed by the request, just curious.

"I borrowed one of the books her name was stricken

from. I thought perhaps you could use your ability and see the history of it. Maybe you'd be able to see the name that way." Generally speaking, Indigo's talent lay in understanding the makeup of something. It was what made him such a gifted craftsman, what would make him a wonderful Stitch Witch when he finally settled on that path, which was inevitable. But he had the ability to view the past of an object as well. Everything or everywhere it had been before coming to his hands. It took more concentration and magic to do it, but Azure had faith that he was at a place in his training that if the name was to be found, he would find it.

She twisted in her seat and reached into the back, pulling the book from her bag. "Do you think you can do that?"

"I can try." Indigo took the book with careful fingers, as if afraid it might burn him. Which, Azure supposed, was fair. What she was asking of him would be taxing, and not everything he saw when he looked would be pleasant. "Are you going to tell me how you managed to sneak a book out of the archives without the minders noticing?"

"Let's just say I've learned a few tricks from Rus these last few months."

Indigo barked a laugh, his face crinkling with joy. "You know, I like the new Az. I think she's fucking awesome, no matter what anyone else says."

Azure hummed her appreciation and nodded toward the book. "Page 345."

"Right." Indigo sat back in the seat, opened to the page, and let his hands and the book rest in his lap as he closed his eyes and hummed softly. His magic settled around him, a warm lavender color, soothing but cheerful just like him. The smell of springtime filled Azure's car. She forgot sometimes how pure Indigo was. How untainted he'd remained through everything. It showed in the way his magic manifested.

His brow creased, mouth twisting in concentration as he pushed further, tried harder to do the thing his sister had asked of him. Sweat gathered along his upper lip. The scent of his magic became more prevalent, threatening to choke Azure in its freshness. Flowers and fresh cut grass and warm air filling her nose. Springtime in a meadow. She cracked the window and thought, not for the first time, that maybe she ought to let Rus ward her car as well, lest the smell draw anything unsavory from the graveyard. But still he pushed. Pushed. And pushed. And pushed. Until blood trickled from his nose and Azure could see that his breathing had become labored.

She reached for him, her hand tight around his wrist. The urge was there to snatch the book away, to end this before it went any further. But she knew the abrupt departure from his connection with the item's past could seriously hurt Indigo, so she didn't. She gave his wrist a hard squeeze and a little shake, hoping to rouse him without having to use her own magic on him.

When that didn't work, she pressed further, used their shared lineage to create a connection between them, and murmured, "Indigo, let go" directly into his mind.

He came back to himself with a gasp, his eyes flying open, now sapped of much of their color, looking almost black. He dropped the book to the floor as if it had burned him. "I couldn't—There was—" He swiped at the blood under his nose, hissing a little. "Whoever burned that witch's name away did it so thoroughly, there is no trace left of her. Whatever she did to deserve that . . . Azure, I think it might be best if you left this alone."

"Yes." Azure took the book before its past could draw

him back in. There wasn't usually a danger of that, but with an item so perplexing, so unusual? One could never be too careful. "Maybe you're right."

"But you're not going to." Indigo said it like he knew that to be the truth, and he was right about that too. Azure couldn't leave this alone, especially not now that the mystery of it had deepened.

"Good night, Indigo." She turned and climbed out of the car, then waited for him to follow before locking it. "Thank you for this."

"Of course." Indigo pulled her into a hug so tight, Azure's bones creaked under its force. When he pulled back, he looked like maybe he was about to cry, but he somehow managed to sniffle it all back. "You be safe. All of you. I love you and your little family, and I don't want to lose anyone else."

It was easy to forget sometimes where Indigo had come from. How he'd been an orphaned child of one of Aunt Maureen's sisters that Aunt Maureen had taken in. How he knew tragedy the same way that Violet and Azure did. Knew loss and being left alone in the world. He hid it so well. But his pain ran just as deep as hers. And the fear of being left alone again sat right alongside it.

"I promise."

"Okay." His smile was watery but bright. Then he spun and fled across the street, shouting, "See you later, Az!"

She waited until he was inside their aunts' before turning back to 157 Mourning Moore. The front door creaked open, welcoming her home in its own way, and Aihuan's head popped up from over the back of the couch in the living room just off the foyer.

"Auntie Az! Auntie Rus made popcorn! Come watch the movie!" Aihuan shouted as if she needed to be heard over the sound of explosions and fight scenes. But someone had paused whatever they were watching, and it looked like a cartoon, not an action movie.

It wasn't the shout that stopped Azure in her tracks, though. Wasn't the loudness of it that had her heart pounding against her ribcage so hard it ached.

Auntie Az.

Auntie Az and Auntie Rus.

Rus turned her head slowly to meet Azure's eyes, and Azure saw the same stricken look there that must have been on her own face. Panic and warmth fought for dominance.

Auntie Az.

"Scoot over and make room for her, Huaner," Meiling grumbled, giving her sister a nudge, not even blinking at the enormity of what her sister had just said.

"Auntie Az," Azure mouthed to Rus, whose cheeks flared red.

"Auntie Az," Rus whispered back, unable to fight the smile that wrinkled her nose, turned her eyes to crescents. Joy. So much joy.

"Come oooooon, Auntie Az, you're gonna miss the best part," Aihuan said, her mouth now full of popcorn.

"Yes, we wouldn't want that," Rus agreed.

Azure nodded numbly and stumbled out of her shoes before making her way over the rug and around the couch. Yes, she was definitely going to fight like hell to keep this.

# Chapter 11

"I love it when you stress bake," Sunila said, stuffing another too-big bite of muffin into her mouth. They were blueberry this time. There had been no chocolate chips in Rus's pantry this morning. Likely because Aihuan had mixed them in with the popcorn for their movie night, then proceeded to pick them out of the bowl when she thought no one was looking. It was adorable. Although they had all noticed, no one said anything.

Thankfully she crashed long before they'd finished their second movie of the night. Otherwise, Azure didn't envy Rus trying to get her to bed.

"I didn't stress bake." She most certainly did. There was a whole rack of muffins and scones and cookies in the back of her car parked on the curb outside Elwood & Co. just waiting to be delivered. In baggies. On trays. Portioned off for the whole of Rus's little family. She'd already dropped off a container of Aunt Carmine's favorite spinach and cheese biscuits by her aunts', along with some brownies for Indigo and egg tarts for Aunt Maureen.

"Tell that to the flour on your shirt."

"I wore an apron, there shouldn't be—" Azure looked to find a streak of white powder down her right side, cut in an odd shape by where the apron had protected the scallop-hemmed black top she wore over a pale-green pleated skirt. How had she missed that? She swiped at it, murmuring a soft spell to make it flutter to the floor where the magic of Elwood & Co. would swallow it. "Fuck."

"Fuck is right." Sunila grinned wider, pulling a handkerchief from the pocket of her seventies-themed floral jumpsuit to clean her mouth then hold it out to Azure. "Wanna talk about it?"

"Do you want to talk about Fernando?" Azure countered, brushing the remainder of the flour off her shirt and handing the handkerchief back, all without breaking eye contact. It was no real secret that Sunila had a bit of a thing for Fernando. It'd started when she'd moved to town to take over Elwood & Co. a few weeks back, gone into Necromancer's for her daily over-caffeinated, over-sugared drink, and come face to face with Fernando Perez. All soft smiles and softer tones. Rus had bragged about watching it happen in real time that evening after they'd put the children to bed, thoroughly embarrassing Fernando. But Azure couldn't say she didn't approve. Because . . . well. She did. "Indigo says you still haven't even asked for his number. In fact, he says you hardly speak to Fernando for more than—"

"Shh!" Sunila leapt across the counter and pressed her finger to Azure's lips, silencing her. "Someone might hear you."

Azure raised a brow but didn't otherwise point out that it was midday on a Monday, and the store was empty. "I have a plate of scones in my back seat you could take over to Necromancer's."

"Why don't you take them?" Sunila shifted, her gaze flicking from Azure's to the big window that sat right across from Necromancer's. The skull in place of the *o* seemed to wink at them, and Azure had to fight not to laugh.

"I just thought maybe you'd like a reason to visit." Azure shrugged. Which was complete bullshit. And if

Sunila had grown up with Azure the way so many others had, she'd see it for the fib that it was. It wasn't that she was trying to play matchmaker. She just didn't want to see Rus, not until she'd had a day to process Aihuan's little voice saying *Auntie Az* last night. They hadn't talked about it when they crawled into bed. They hadn't talked about it over the breakfast table as they got the girls ready for school. And they hadn't talked about it before Rus jetted out the door with Fernando on her heels to head into work. Which maybe should have bothered Azure more, but it didn't because she needed space to wrap her head around it, and she was sure Rus did too. The implications—

"Well, aren't you just the sweetest little matchmaker," Sunila said, sarcasm heavy in the words. Azure couldn't tell if she saw through what Az was doing—she didn't know her cousin well enough—but she didn't care.

"I am. I'll go get them." Azure pulled away from the counter, completely ignoring Sunila's grumbles about nosey family members on her way out the door, a smile quirking up her lips. She supposed maybe it was different for Sunila when she wasn't in Moondale. Although she'd come from a large Elwood family, they didn't live around any other Elwoods, and they weren't in a small town. Meaning there was no one to tell Sunila's business to her family so they could stick their noses in where they didn't belong.

Sunila would get used to it. They all did.

"I JUST CAME to bring some muffins," Azure said, resisting the urge to shrink in on herself under the combined weight of the knowing gazes of Cagney, Nesta, and Greer. She hadn't really expected them to all be together, although she wasn't sure why. It was lunchtime, and these days it seemed unlikely that she'd see one of the trio without the other two. Still, she'd come to the sheriff's department to drop off the platter of baked goods, not thinking for a single second that Cagney and Nesta would also be there. "And ask about what Evander found about the Elwood in the graveyard."

"Of course you did." Cagney's green eyes were narrowed on her, not the platter of goodies, which wasn't helping the feeling of being pinned to the spot. Although Azure wasn't sure what Cagney could see from that vantage point. Cagney didn't know her well enough to know what was going on with her. Nesta and Greer, on the other hand—

"I didn't find anything. Sit," Greer said, his voice suddenly too close, making her jolt. She hadn't realized he'd joined her in the doorway. "I'll put the kettle on."

"I really don't have time to—"

"We didn't ask." Nesta shrugged, unbothered, and kicked out the chair across from them at the table while Greer took the platter to set on the counter. The two of them worked in concert in a way that Azure had to admit she was a little jealous of. She and Rus had been like that once upon a time. A unit. Moving around each other like they'd lived together all their lives. There was a lot of bumping into each other going on in the kitchen of 157 Mourning Moore these days. It would take time to relearn each other's patterns. Time Cagney, Greer, and Nesta had had because they weren't fighting for their fucking lives every other month. Lucky them.

Cagney tilted her head, red hair falling into her face. She nodded once, and the door to the break room shut, blocking out the sound of the bullpen beyond. Great. Now Azure was stuck in a room with these three. And they were going to pry this out of her or keep her there until things became uncomfortable for all of them.

"Spill," Greer said, setting a mug in front of her and pulling out the chair on the other side of Nesta so he could sit across from Azure as well. And then three pairs of eyes were on her, waiting and expectant.

Azure lifted the mug to her lips to take one burning sip in the hopes that it would waylay the inevitable. Because the truth was, she *wanted* to talk to someone about this. She needed to say the words out loud to fully process them. But Indigo was busy with classes. Violet wasn't speaking to her. Fernando was way too close to Rus. And Rus was out of the question, because it was *about* Rus. That just left . . . *these* three.

"You know I could have Evander handcuff you to your chair," Cagney threatened, tone conversational, her smile all teeth.

"Now, now, rosebud. We don't need to resort to such things." Nesta patted Cagney's hand gently, leaning their head in to bump lightly against Cagney's shoulder in reprimand.

"They're right," Greer agreed, his grin as sharp as Cagney's. The pair of them looked like two feral guard dogs, just waiting for one right word from their master to attack. "Azure is going to tell us what's going on. Aren't you, Azure? Because if not, we'll ask Ashthorne."

Greer was bluffing. He'd sooner rip out his own teeth than try to have a friendly chat with Rus about her and Azure's relationship. But Cagney and Nesta wouldn't hesitate to do so. Azure took another long, burning sip from her tea, and lowered the mug to the table.

"Huaner called me Auntie Az last night," she blurted before she could think better of it. Because no, she didn't have anyone else to tell, but that didn't mean she wanted to tell Nesta, Cagney, and Greer. They were friends of a kind, but they weren't close the way she was with her siblings, with Rus. Second thought, maybe it would have been better had she discussed this with someone else. Like Phyre. Shit.

Greer's lips twitched into a smile—a real one—seemingly without his knowledge as his brows raised high on his face.

Cagney let out a soft "Well, I'll be."

And Nesta merely smiled as if they knew it all along. Maybe they did. They were a cupid after all, which meant a certain amount of love knowledge. Although Azure had always thought it was restricted to romantic love, but there was no actual evidence to prove that. And now that she was thinking about it, it made sense that a cupid, especially one like Nesta who specialized in finding homes for people, would be able to see something outside of the romance between her and Rus. They'd see the potential for familial love there too.

"And you're freaking out about it," Greer said, like he was guessing, but Azure knew whatever she was thinking showed on her face. At least, it showed enough that someone close enough to her like Rus would have been able to see it. Maybe Greer couldn't.

"I wouldn't use the term *freaking out*." Because Azure didn't use that term ever. She didn't know why, but it felt so . . . strange in her mouth. Like it didn't fit there. It seemed more the kind of thing Rus would say. "I'm just—" All right, so she *was* freaking out. But she certainly wasn't going to call it that. "I'm trying to sort out how I feel about it."

"Besides ecstatic, you mean," Cagney said, her tone flat,

but the smile had slipped from her face, her brows drawn in, as if she were on the verge of being well and truly upset. Azure could only guess at what she was thinking—that Cagney thought maybe Azure *wasn't* happy. The protective instinct of Rus's best friend was about to rear its ugly head, and Azure couldn't afford that, not right now when her own emotions were so . . . mixed up.

"Obviously." Azure breathed, tightening her grip around the mug in her hands lest she be tempted to reach over and grab the three of them in an attempt to make them see. It was hard to get the words out. Hard to turn the feelings brewing inside her into tangible things that another person would understand. And then it struck her—what was bothering her about this whole thing. "Rus also asked me to move in with her."

"That's great!" Greer cheered, momentarily seeming to forget the feud between himself and Rus. "Isn't that great?" He deflated at whatever he saw on Azure's face. "Why isn't that great?"

"Because I'm not sure that's what *she* wants." And there was the root of it. The problem. In her post-orgasm haze, so elated with having Rus in her arms again, Azure had missed the signs. Missed how Rus had asked her what *she* wanted, but when Azure turned the question around on her, Rus had shrugged her off. Now, Aihuan's words cast everything in a different light. Had Azure overthinking things she usually would have ignored.

"Why wouldn't she?" Greer blurted, but Azure noticed how Nesta and Cagney stayed silent. How they seemed to draw in on themselves in thought.

"I don't know. But when I asked her if she did . . . I just . . . I would have liked a more clear-cut answer. A yes or a no. A maybe even. Something other than a shrug." It was the shrug that bothered her. The way it had seemed . . . indifferent. Like it didn't matter one way or the other what Rus wanted. When such a big step really *should*. Especially to a single mother.

"I'll talk to her," Cagney volunteered, and Azure could have sagged under the relief. "I need to get her and Phyre in a room together anyway to talk about what happened with the Board a bit ago. Why not hash a few things out while we're there?"

Oh, Rus was not going to be happy about that. "Just don't tell her I told you."

"Please, I know how to be discreet."

Nesta and Greer both choked on a laugh, and while maybe that did lessen Azure's confidence in Cagney's relative ability to be discreet, it also lightened the tension. Let her shoulders droop down from around her ears. She settled back in her chair, finished off her tea, and asked, "So, what's it like living with these two?" to no one in particular, and watched the chaos ensue.

# Chapter 12

"What the fuck is this?" Rus asked, scowling at the postcard Cagney had just slid across the counter of Necromancer's for Rus to get a closer look at.

"It was bulk mail," Phyre almost whispered, giving Rus a small wave that screamed of uncertainty. Which, considering they hadn't spoken since Phyre sold them out to the fucking board a couple months back by telling Brant that Rus had almost summoned a demon, made sense. "Hi, Rus."

"Phyre." Rus nodded before ducking her head to look at the postcard again. She'd kind of hoped they could avoid this confrontation all together, maybe until one of them died. But that wasn't really fair to Phyre or herself, and although she knew that, she hadn't been planning to do anything about it. Clearly Cagney was over them skirting each other. Meddling druid. "Okay, it came through bulk mail, but what *is* it? What am I looking at?"

The bit of bulk mail in question was made of shiny cardstock with a skull and crossbones set in white on a black background on the front that looked eerily similar to the Necromancer's sign living over Rus's coffee shop. When she flipped it over, in big bold print were the words "KEEP THE DEAD OUT OF MOONDALE." There was a QR code underneath that, likely led to a webpage that listed all the bad that having a necromancer in their community could have.

It would have been funny, if it weren't so annoying.

A twinge settled into Rus's temple. They didn't need this. They definitely did *not* need this. Not with everything else going on. They couldn't afford for the community of Moondale to turn against them on top of the handful of board members looking to chase her out of town all over again.

"We don't know who sent them," Cagney said. Her fingers twitched against the counter as if she wanted to snatch it from Rus's fingers and light it on fire. A sentiment Rus wholeheartedly agreed with. "But we have our suspicions."

"Let me guess." Rus scrubbed at her face, dropping the offending bit of closed-minded drivel to the countertop. Her fingers itched from having touched something so bigoted, as if the small-mindedness could seep into her bloodstream via skin contact alone. "The website is all about how I'm poisoning the well and turning their children to the dark side of magic." She gasped, high and sotto, clutching her chest. "Soon little Jimmy will be summoning spirits over dinner. Goddess, what is this, 1850?"

"Something along those lines." Cagney snatched the postcard from the counter and stuffed it into her pocket.

"Brant's behind it, I'm sure of it." Phyre leaned back on her heels when Rus's gaze cut to her, as if she could shrink in on herself and disappear from Rus's notice.

"Just Brant?" Rus scoffed.

"The website is too high tech for him." Cagney shook her head. "My guess is Taryn, honestly. This has her all over it. Remember when we both ran for class president in high school?"

"Yes." Although Rus hadn't thought about that in years. But the smear campaign Taryn ran against Cagney was legendary. It had almost been enough to get her suspended, but had somehow toed the line just enough, been just vague enough that none of the teachers could prove that the rumors going around had originated with Taryn. "Right. So why is Taryn trying to get rid of me?"

"Maybe she thinks putting her lot in with Brant is the way to go. He's never minded throwing money around." Cagney shrugged, dismissing the idea. "Plus, he's easier to control than some of the others."

Phyre took a deep breath suddenly, drawing herself up as if readying herself to say something. She met Rus's eyes head on, and Rus didn't shy away from the fierce look. "I'm . . . I'm sorry about the part I played in all of this."

Rus frowned, rubbing at her twinging temples before pinching the bridge of her nose. She knew why Phyre told Brant Ironwood about Rus being arrested a town over, but that didn't mean it hadn't hurt. Didn't mean Rus wasn't still aching a little with the knowledge that her own sister had sold her out.

"Can you ever forgive me?"

"In time, I think so. But we're not there yet." Rus wasn't sure when they would be there, but she supposed she could look past what Phyre had done eventually.

They could grow past this as they'd grown past so many other things throughout their lives. And besides, it was hard to stay mad at someone like Phyre. Someone who had been there for Rus since the very beginning. Her first sister. The one who had held Rus when she was alone, contacted by her first spirit, and so fucking scared. Phyre was the only child in the orphanage who hadn't shied away from Rus.

"Just . . ." She blew out a breath, running a hand through her hair. "Don't pull that shit again."

"Of course not." Phyre nodded firmly. She looked like

she wanted to launch herself across the counter and sweep Rus into her arms. They weren't there yet either, but Rus longed for it just as badly as Phyre seemed to. For the connection and the reminder that she wasn't alone. "I know where my loyalties lie."

"Well, I'm glad you've both finally seen sense." Cagney bumped Phyre lightly. "But that's not the only reason we're here."

"Lovely." Rus didn't like the look in Cagney's eyes, but there was no way to stop whatever was coming next. "What now?"

"We know you asked Azure to move in with you." Cagney's smile turned sharp, and while Phyre's didn't mirror it, she was grinning too.

"Okay. And?" Flexing her toes in her shoes, Rus refused to look at either of them. They both looked far too proud of themselves.

"She's worried you don't want her to move in with you. She thinks you just asked because it's what she wants." Cagney was always brutal in her efficiency to flay Rus alive and leave her bleeding. Rus's heart dropped to her feet, stuttering in fear. "Tell me you aren't being stupid again."

"I don't think that's any of your business." Tilting her chin up, Rus prayed to the Goddess that Cagney didn't see the way she faltered.

"Goddess, Icarus!" Phyre chided, shaking her head. "You need to tell her that you want this. It's been eleven fucking years—"

Rus gasped. "Language!"

Phyre rolled her eyes and continued as if Rus hadn't interrupted her at all. "You can't expect Azure to read you like a book like she used to. You need to *tell* her how you feel."

Phyre was right, of course she was. There was hardly a time in their lives when she hadn't been, except for when she'd told Brant about Rus almost summoning a demon in the next town over. And she was very much correct in her assessment that it had been eleven years, and Rus and Az had both changed. It only made sense that those changes would result in a need to communicate better. It was just . . . Rus didn't want to ruin this for herself by wanting it too much.

"Don't be an idiot," Cagney said, as if she read what Rus was thinking without her even having to say it. "Moondale isn't going to let you slip through her fingers again. You're stuck here now. Might as well get what you want in the meantime. Right, Phyre?"

"Right."

Rus laughed a little, shaking her head. "Yeah. Maybe. I'll . . . uh . . . I'll think about it." It was the most she could promise them. The best she could do.

Phyre reached out, taking Rus's hand, a soft smile on her face. "Let yourself be happy. Please. You deserve it."

Her heart in her throat, Rus nodded and tried to sniffle back the tears in a way no one would notice. If the look Cagney and Phyre gave her on their way out the door was any indication, she hadn't managed, but at least they didn't mention it.

"Hey, guys." Sunila waved to them on her way inside. There was a tray of something in her hands, and when she turned to look at Rus, she frowned. "You uh . . . you good?"

"Yeah. Fine." Rus scrubbed at her eyes with the back of her sleeve. "You here to see Nando?"

Sunila blushed brightly, her eyes flicking from Rus to the empty space behind her where Fernando usually stood, ready and waiting to fill orders. "Is he . . . is he in?"

"He's on lunch. But he should be back soon." A smile tickled the corners of her lips, drawing them upward into a soft smile. It was nice to see someone paying attention to Fernando. He so often faded into the background with Rus because she was so loud and in a person's face. She appreciated that someone had noticed her friend, finally.

"Oh. Of course! Well. I just . . . Azure wanted me to deliver these." Sunila laughed, holding up the tray of baked goods.

"I'll bet she did." Rus shook her head, chuckling. Of course, Az would try to play matchmaker. "Nando will be back any minute. He can tell you where to put those. I can't leave the register."

Sunila let out a soft *meep*, but then cleared her throat and said, "Right. Thanks."

"He likes you, you know," Rus pressed, because she never did know when to keep her mouth shut.

"Obviously." Sunila scoffed. "*Everyone* likes me."

"Right. How silly of me." But Rus noted the way Sunila had gone even redder. Of how when Fernando did make it back from lunch, Sunila's eyes followed him. How their hands brushed as they both worked to fill the pastry case. Silly indeed.

# Chapter 19

"**B**ut I want to go to school with you and Auntie Az," Aihuan whined, kicking her feet where she sat in her car seat.

Blue rumbled around them, displeased by the child's displeasure.

But that wasn't what was making it hard for Rus to think, much less breathe. She didn't know which of the girls had been the one to say it first. If perhaps Meiling had said it when she hadn't been around and Aihuan was just repeating it. Or if someone else had started it and Aihuan had picked it up. She was at that age where she did that. Usually, it was curse words. Which could be funny and embarrassing by turns, and always resulted in Rus and Fernando taking bets about when Aihuan would say her new curse word in front of someone she really shouldn't.

But this . . .

*Auntie Az.*

It wasn't the term *aunt* that was getting her, catching in her lungs. The girls called Cagney and Phyre aunt. Fernando was uncle. Nesta had been termed Bibi Nesta. And even Greer had been gifted Uncle Vander. Az being called Auntie wasn't actually that monumental. Meiling and Aihuan had spent years understanding that a family wasn't a matter of birth or bloodlines, it was a thing built and found. Forged in fire, and able to withstand even the harshest storm. So of course they would adopt the family Rus had in Moondale. The people who had welcomed her home as if she'd never left at all. That only made sense.

No. It wasn't the words themselves, it was the way they were *said*. The way *Auntie Az* rolled off the tongue the same as *Auntie Rus* did. Like they were seeing Az as their guardian, their mother in a sense. It was *that* that made it hard to think. Made Rus's lungs constrict around a breath. There was possibility in it. Hope. *Things* that Rus didn't know she'd wanted all her life until Aihuan had spoken them into being. Goddess, it was going to be the death of her.

"I'm afraid you can't, Huaner," Az said, her voice a soft rumble, and when Rus looked over at her from the driver's seat, she found Az looking just as shell-shocked as she felt. It had taken Az by surprise too when Aihuan first said it as if it was nothing. As if it didn't slot the final piece of a puzzle Rus hadn't known she was putting together into place.

Rus melted down further into her seat. Maybe if she made herself small enough, she could hide from the enormity of what Aihuan was actually saying with those words, disappear before Az could fix her with that searching expression once more. She didn't have answers for Az. Likely wouldn't ever. Which made her almost grateful that the girls had kept them pretty much too busy or too tired to sit down and have an in-depth discussion about this. She didn't think she wanted to know what was going on behind Az's beautiful brown eyes.

"Why noooooot?" Aihuan whined again, growing increasingly unruly. She had been doing that lately—testing her limits, seeing how far she could push the adults in her life before they snapped. It was a typical part of growing up, like a puppy seeing how hard they could bite their siblings before their siblings stopped playing with them altogether. Rus hated it. It made her feel weak, and cruel. Because while she knew she needed to stand firm, she was crumbling under the constant onslaught of Aihuan's unhappiness. It hadn't been this hard when Meiling went through the same phase. But their parents had been alive for that, and the part Rus played in all of it was mostly the fun auntie who got to give in to her temper tantrum.

She didn't feel fun now when she said, "Because we're going to the adult school, little monster. And you need to go to the little kid school."

"But I'm not little!"

Rus pinched the bridge of her nose. Fuck, she was tired. Even with Az next to her, she wasn't sleeping. Nightmares plagued every moment of rest she managed to catch, images of Moondale overrun with the slowly deteriorating dead. Her whole body ached on a cellular level. And her waking hours were spent trying to contact the Elwood witch from the After again or sort out the ever-growing list of things she needed to start a coven.

Historically, covens built over the course of years. They started with a couple of witches and had the chance to grow slowly. They were given time to flesh out their numbers, find a coven house, and make themselves a staple of the community. But the Forgotten were not being given such a leisurely timeline. They had to have everything ready *now*.

Their only saving grace was that Rus wasn't alone in this. That she had a support system baked in when she moved back to Moondale.

It took a village to raise a child. It took a village to build a coven. And even her friends who weren't among the Forgotten had begun to chip in. Cagney was planning to spend the day digging through her shed for something "useful" this week. What useful meant, Rus had no idea, but Cagney seemed to know what she was looking for. Fernando had taken to making the girls' lunches so Rus could focus on other things. Even Greer had offered to pick Aihuan up from school in the afternoon.

"I know that, little monst—"

"Not little!" Aihuan glared at Rus, her brown eyes narrowed and hard where Rus could see her in the rearview mirror. Rus didn't know where this was coming from. Were the kids at school picking on Aihuan because she was so small? She *was* slightly undersized, but that could be expected from the fact that she was reanimated. Dying and being brought back by a necromancer was enough to stunt anyone's growth. Especially when it occurred during such early years. Aihuan had been fucking *two*, so it was going to have an effect. Not that anyone outside of Rus's inner circle could know that. It was too dangerous.

Hence the Coven of the Forgotten.

Hence the ever-growing list of tasks.

Hence the uphill battle.

"No, you're not," Az agreed, her voice calm. She'd reached over at some point and was squeezing Rus's thigh, comforting. "But we won't have time to show you around today as we have a lot to do. So, maybe we could plan another time for you to come to my school with me? Maybe this summer, when you don't have your own school. All the flowers will be out then. It's very pretty."

"What kinds of flowers?" Aihuan asked, her lower lip pouting. But at least she wasn't throwing a fit anymore. Rus would take the win.

"All kinds. There's a druid and a Weed Witch on staff. Maybe we could meet with them, and they could show you their favorites?" Rus wasn't sure how Az was going to pull *that* off, as Az hated interacting with people unless she absolutely had to. But maybe having the dean on their side would make it easier. "What do you think?"

Aihuan tilted her head, thinking about the proposal, her nose wrinkled, then she grinned. "Okay, Auntie Az."

"Okay," Az said, her voice almost breathless. Rus was sure being called Auntie that way had hit Az square in the chest exactly how it had Rus the very first time. Aihuan had them wrapped around her finger, didn't she? "But you have to be good for us now and go to school. Do you think you can do that?"

"Yup!" Aihuan's grin widened.

"Perfect. Now, do you have your necklace?" Az asked, turning around more in her seat so she could check in with Aihuan. Rus had seen this routine enough times recently to know this is how it went. Rus always checked, made sure Aihuan had the things she needed to keep herself safe outside of the protective wards of 157 Mourning Moore. That involved a pendant that would keep her from being possessed until she was old enough, and her magic was developed enough, to do that for herself.

Aihuan pulled the long chain from under her shirt to show them both, then lifted her hands to cover her eyes and said, "Eyes off. All good."

"All good." Az nodded approvingly and slid from the car to begin helping Aihuan out of her car seat.

She waited until Aihuan joined the cluster of other kindergarteners before dropping back into the seat beside Rus. When she'd buckled again and they were on their way, Rus relaxed a little. Just a little.

"You didn't have to do that," Rus said, her eyes firmly on

the winding road through the forest and up the mountain. "But thank you."

Az hummed but didn't say anything. Likely for the best. Rus didn't think her heart could handle a serious discussion about what was going on with the girls right now. Blue—the bitch of a car that she was—began flipping through the radio stations. Rus could only guess at what Blue was trying to do with that, but thankfully the mountains foiled her plan by providing snippets of songs interspersed with mainly static for a few minutes. Until Blue gave up entirely, and they were forced to sit in silence for the rest of the ride.

It was almost a relief when they reached the campus and Az departed for her classes, while Rus followed the path she'd taken many-a-time while she was at Moondale U toward the dean's office. Honestly, it was amazing she'd even managed to graduate with how many times she'd been in to see the dean about everything from her behavior to her "unethical" views on spirits.

"Come in," Vanessa Cochburn called from behind the door when Rus knocked. Rus let herself in. The dean of Moondale was a tall woman with bright red hair, freckled cheeks, and wire-framed glasses perched on her nose. She looked like a stuffy librarian. But the wide smile she fixed Rus with as Rus settled into one of the chairs on the other side of her desk was friendly and kind. Much less like she'd shout at Rus for being too passionate in the library than any librarian Rus had ever known. "Miss Ashthorne. Welcome. So you've come to accept my offer?"

"Rus, please. And yes." Rus shifted, the leather creaking beneath her. She still wasn't sure how comfortable she was with this. Making the time to guest lecture was going to stretch her thin, but Az was right—they needed Vanessa's help with the prophecy, and they needed to start taking recruitment seriously. "I'd be happy to do a couple of guest lectures, I'll just need to work it around my schedule. As I'm sure Az has told you, we've got a lot going on right now."

"Of course. We need a couple of weeks' notice to set up a classroom and advertise the lectures for students. Maybe just after the students have finished their exams? Then they won't be so bogged down with everything else." Vanessa looked down at some piece of paper on her desk, maybe a calendar for the semester. "It looks like they're finished on the seventeenth of May. How would the following Wednesday be? The twenty-second? It'll give the students the weekend and a couple of extra days to reorient themselves to learning before taking your course. I was thinking maybe it could be a couple of sessions?"

May 22? That was just about two weeks, exactly. Could Rus pull a lecture together that quickly? She didn't know. But the feeling of the noose tightening after the events of this weekend reminded her that she didn't have much more time than that to fill out her coven. Not if what Nixie Virnan said was true and some of the elders were already planning to try repealing the decision made by the board.

"I think I can make that work." She'd have to.

"Perfect. I'll pencil you in and send the paperwork over."

Great. *More* paperwork.

"In the meantime, Azure said there was something you both wanted me to look at. A prophecy?" Vanessa scribbled something on the piece of paper in front of her and looked up to fix Rus with a searching gaze. "I'll admit, that wasn't my primary focus when I was doing my studies, but I'll do what I can."

Rus nodded and pulled a legal pad from her bag. Az had written everything they'd learned so far in her neat, steady handwriting. After flipping to the page with the prophecy, Rus slid the pad across to Vanessa.

"May I?" Vanessa asked, tapping her pen on the paper.

They'd left the page mostly blank aside from the prophecy. To allow room for notes and to keep Vanessa from inadvertently seeing anything that might influence what she found there. It was better if she read it without the knowledge of everything else going on.

"Of course."

"Right. *And on the eve of the 500th year our heart will be open, and while the shadows of our past walk amongst us, all who are closest to our heart and seek its strength may receive it.*" Vanessa's pen scratched against the page as she started writing. "So the eve of the five hundredth year clearly puts this into the context of the fifth centennial of Moondale."

"We figured that much." Rus resisted the urge to roll her eyes. It wouldn't do to get herself on the wrong side of someone who was trying to help them and who was about to be her employer in a manner of speaking.

"As for the heart," Vanessa continued as if Rus hadn't spoken at all, which might have been for the best, "I believe there is something called the Heart of Moondale in town, correct?"

"Of course!" Goddess, why hadn't she thought of that? The large ore deposit in the mountains that connected to all the lei lines in Moondale was the *first* thing any folk in town learned about. The thing that kept the wards sustained. That made the land so rich with magic that it was almost too easy for things like houses to become sentient, even those inhabited by humans. Between she and Az, they should have realized that's what the prophecy meant by *heart*. "So, it's talking about the influx of magic we're expecting to see at the centennial."

"Very likely." Vanessa nodded. "I'm unclear what it means by 'the shadows of our past walk amongst us.' That could be anything. A secret about Moondale before it was formed. The mistakes of everyone in Moondale coming back to haunt them."

"Or it could be more literal," Rus said, following along. Now that her brain was going, she was seeing the prophecy from a new angle. Understanding it differently. Sometimes it just took another person to talk to for her to see things in a different light. "It could mean the dead will walk among us."

"Maybe." Vanessa's hand hadn't stopped moving, adding everything they said to the paper so Rus could reference it later. "As for 'those who are closest to our heart'—"

"It might mean proximity, or it might mean the elders."

"Right." Vanessa lifted her head to grin at Rus, clearly also excited by the way they were feeding off each other. Two like minds working together. "But I'm sure there is some ceremony that will be done on the eve of the centennial, something that's tradition?"

"There is. And it'll put all the elders in proximity to the heart. So they'll all receive a boost in magic for them and their covens." Rus wondered if any of the others realized this. If they knew what was coming. Maybe the other elders didn't, but Taryn clearly did. It's why she was cozying up to Carmine. She was hoping to be there for the ceremony, to receive the boost directly instead of passed through the elder of Jade Waters.

"That would make sense."

Rus frowned, scrubbing at her nose. If that was the case, Taryn posed a bigger threat than they'd originally thought.

And it put their Nixie-posed timetable more into perspective. They needed Az to be an official elder of the Board of Magic before the centennial or risk being cut off from the magic of Moondale entirely. Fuck.

If the prophecy was referencing some secret from the beginning of Moondale, then it might be whatever happened to Az's ancestor. The nameless witch who had been scrubbed of all Elwood records might be the key to this whole thing.

But she needed to deal with the imminent threat first: Taryn.

She looked up from where her gaze had fallen to watch her fingers tap against her legs. "You don't happen to have a place on campus where I could try contacting some spirits, do you?"

"Not that I know of, but perhaps one of our lab techs would." There was a gleam in Vanessa's eyes like she was up to something, and Rus didn't care for it. She'd learned a long time ago that when certain types of women had that look about them, they were usually about to do something bothersome. "I'll give you the building number."

THE STICKY NOTE Vanessa had given Rus led her to a squat brick building, down a hall lit by yellowed bulbs, to a door that had a sign hanging crookedly from a hook on it. The words "Delacroix Labs" in all caps were emblazoned in red paint.

"Of course." Rus scoffed and rolled her eyes, but she was already here, so she might as well see what Hunter had to say about contacting spirits on campus.

"Can I help you with something?" a voice echoed from further up the hall. Rus turned, her eyes landing on the shadowy figure of one Hunter Delacroix. She recognized him immediately from when he'd come to see her about the Ghost Tracer, even in the sweeping white lab coat, and with his long curly dark hair pulled into a messy bun.

"Yeah. Dean Cochburn said I should stop in and ask you about something." Rus tilted her head, pasting on a smile as Hunter got closer. "Also, hi again, I guess."

Hunter blinked at her a moment as if starstruck, then took several long strides toward Rus and held out his hand. "Icarus Ashthorne! What an absolute honor to have you at my humble lair."

Rus shook his hand, laughing to herself. "No need to stand on formality. I'm just your everyday necromancing Crow Witch. Nothing special."

"Pft. Nothing special, she says." Hunter rolled his eyes, rocking forward on his toes as if he wanted to press in closer to her space but wasn't sure he ought to. "Honestly, the Ghost Tracer is . . . it's . . ." He hesitated as if the word evaded him, then snapped his fingers in excitement. "Revolutionary."

"Oh, it was really—"

"Really amazing," Hunter pressed, not letting her take a breath to talk down her own accomplishment. "Anyway, you said Nessy sent you?"

"Oh yeah. She said you might know someplace where I could do a little channeling on campus."

Hunter frowned, his nose scrunching up, the glasses on his face moving with the expression. "'fraid not. Moondale U is bound up too tight for all that."

"Shit." Rus sighed. She'd have to do it back home then, she supposed. "All right then. Well, I should—" That hadn't really been why Cochburn had sent her here, had it? No. She was up to something. She'd wanted to put Hunter in Rus's path for a reason. Likely hoping Rus would pull Hunter in, just like Az was. Well . . . no harm in talking, was there? "Actually, you know what? I heard you're covenless."

"Yeah. What of it?" His shoulders grew tense, as if he was preparing for a fight. He drew himself up to his full height, which dwarfed even Rus's taller than average.

"Az and I are starting our own coven. In Moondale. I uh . . . I don't have any information on hand, but if you wouldn't mind, could I send you some stuff? You can look it over, and if it's a no, I swear I won't bug you ever again."

Hunter blinked at her, his dark eyes wide, then he smiled big and unrestrained. "Sure. Here," he said, stepping through the door with the crooked sign on it. "Lemme just grab you a business card."

"Great."

# Chapter 14

The process of reaching out to the unsettled spirits of Mourning Moore was maybe a little too easy. Rus had borrowed their strength so much over the last few months that they came willingly. It was, however, not something that could be done while on Moondale University campus—the wards in place wouldn't allow it, or so Hunter explained after they'd chatted a bit more. So she had to wait until she returned home and locked herself away in the house next door.

Az had only looked at her askance once when Rus said she was going to swing by 155 Mourning Moore to check in with the spirit of the house. The door didn't creak, but she felt welcome this time. Like the house was gradually adjusting to her presence there. Maybe it *was* shy, like Nesta said. A strange concept for Rus, who was so used to 157's extroversion.

Still, it was nice to not be outright rejected by the place.

She settled into the middle of the front room again, closed her eyes, and waited.

There were no barriers between her and the unsettled dead of the graveyard beyond these walls. No After to contend with. Just the thin film that separated the world of the living from limbo. So flimsy, she could easily have punched a hole through it and ripped out any spirit she wanted. Especially with how experienced she was at doing just that.

But what she was doing now would not require brute force, nor the energy necessary to provide the spirits she wanted to use with bodies.

*Spies. Spies. Spies. Spies.*

The spirits' voices rose around her, whispering, repeating, giving voice and direction to what Rus needed. They wouldn't even need to properly take form. It'd be better if they didn't, actually. She made that clear to them in her intention.

To an outsider, the way Rus dealt with spirits might seem strange. How she was able to think what she needed versus speaking it. How directions flowed in a form of communication that was less tangible to the living. Like describing an apple to someone who had no idea what an apple was. Or the color red. Or what the word *tart* meant. The language of spirits was like that, only more so.

*But who? But who? But who?*

This part was simple enough. All Rus had to do was picture Taryn Elwood and broadcast that signal to any spirit that would listen. The only bit of this that would be difficult was when the spirits came to collect their due.

Each would have a price for their help.

Some might simply want their graves tended.

Others might ask that their unfinished business be seen to, although that was uncommon. Most spirits didn't remember their lives clearly enough to want for anything of that kind. Maybe those things had been what kept them there, originally, but after so many years of roaming the world as a disquiet shade? They tended to forget the trifles of the living.

Most of them would simply want Rus to help them over to the After, to bring them peace.

This, she could do. Would do. It was no hardship aside from the strain it put on her body and magic to deal with such an influx of spirits to give safe passage. If she wasn't the only necromancer in their coven, that would help. But Rus was willing to bear the brunt of this burden, at least until the girls were of age to help her.

With her spies given their marching orders, Rus rose and stretched.

The house groaned around her as if trying to communicate, but Rus didn't know this place and couldn't speak the language of it the way she could with 157 Mourning Moore. A shame, really. She was sure this place had plenty to tell her.

"You'll be a good home for someone soon," she assured it, hoping that would ease its spirit.

When Rus reached the front door, she found the knob stuck fast. Not like it was locked—more like someone was holding it from the other side. The house trying to keep her. With a sigh, she whirled around to address 155 Mourning Moore as a whole and found that the front room she'd just vacated had been repainted. Where before the walls had been a neutral cream color, perfect for any new homeowner, now one wall was a stunningly familiar shade of lavender, and the surrounding walls were a deep, dark gray. A mirror of her living room at home.

Rus hummed thoughtfully, watching as every wall in the house shifted to mirror those of 157, as if the house was trying to convince her this was home.

"I'm not saying yes," she told it, but she scuffed through the foyer to check out the layout of the first floor. "But you raise an interesting point."

The house creaked, and Rus wondered if that was a sound of joy. The first floor was a mirror image of 157 Mourning Moore now, everything the same but flipped. The second had more rooms, but they were smaller, broken down to allow for more guests, if need be. The attic space had gone completely untouched, left merely for storage, but there was potential there.

"Okay," she said to the house again, having returned to the first floor. "But do you have a basement?"

The house shone a light on a door under the front stairs. What she found below was another unfinished storage space.

It certainly wasn't as grand as the Jade Waters coven house. Nor was it tucked away secure in the mountains the way the Crimson Tides house was. Nor as gilded as the Silver Flames one. But the Forgotten weren't near as large, or as self-important, as the other covens. They were small.

A fledgling coven. And what better place for a coven with a necromancer at the helm to call home than a place that abutted one of the oldest graveyards in Moondale?

She couldn't believe she was doing this, but Nixie did say having a coven house would give them a better foothold in the community. And with the clock ticking loudly toward the centennial, they didn't have a fuckload of time to find one. So Rus dialed Nesta, and before they could even say hello she said, "Are you at your office?"

"Yes. Why?"

"I'll be by in ten. I want to go over the list Az sent you about our requirements for a coven house."

"You have some place in mind?" Nesta sounded like they had fallen completely still on the other end of the line. They also might have been smiling, but it was hard to tell. Either way, Rus was under no illusions that Nesta hadn't orchestrated this somehow. Meddling fucking cupid.

"Have all the specs for 155 Mourning Moore waiting for me" was the only answer Rus felt up to giving them, then she hung up.

The house groaned around her, and the front door popped open with a soft creak.

"I suppose you're very happy with yourself, aren't you?" Rus asked it. It didn't answer, just sat silent and smug the way 157 Mourning Moore did sometimes. "Well, don't get your hopes up. My partner has exacting standards, and you might not live up to them."

The lights in the front room blinked on and off once as if the house was laughing. Rus shook her head and left the house to head for her car with a long sigh.

Because another sassy house was *exactly* what she fucking needed.

AZURE FROWNED AT HER PHONE. She didn't think she really understood what Rus was up to, but she trusted her. Rus wasn't going to dick around when it felt like the proverbial cauldron was bubbling over. She knew what was at stake: Their home. Their family. The life they were building together. So if she said she had a hunch about a coven house, Azure was going to leave her to it.

In the meantime—

"A'ling," Azure said, knocking softly on the teenager's door. Meiling was sprawled across her bed, half hidden by the gauzy canopy, reading a book. Her feet kicked in the air behind her, a pen dangling from her lips as they moved while she read. It was so heartbreakingly familiar to the times Azure had walked in on Rus studying at the orphanage that she had to stop for a moment to process what she was seeing, to force herself to breathe past the ache of years lost that clutched her lungs. To not see the image of Rus instead of what was right in front of her.

"Hm?" Meiling asked, not even bothering to look up from her book.

"I need your help with something." The strap of her bag cut into Azure's shoulders, the supplies in it feeling far heavier than they ought to for their weight. It had been a long time since she'd done this. And never without Rus there to facilitate. "I want to hold a séance."

Meiling's head jerked up, her eyes wide. "Without Aunt Rus?"

"Yes." Shame settled into the base of Azure's spine, threatening to bow her to its weight. She didn't like the idea of doing this without Rus. It wasn't right. But something had spooked Azure's elder when she spoke to Rus, and even before that the connection had been tenuous at best. A connection born by blood was less likely to have those complications.

"Why?" Meiling narrowed her eyes on Azure, pinning her to the spot as if she could see down into Azure, read all of her insecurities. Goddess, had Rus been that perceptive as a teenager? Probably.

"Because something frightened my ancestor off when she was speaking with Rus, and I think using Elwood blood will make it easier to hold the connection." Rus was going to skin Azure alive for this, probably. But she'd understand. Eventually. "Can you help me?"

"Fine." Meiling rolled off her bed, adjusting her sweat-shirt once she was standing. "But I'm in the protection circle with you. I don't want my own. I want to be *with* you."

Azure shook her head. "You won't be there. I just need help with the messaging. I can do the rest. Once I've got it translated into something they can understand in the After, you're coming back to the house."

Meiling's shoulders relaxed, her posture going looser. Azure hadn't noticed her winding herself up, trying to make herself appear bigger and braver than she was until that moment, and it made every bone in Azure's body ache with something she didn't quite understand. Had Rus done that as well? Had she spent years puffing herself up to look bigger and braver than she was? To appear stronger and more frightening in the face of everything? Azure had always thought of Rus as untouchable, a veritable badass, but how often had she just been a scared kid when they were younger? How often was she scared now?

"Where are we doing this?" Meiling asked, suddenly standing beside Azure.

"Grab a blanket. We're going into the graveyard."

IT WAS WARMER than it had been in several months as the sun slowly faded from the sky, but Azure felt the chill of the graves around them brush her skin. Shades and spirits that had long forgotten why they stayed behind passing by her unseen but felt.

Meiling shifted closer, clearly unsettled with being surrounded by so many of the dead. All of whom she could likely see where Azure could not.

"You'll be all right," Azure promised. "I won't let anything happen to you."

She wouldn't. But that didn't change the fact that she wished they had brought Rus with them. Azure could protect Meiling, and she would. But Meiling might feel more comfortable with this if Rus were there. Meiling agreeing to help and stepping into the graveyard with Azure after only a moment of hesitation showed growth though, and showed Meiling's ability to overcome her fears when it meant helping others. She was going to make one hell of a necromancer once she set her mind to it. Azure hoped this experience was the first of many good ones for Meiling when it came to the spirits of the After. It also showed that Meiling trusted Azure to keep her safe, to look after her. Azure was going to prove she deserved that trust if it was the last thing she did.

"This is it," Azure said, stopping in front of a marker that was devoid of anything apart from dates. There was no name, no indication that anyone had even tried to etch one into it. But connection tugged at Azure's blood, a line pulled taut. Blood calling to blood. Yes, this was definitely an Elwood burial site.

"How do you know?" Meiling asked.

"I just do."

"She might not answer." Meiling pulled the blanket from her shoulder, and they spread it between them in front of the headstone on the ground over where a body would have been buried if there was one. Azure had no way of being sure if this was where the mysterious Elwood's bones actually rested, but the marker would be enough. Especially as there were traces of Elwood magic lingering behind. As if someone had spent time there tending to the gravesite afterward. Maybe the witch's siblings had visited, unable to let go of their sister even if she'd been burned from their coven. "And without a name, we can't compel her to."

"She'll answer."

"How do you know?"

The blanket placed, the protection circle traced in salt, the characters pinned carefully to the blanket with iron nails, adding to the protection, Azure settled at the center of it all and smiled up at Meiling, who was shifting awkwardly in the dry grass. "What is it Rus always says spirits want more than anything?"

"For someone to listen to them." Meiling scrubbed at the tip of her nose, a habit she'd inherited from her aunt. "But she also says that the first rule of necromancy is that spirits lie."

"Then we'll take everything she says with a grain of salt. Now go on, back to the house." Azure shooed her and waited until the back porch door shut behind Meiling before she began to hum the lilting, haunting tune that would open a line to the After.

It took her longer perhaps than it might have taken Rus to make the connection, but once she did, it was strong, Azure could feel it. And when she opened her eyes, her nameless ancestor knelt before her, brows raised high on her face.

"Has the Elwood line finally produced another necromancer?" the witch asked, her voice echo-y and warbling as she leaned in closer to get a better look at Azure. She couldn't pass the barrier of the protection circle, but she came very close.

"Not as such." Azure sat up straighter. "I'm Azure Elwood, and your name is?"

The witch tilted her head. "Mazarin Elwood. If you

aren't a necromancer, how did you know how to contact me?"

"That's not important." Azure shook her head. She didn't think she wanted to tell Mazarin about Rus. It might spook her. Then there was the matter of Mazarin asking if the Elwood line had finally produced *another* necromancer. As if it had happened before, when no records Azure could find showed that the Elwoods had ever dabbled in anything to do with the dead. "What is important is the centennial. What's different about this one than the others before it?"

"So not a necromancer then, but in love with one. Interesting." Mazarin had keen eyes, although Azure wasn't sure what color they were through the gloom of the After. Keen eyes, and a cunning mouth. She was dangerous. "It's the fifth, is it not?"

"It is."

"Five in numerology represents change. Not all change is good." Mazarin rocked back on her heels, allowing some distance between her icy presence and where Azure sat.

"The prophecy says that those closest to the Heart of Moondale may receive its strength." That had to be a good thing, right? That had to mean that the changes coming to Moondale would be for the better. But there was no way of really knowing. What could that strength add up to? And what could power like that make people do to get it? And how would they use it after they had it? Moondale had never been a place for the power hungry before. It was founded on the principles of equality, of all finding a home away from the wider world—both folk and human alike— that often sought to use and abuse their gifts.

"This is so." Mazarin conceded. "It also states that your shadows will walk amongst you. What do you think the shadows of our family will do with their time on earth?"

More word games and riddles. Azure resisted the urge to roll her eyes. She was just about to tell Mazarin to cut the shit when—

"You must be cautious of the dead who walk with you." Mazarin's eyes had hazed over, her features going blurry. They were losing the connection, and Azure wasn't sure why. Was something interfering? Something or *someone* that didn't want Mazarin to tell her story? Or was this merely a consequence of the thickening veil due to the changing seasons? Soon it would be the longest day of the year, and the After would be as far from this plane as it could get.

"What dead who walk with me?" Azure was getting real fucking tired of the vagueness. Why couldn't everyone say what the fuck they meant?

"Cling close to your necromancer, Azure Elwood." Mazarin leaned in closer again, her voice a whisper as if she was afraid someone might overhear them. "She might be the only one who can put to rights the wrong I unleashed on Moondale."

Then she was gone.

# Chapter 15

"So let me get this straight," Rus said after Azure told her everything she'd learned from Mazarin. Which wasn't much, admittedly. More vague warnings and blurry threats. There was nothing concrete for them to fight against. Not yet. And Azure hated that more than anything. How was she to prepare a defense when she had no clear indication of what the offense might look like? "There is some ancient wrong that your ancestor let loose on Moondale five hundred years ago, and she thinks only I can fix it?"

"That is correct." If Azure didn't have a headache after opening a line to the After, she sure as shit did now. The tension that resided in Rus's shoulders, pulling them up around her ears as she hunched forward over her desk, perfectly mirrored the tightness that had settled into Azure's own muscles. A spring winding itself up and up and up with no release in sight.

Fernando shifted in the seat beside her, Cal—his familiar—was tucked into the hood of his sweatshirt and poking her nose out to sniff the air. They'd both been silent thus far, letting Rus and Azure hash this out as best they could. But that almost made things worse, in Azure's opinion. She could use his calming presence now. The easy way he was able to make any problem seem small.

"And," Rus continued, her tone going up another octave

as panic clearly set in, "we also have to worry about, and I quote because fuck me this is a lot, '*the dead that walk with us*'?"

"Yes."

"Great." Rus's voice cracked on the word, and Azure had to fight every fiber of her being not to go to her. To comfort her. To try to shield her physically from everything that was coming. "Just super."

Wait.

She didn't have to war with herself about comforting Rus. She was allowed that now. She had been gifted permission to be everything Rus needed now. So Azure rose from her chair and made her way around the desk. Rus leaned toward Azure, seeking her warmth the way a sunflower seeks the sun, and Azure curled around Rus's seated form. Azure pressed her nose to Rus's hair, inhaling slowly.

"Add it to the fucking list." Rus let out a broken chuckle, pressing her face into Azure's stomach. "Right alongside finding two more members, your aunt being sick, and whatever the fuck Taryn is up to."

"And the appeal for our covenship likely coming," Fernando added, which was not at all helpful, but he wasn't wrong. That was a very real concern as well.

"Is there any *good* news?" Rus asked, the words muffled by Azure's sweater. She was glad the girls were in bed. Glad they couldn't see their guardian like this—lost, hopeless.

"You said you found us a coven house." Fernando leaned forward more. His face was less drawn than it had been a moment ago, but Azure didn't know him well enough to know if he was forcing the smile.

"You did?" Azure pulled away so she could look down at Rus's face. "Where?"

Rus smiled, sly and smooth, so much of the old Rus

shining through that Azure could almost forget about their current problems. "It's not for sure yet. Nesta has to check to see if I can get the permits to change a property that's residential to coven, and of course I'll need to see if we can get the loan for it."

"Residential?" Azure blinked at her, then she was laughing, delight fizzing through her veins and making everything else seem insubstantial. "Next door?"

"Like I said"—Rus shrugged, sitting up straighter—"we'll see. But I've started the process of seeing if we can swing it. Nesta is going to keep this all under wraps until they're sure we can. Otherwise . . ."

"The Board of Magic might try to stop you." Azure nodded. She leaned back, resting her butt against the desk. "I could see Brant scooping up the property just to ruin our plans."

"Exactly."

"You don't really think they'd do that, do you? They gave you permission to start a coven." Confusion drew Fernando's brows together. Which was sweet, almost. Like he didn't understand the cutthroat behavior and pettiness that went on in a political landscape as tightly knit as Moondale. Maybe he didn't. He wasn't from here, after all. But Azure had spent her entire life among the sharks, and she knew what they would do. She knew what kind of frenzy came from a drop of blood in the water.

"Brant didn't agree with the decision, but he was over-ruled. Now that Gilroy is back from his hibernation, he's taken Brant's side." It was only a matter of time before Brant and Gilroy had poisoned others against them.

"Gilroy Herne?" Rus asked, a delighted smile curling the corners of her lips, which was infuriatingly adorable. Why Rus found it funny that Gilroy had it out for her,

Azure may never know. "That old bastard never did care much for me."

"He thinks your magic is against the natural order of things. That it upsets the balance." Azure had heard those exact words enough growing up to know that was the logic Gilroy and Brant would use. It was the same things they'd whispered about Rus when she'd first started raising the dead. Azure had realized it was closed-minded drivel in the months since Rus returned to Moondale, considering how careful and in tune Rus was with the balance. It would be laughable if it weren't so fucking dangerous to their position here.

Rus *did* laugh, her head tilted back, the sound filling the office, bouncing off the walls papered in a black and gray forest. When she was finally through, she wiped a tear from the corner of her eye.

*Dramatic bitch. Goddess, she's beautiful like this.* Bursting at the seams with so much Rus-ness. Azure wanted to take a bite out of her, hold the last of Rus on her tongue and savor it. Maybe later.

"I'm sorry, I just find a lecture on balance funny coming from a druid who once introduced an invasive species to Moondale so he could choke out a plant he considered a weed." There was a sharp malice to Rus's words, a bite that could cut. She wasn't incorrect though—Gilroy had done that. It had been many years ago and he'd learned his lesson, but he'd done it just the same. "All the while, I bleed to keep the balance in place."

"He's uneducated," Azure tried to reason.

"He's an asshole," Rus sniped dangerously.

"I'm not arguing that he's not." Azure shook her head because Rus was right. Gilroy was an asshole. It was honestly kind of amazing Cagney hadn't tried to unseat him yet. But druids lived much longer than witches, and Cagney was still a baby by their standards. "But he is a real danger to us."

"You think he could turn the tide," Fernando said. It wasn't a question. He didn't sound frightened though, which was good. They couldn't afford to be afraid now. They had to present a united front. To stand against this together. Not one of them could show hesitation. Azure knew she could count on Fernando and Rus for that.

"I think it was easier to drown out a single voice, but it'll be much harder when there are two. Some of the others who were on the fence, or maybe kept their disagreements silent, might come forward now and stand with Brant and Gilroy." Azure tilted her head back so she could look at Fernando, gauge the resolve on his face. He tilted his chin up and met her gaze with determination. Good. That was good.

"What are you going to do about him?" Rus asked.

"I'm going to set up a meeting with Hunter Delacroix. I don't think we can wait until your lecture series to add to our numbers." Azure stood, smoothing her hands down her clothes, tidying up her appearance. "You and Nesta are going to work on the coven house paperwork. When it comes time to purchase the property, let me know. I'll help with the loan."

"So, just keep going as we are and hope it all falls into place?" Rus didn't look convinced, her brows raised high on her face. "I don't know, Az. Maybe we should speak with Gilroy? See if we can strike some kind of deal?"

"That wouldn't help." Azure shook her head. "It would only vindicate his belief that you're bad for Moondale if he thinks you're willing to do anything to get a foothold on the town. He'd call it bribery. We have to do this through the correct channels. Once we have two more members, I'll petition to have the probationary status dropped, and then start my bid for an elder seat."

There was so much to do. Too much. And they didn't have enough time to do it. Not if Gilroy and Brant were going to make their move before the next official Board of Magic meeting at the full moon. Two weeks. They had two weeks to make this all work. All Azure could do was pray to the Goddess that Hunter had a friend or two who also needed a coven.

"And in the meantime, we keep an eye on this dead walking business?" Fernando suggested. "Because that's still an issue. Should you maybe tell the board what you've found?"

"No," Rus and Azure said at the same time.

"They'll either dismiss it . . ." Azure said.

"Try to use it to their advantage, or blame me for it. There's too much possibility for a total power grab here. We have to be more careful than that." Rus nodded in agreement. "We sit on that information. No one outside of the coven knows, not until things are more settled and we better understand what is going to happen with the centennial."

"I should get going. I have a board meeting in a half hour. I can't be late." Azure pulled out her phone to check the time and sighed. She didn't want to go sit in a room full of people who didn't trust her or her coven, but it was the best way to keep them all safe. At least for now. She straightened her clothes again, a nervous habit, and turned to head for the door.

"Az." Rus grabbed her by the wrist. Azure hadn't even heard her rise from her chair, she was so caught up in the dread of another meeting. But the warmth from Rus's grip eased some of the strain, as if she were shouldering some of the weight loading Azure down. Rus's thumb brushed over the thin skin on the inside of Azure's wrist, the callouses rough but comforting. "I'll pick you up after, all right?"

"I'd like that."

MAKING nice with Taryn was honestly the hardest part about organizing the centennial celebration. Everything else came as if by instinct: the schedule for the events, the number of vendors, where certain things should be held in town. Azure had been raised to know all of these, to be ready for this exact event, and she was. But smiling politely and pretending like she wasn't deeply suspicious of Taryn and her motives was a struggle in futility.

"I was thinking perhaps we should have the vendors set up near the docks, instead of on Main Street," Taryn said, tapping her pen against the map sprawled out between them.

"There is more space there," Brant agreed all too readily.

Azure wasn't sure why, in the name of the Goddess, Brant had shown up to this meeting. It wasn't for the elders; it was for the people who were planning the normie events. But she supposed someone needed to oversee their progress, and he had volunteered. Just to be a pain in her ass, specifically, she was sure.

"The flow of energy would be all wrong." Azure frowned, resisting the urge to sigh. Were they *trying* to turn this event into a disaster?

"How do you know what the flow of energy would look like?" Brant sneered. "Did you study energy patterns? Or the geographical makeup of Moondale? Do you have a PhD in—"

"It would flow directly toward the water, then downstream toward Ironport instead of up to the Heart of Moondale." Azure was not having a good time, not at all.

Brant's face turned red at being cut off, and he opened his mouth to argue further.

"Azure's right," one of the other protégés offered, but they kept their voice soft, as if wary of getting between warring family members. "Main Street runs right into a major vein from the Heart. It'll provide the best feedback."

"Then why have the seafood feast on the docks?" another asked, a snide tone to the question. This was Brant's protégé, and honestly, Azure was so fucking tired.

Goddess, she just wanted to be done with this already. If it were solely up to her, everything would be organized and they'd be collecting vendor applications and contacting everyone they needed to by now. But because the planning was done by committee, it was all going to take so much fucking *longer*. And while time wasn't short for them to organize this, it *was* short for her to get her shit together and keep the Coven of the Forgotten from being disbanded before it'd really begun. She didn't have time to argue with people who clearly didn't understand how negative and positive energy flowed.

Damn Nixie Virnan and her infernal debts.

"Because there is negativity associated with the death of so many animals as well. It makes that particular event almost null in terms of energy flow." Was every folk the elders had chosen to act as their protégés a fucking novice? Azure was sure even Aihuan would understand the connotations of a non-vegetarian feast. Not that she held anything against people who wanted to eat crabs in the summer—it was what Maryland was known for, after all. But when it came to what would work best for their needs, the potential for unsettled crustacean spirits had to be taken into account.

"There won't be space for the vendors to be set up on Main Street," Taryn argued, stabbing her finger on the map. "We need at least a ten-by-ten for each vendor, and we have over a hundred confirmed. I'm not going to go through and cut the list, not when they've all already paid their table fees. Are you?"

"We'll have to coordinate with Sheriff Greer to close the road through that area." An act Azure knew would cause some frustration—and thus negativity—from the people who were rerouted, but she had taken that into account. Factored it in by placing the parking for it down by the water where any bad feelings, like any potential lingering crustacean spirits, would be swept downstream. Plus, hungry people would be closer to the food, and thus less likely to remain grumpy as they walked around town.

"What about the carnival?" Dillan Holyore—Nesta's sibling—asked. He was young yet, much too young to be a potential for the Clan of Crescentia elder seat, but as Azure looked around, she realized that they all were. Only she and Taryn were even close to the right age to be taking over for a retiring elder. In all likelihood, none of them would be chosen as elder for their clan when the time came. It would be someone else, someone who maybe wasn't even born yet. Which made this whole thing worse, honestly.

"That, I was having a difficult time finding a place for. I'm unsure what kind of energy we can expect from it, and so placing it is a struggle. Plus, we need an area of town that's wide open to allow space for the rides and games." In truth, Azure didn't think they should have a carnival. It cheapened what they were doing. And it wasn't something that had been done at the first four centennial celebrations, making it a wild card she didn't care for. There was no way to know exactly what kind of energy it would produce and how that energy would affect the overall landscape of Moondale's natural patterns. But Taryn had proposed the idea, and the other elders had seen the benefit of more potential revenue with the games and such drawing in a younger crowd that may not have otherwise been interested.

"I suppose we can't use the fairgrounds?" Taryn raised one dark brow, either in question or mockery. Maybe a bit of both.

"The fairgrounds are so far out of the regular grid . . ." Azure wore on her lip. "It might be viable. Maybe it would be detached enough from the main lines that it wouldn't really have an effect, negative nor positive."

"It's the only place that has enough room. I'm putting it there," Taryn said without waiting for any further argument as she scribbled it onto the map they were working from.

Azure's eyebrow twitched.

From there, the discussion ebbed and flowed. They agreed and disagreed in turn. But within a couple of hours, they had a plan in place. An order of events, and placement for everything that needed placing.

Productivity relaxed Azure. Some of what was going on around her was out of her control, but not all of it. She'd proven tonight that she would make a fine addition to the Board of Magic, even if the only one who'd been there to see it was Brant Ironwood, and now she could go home to Rus loose limbed and tired. Rus would curl around her and remind her that she had done her best. And it would be enough.

Rus, who was waiting for her right outside those doors,

ready to take Azure home. *Home.* The thought of it made Azure smile.

"Elwood," Brant said, moving up beside her at the now empty table in the middle of the room. She'd been gathering the papers together, planning to make copies of them for everyone so no one could claim they didn't know what was going on.

"Brant." Azure straightened her back, lifted her chin, and gave Brant her full attention. Not out of deference, but because she'd learned over the last few months that one didn't turn their back on an enemy.

"Is it even *right* that you're helping plan the centennial when technically you're not a part of a Moondale coven anymore?" Brant leaned in closer, his eyes sharp and cutting. "What you and that . . . death dealer are doing in our town, it's sickening. Scooping up viable real estate. Spreading your twisted views on magic to our children."

Azure opened her mouth to argue, to put him in his place. Someone needed to—he was getting rather full of himself with all of this. As if he had any authority at all to contradict her place when the board had agreed to let her coven have a seat at the table.

"Don't you have any shame at all?" he pressed, not giving her a moment to speak as he loomed over her. His muddy green magic had settled around him. A threat. Intimidation. Azure wondered idly what he thought he could do with that. If he thought he could attack her in the middle of the Board of Magic building and no one would notice. No. Likely not. He was arrogant, not stupid. "Walking around, dragging your family's name through the mud. If you were my child, I'd—"

"You'd *what?*" a new voice asked from just behind Brant.

He flinched, face going suddenly pale, and whirled around to find Rus standing behind him. Very close. Close enough that it was a wonder he hadn't felt her breath on his neck. A wonder that Azure hadn't noticed her there.

"Elder Ironwood." Rus dipped her head in cold politeness and paced carefully around him to stand at Azure's side, never once turning her back on Brant. Her hands were behind her, and the soft whisper of unsettled spirits accompanied her when her hip brushed against Azure's. There was no glowing hiss of her magic, but the threat was there, imminent and far more terrifying than anything Brant Ironwood could do.

"Ashthorne," Brant grumbled. His eyes narrowed on Rus, his lip threatening to lift in a snarl.

"As I seem to recall," Rus said, keeping her tone light and cordial, "we earned probationary status for the Forgotten thanks to Az's excellent rhetoric and my ingenuity. I believe that means we earned that spot fair and square, don't you? Or"—she leaned forward, and Azure swore her eyes glowed—"are you saying that you haven't benefited from the use of my Ghost Tracer?"

"I never said—"

"I didn't think so. From what I've seen," Rus continued, not giving him a single moment to interrupt, "your coven used that data a mere month ago to plan your spring rituals."

She paused and waited for Brant to contradict her, to argue, it seemed, and holy shit, Azure wanted to grab Rus by her collar and kiss her until they both couldn't breathe.

When he had nothing else to say, Rus offered him a cold, cutting smile. "It's hardly right for a man of your station to hold grudges and make petty threats, isn't it? What would your coven say?" Rus clicked her tongue disapprovingly, shaking her head. "They might think someone else would be better suited to the post. Your niece, perhaps?"

"I'll see myself out." Brant's face had gone deathly pale, more afraid of the vague threat of being overthrown politically than the magic that Rus would more than happily utilize against him. "Good night, Elwood."

"Good night, Elder Ironwood." Rus waved cheerfully at his back, her gray eyes bright.

Azure didn't give her a moment to think, much less turn to face her, before she grabbed Rus by the collar and slammed their lips together, pivoting them until Rus was backed into the table. Rus let out a soft yelp of surprise but melted into the kiss. Going pliant and easy under Azure's weight.

Goddess, Azure loved her like this. Dangerous and deadly necromancer putty in Azure's hands. Weak for the touch of Azure's mouth. It was a rush.

"Take me home," Azure said against Rus's lips, only pulling back long enough to grab her purse and start stumbling toward the door.

# Chapter 16

Usually, Azure liked to be in charge, in control. That's how her dynamic with Rus had always functioned from the inside. Which was funny because from the outside people seemed to assume that Rus was the more experienced of the two of them, the more adventurous, the more dominant. It wasn't true. Rus could flirt and charm with the best of them, but when it came to sex, things were different. Behind closed doors, Rus seemed happy enough to make out a little and not push things further until Azure nudged them along and hinted that *she* wanted more.

So yes, Azure was used to being in charge, and she liked things that way, honestly. But there was something about the Rus who had come home to her after eleven long years. This Rus was older and more powerful. This Rus knew her strength and didn't shy away from flaunting it. This Rus would not be shamed by others simply because of how her magic had manifested. *This* Rus made Azure want to get down on her knees, give Rus the reins, and worship at her feet.

Especially after the way she'd put Brant in his place so soundly.

So when Azure's back hit the wall beside their bedroom door with a *thud*, and Rus's thumb dug into the hinge of her jaw to angle her head up for better access to her throat, she didn't fight it. She didn't try to wrest control back from Rus.

Instead, her breath caught in her lungs, her skin prickled with heat, and she did her level best not to melt into a puddle on the floor.

She was pinned down, held in place by the pressure of Rus's fingers on her jaw and nothing more. Because her knees were fucking jelly, melted under the warmth that had settled into her veins, and she couldn't seem to remember how to tighten the muscles to shore them up. It was amazing they'd made it to the house at all with how hot Rus's hand had been sprawled across her thigh from the driver's seat. Even more amazing that they'd made it up the stairs to their bedroom.

Rus bit another kiss into the side of Azure's throat, her teeth blunt and aching through the skin, drawing a whine from Azure that she didn't think she'd ever heard from herself before. This was new territory for her. Letting someone else be in control. Letting herself be submissive like this. She wasn't sure how she felt about it, but her mind had gone fuzzy the moment her back hit the wall, and she couldn't seem to get a thought through it aside from sensory things.

Rus's teeth against her skin. Her hands bruising tight around Azure's hips. Azure's bra constricting her lungs even more, making it hard to draw in a full breath—not that her body seemed intent on trying with the way her chest heaved. The cold burn of magic along her skin where Rus's green flames still twisted and settled into Rus's scarred arms, pressing against Azure almost by accident. The chafe of her skirt against her thighs where Rus was close, so close, but not close enough. Where Azure arched her back to press her hips against Rus's own, trying to gain some traction, some friction, asking for what she needed, pleading without saying the words.

"No," Rus murmured softly, tightening her grip on Azure's hips so her blunt nails dug into the skin through Azure's clothes. The wallpaper was rough through her thin collared shirt, the button at the top of her spine digging into the bone. But Azure stilled just the same, went wide eyed and frozen at the gentle but firm tone.

"No?" The word tumbled from her lips, unbidden. Azure didn't want to question Rus. She didn't want to push for the tables to flip. She wanted to see what this new Rus would do with the control Azure had all but thrust at her.

"I don't—" Rus stopped, swallowed roughly, and lifted her head so she could meet Azure's gaze, finally, finally showing Azure the emotion sweeping across her face. It was complicated. Rus's brows drawn together, her mouth twisted a little. An expression Azure usually associated with Rus worrying she'd disappoint someone. With her being self-conscious. Which was jarring considering how she'd been a moment ago. Rus faltered, her eyes darting to the wall just over Azure's shoulder.

"You don't what?" Azure pressed, not wanting to stretch the moment any further lest it break. Whatever this was, whatever had drawn Rus up short, they could work around it. They'd always be able to work around it. Rus just needed to talk to her.

"I don't feel—" Rus sighed, but she hadn't dropped her hold from Azure's jaw, her thumbnail—bitten to the quick— still digging in lightly to Azure's skin. It felt good. As if Rus didn't want to let go. As if she couldn't tear herself away, even as she struggled against whatever intrusive thought had pulled her to a stop. Rus hummed for a minute, thinking, then nodded to herself. "I don't want it right now."

It took Azure an embarrassingly long moment to realize what Rus meant when she said "it." Her brain was slow from the warm buzz that refused to dissipate so long as Rus had her hands on Azure the way she did. Dominating. And then she understood, fully. Rus's desire for intimacy between them was always fairly consistent, but her desire for the physical act of sex waxed and waned like the moon. It always had. Some days, she wanted it as badly as Azure did. Some days, the need burned so hot beneath her skin that Azure swore it would set them both alight. Other days, Rus was happy enough to let Azure find her pleasure without caring for any herself.

It had never been an issue between them.

It wasn't one now.

"You're in charge," Azure murmured, leaning back into the wall and lifting her chin to bare her neck to Rus fully. "We do what you want. If you don't want me to touch you, I won't. If you want to stay dressed, you can."

Rus blinked at her, her cheeks flushed, her gaze flicking between Azure's eyes, uncertain. As if no one had told her that recently. As if all her partners since Azure had tried to change how Rus was. As if someone had told her there was something wrong with her. There wasn't. And Azure would like to burn every person who had made Rus believe otherwise. Reduce them to cinders and scatter the ashes to the wind.

"You're in charge," Azure repeated, letting her body go lax, her hands falling to grip the wall on either side of her hips instead of where they'd been on Rus's waist, trying to pull her in. The frenzy had died away. The need to push, to pull, to be closer, closer, *closer*, a soft buzz. But the heat remained, simmering low in Azure's belly. Easy enough to think through now, but not gone.

Rus let out a soft, strangled noise, the flush rising higher on her cheeks, burning red, and ducked forward to press her face into Azure's neck where she let out a delighted chuckle. "You're the best. Really, Az, just the fucking best."

Azure bit back a laugh and rolled her eyes. "I know. But don't tell me." She tilted her head further, her hair snagging on the wall and pulling a little as her back arched. Not enough to press against Rus, since that was clearly not what she wanted, but enough to drive home the invitation. *Touch me. However you like. You haven't scared me away. You never could. Not even if you tried.* "Show me."

"Okay. Yeah. Okay. I can do that." Rus pulled her face away from Azure's neck to fix her with a smile so sharp, it felt like a blade against Azure's skin.

Azure closed her eyes, took a breath, and waited for Rus to tell her what to do, where to go. She'd thought maybe they'd move to the bed, maybe Rus would pull away and leave her cold for a moment as they got somewhere more comfortable for both of them.

Rus seemed to have other ideas.

Instead of pulling away, Rus leaned in closer. Not close enough to press her body against Azure's, but close enough that Azure swore she could feel the warmth of Rus's chest right along with the cold burn of her magic rising. It sizzled along Azure's skin. Made her squirm. Her heart ratcheted up in speed, slamming against her chest, and the fire in her belly sparked anew.

Rus pressed her knee between Azure's thighs, nudging them apart slowly as she nosed at Azure's jaw, her warm breath burning hot against the overly sensitive skin. Azure shifted easily and let Rus adjust their position.

Sharp teeth sank into Azure's earlobe, drawing out a muffled gasp and sending a shudder down Azure's spine that made it harder to keep her hands to herself. A dark chuckle left Rus, rumbling through her chest as she rubbed her thigh against Azure through her skirt, smearing the wet there and making Azure shiver.

"I want you to ride me," Rus said, tone deep and leading. Like a siren calling Azure to the sea, luring her toward surrender. Every hair on her arms stood on end, her body humming with want. "Do you think you can do that, Magpie?"

*Magpie.* Goddess, how long had it been since she'd heard that particular nickname out loud? It had only been in dreams. In idle imaginings that she used to get herself off for fucking *years* that she heard Rus call her that. *Magpie.* It should have felt almost like an insult. After all, magpies—like crows—were thieves, stealing shiny things to build their nests. But it never had. Not when Rus said it that way. Not with the possessive edge Rus liked to use. With reverence. As if she was thinking instead of the Magpie Bridge. Of the beauty of being reunited with someone beloved after so long.

*My magpie* had been how Rus had used it first. But after that it was shortened to just Magpie, or Maggie, the "mine" unspoken but no less understood. And honestly, if Azure had struggled to get back into the moment, just *that* would have sent her over the edge.

She melted back into the wall, going almost boneless so the only thing holding her up was Rus's thigh, which didn't move. Didn't offer any further relief to Azure's aching core. Just stayed there, soft with muscle and hard with bone.

Rus was humming softly against her neck when Azure got her head back on enough to listen. The sound sent vibrations into her chest. Rus's thumb no longer dug into Azure's jaw, but rubbed against it in a slow, methodical motion. As if soothing an erratic spirit. "Back with me?"

"For the moment," Azure said, but the words scraped

raw against her throat as if she'd been running for miles in the cold. "What were—what were you saying?"

The chuckle Rus pressed into her throat was dark and liquid. Dangerous. And it pooled hotter in Azure's belly than anything else had thus far. "Do you think you can ride me, Magpie?" Rus repeated, her hands falling to grip Azure's hips so firmly, they felt like a brand against her soft skin. "I'll help."

She gave Azure's hips a sharp tug, dragging her mound, wet folds, hot clit, and all against the fabric of Rus's jeans. The seams scraped rough at Azure's thighs, but it didn't matter. None of it mattered. Because that friction was exactly what she needed, pressing hard and unyielding, a slow grind that made her toes curl against the floorboards. Rus set the pace. Her fingers tight against Azure's skin, not letting her speed up or slow down. Moving her exactly as Rus wanted.

And Azure . . . Azure was fucking helpless but to go along. Soft gasps and whimpers ripped from her throat at every push forward, as Rus changed the pressure, lifting her thigh higher, easing off. Driving Azure slowly to a cliff she was sure would leave her shattered.

"That's it. That's my girl," Rus cooed against her throat, her breath so hot Azure was sure it would blister. A shiver slid down her spine like a caress. "My Magpie." Rus hummed almost idly. "Keep going."

She pulled her hands away from Azure then—leaving Azure to continue the movement of her hips, chasing her own release—and lifted them to begin working Azure out of her shirt. The button at the top of her spine got caught in her hair, snagging through the braid, and Rus grunted, annoyed. But with a soft murmur of magic, it came undone and was tossed to the floor. Leaving Azure in just the strapless bra she'd been wearing underneath, and the skirt that was gradually becoming uncomfortable with how it got in the way of her movements against Rus's thigh. She pressed her clit harder against Rus now that she was left to her own devices, but she didn't increase speed. That would be too noticeable. Rus might stop her then. She didn't want to be stopped.

Cool air hit her chest when her bra was cast aside as well, making her skin pebble. But Rus didn't leave her cold for long. Her calloused hands slid from Azure's waist to brush over her breasts. Thumbs scraping her nipples, making her keen and arch into Rus's touch further as Rus's cutting smile pressed knife-sharp against her collarbones. "I still know what you like."

"Mm-hmm," Azure agreed idly and gasped, rocking hard against Rus's leg as she felt the first warm press of Rus's mouth against her breast, lifting Azure onto her toes for better access to her chest. Azure let out a soft noise of protest as the new angle made it near impossible to work herself against Rus.

"I've got you, Maggie," Rus murmured against her skin, teeth rolling gently over her nipple. Her free hand slid under Azure's skirt, fingers making quick work of pushing her underwear out of the way so she could work Azure's clit with her thumb, following the same slow, building rhythm as before. Two fingers slipped inside Azure's wet entrance, meeting no resistance apart from the way they had to fit between Azure and Rus's leg. Rus rubbed her thumb in slow circles against Azure's clit while her mouth went back to work.

It took what felt like years and seconds all at the same time for the relentless pressure on her clit, the biting hot kisses on her breasts, and the press of Rus's fingers inside of her to drive her over the edge. Her orgasm crested and slammed into her, her walls clenching down hard around Rus's fingers, and a choked sob ripped from her throat.

Rus worked her through it. Stayed pressed inside her, switching to soft kitten licks against her breasts as Azure floated, warm and sated. Azure grumbled when Rus pulled away, but it was only far enough for her to squat down and lift Azure onto her hips, a feat that arguably should have been impossible. But what was magic for if not to manhandle one's girlfriend to the bed? Azure approved of its use, and even more of the way the covers felt against her bare skin after Rus helped her out of the rest of her clothes and covered her then went to the bathroom for a washcloth to clean her up.

It took what felt like forever for Rus to come back and curl up beside her, now down to her own underwear and a thin cami. But Rus pulled her in close, curling around her back and nosing at Azure's neck softly.

"Good night, my magpie." Rus's breath coasted warm against Azure's skin, and Azure shivered, closing her eyes.

"Good night, Icarus."

# Chapter 17

Rus recognized that it was just nerves. Just old anxieties rising to the surface, telling her that no one would want to join her coven, no one would want to be her friend, she had nothing to offer. For so many years, that's what the adults of Moondale told her. She'd grown up hearing that her magic was of use to no one. That her ideas were ridiculous. That she'd never make it in the world by following every harebrained idea that struck her. She'd been a pariah by the time she left, after bringing Darcy back. And everyone told her, excluding Az, that no one would ever want anything to do with someone who played with the dead. That the smell of corpses and grave earth would follow her forever.

She'd proven them wrong, over and over again, out in the world at large. Come back to Moondale a success, in some minor terms. An accomplished necromancer who understood her magic, who felt settled in it, who finally saw the value in it. Had built a family for herself. Found people who loved her not in spite of what she was, not because of it, but because of *who* she was. Necromancy was just another thing about her, like her gray eyes and the freckles along her nose.

But . . . well, being back in Moondale had a way of drawing out her old hangups. And the insecurity of it made her skin prickle.

"You'll be fine," Az said from where she was sitting on the couch, watching Rus pace. She hadn't tried to talk Rus off the ledge, which Rus was grateful for because they both knew if she did, it would just make Rus feel more out of control. More wound up.

"I'll make tea," Fernando said, rising from one of the armchairs to head to the kitchen.

The house was quiet around them, devoid of the girls Indigo had ushered across the street about twenty minutes ago to visit with Aunt Maureen and Aunt Carmine. It was strange, but Rus thought perhaps the girls were starting to see the two women as their grandmothers. Nice, because they didn't have biological grandparents, but strange . . . still. Every minute Az spent at 157 Mourning Moore, her family was blending with Rus's, slowly becoming one. Rus thought maybe she ought to be more resistant to that, but she didn't want to be. It was a relief to not feel like she was in this alone anymore. And there was a selfish, grasping part of her that wanted to snatch every bit of goodness, every shining thing on offer and hoard it away for herself. Like the crows she was associated with.

"What if they don't like us?" Rus asked. She spun on her heel to walk the stretch of the living room again. "Or what if they like being covenless? I liked it before . . . everything."

Az hummed thoughtfully but didn't respond. Probably for the best. Anything she said, Rus would simply argue against. And then they'd get into a fight. And then the tension in the air would be so palpable that Hunter and his friend wouldn't want to be around them at all, much less join their coven. Oh Goddess, what if the energy was wrong? What if they just didn't *mesh*?

"Why don't you sit down?" Az patted the spot beside

her on the couch. She met Rus's gaze with an expression that Rus could only identify as coaxing, leading. And Rus had spent so many years without that expression in her life, without those brown eyes looking at her as if they wanted nothing more than to draw her in, that Rus crumpled under the weight of them. It had always been a struggle in futility to say no to Az, but their time apart had only made that more true. "Tell me what's really worrying you."

"What *isn't* worrying me?" Rus laughed. She leaned forward, bracing her weight on her knees. She'd tugged on one of Az's sweaters this morning. It was too hot for it, but she needed that layer of cozy comfort, the smell of Az near her nose, her arms and scars hidden away by something softer, prettier, unable to be touched by the air-conditioned air. It was probably expensive, cashmere or Angora or something—had to be for how nice it felt. And it was a pale blue-green color that might have been mint if it didn't have so much blue in it. Rus didn't know colors as well as some might, but she knew it looked damn good on Az, and it felt nice to be surrounded by something that screamed *Azure Elwood.*

"I see," Az said, and Rus thought maybe she did. It was scary sometimes how Az could see into the core of her. How even with eleven years apart, over a decade of experiences separating them, Az still *saw* Rus. There had been a time in Rus's life that she'd thought her and Az's paths would never cross again. That they would continue to drift further and further apart, like continents. But like any large land mass, a seismic shift could push them back together, and it had. Her girls. Her beautiful, perfect, sometimes bratty girls. Goddess, she'd gotten so lucky.

"Try putting them into words," Az encouraged. "They may seem smaller once they're out in the open."

They might, but Rus couldn't really apply language to the vague sense of panic in her belly. She tried, and what came out was "What if they don't like *me*?" Which was childish and immature, and she recognized it for what it was but couldn't take the words back now that they'd been said. "What if I can't convince them and we have to start over?"

Az looked like she maybe wanted to roll her eyes, but she didn't. Instead, she said, "Hunter has already met with you. You two seemed to have a very good discussion about the Ghost Tracer. It seems to me that he already likes you."

"Tea," Fernando said, reappearing before them with a tray. "It'll help with your nerves."

Az pressed a mug from the tray into Rus's fingers. One of the basic bitch gray ones from the cupboard, although these days there seemed to be less and less of them. The gray in Rus's world, her home, slowly being eclipsed by Az's soft colors. Strangely, it made 157 Mourning Moore feel more like home, not less. Rus didn't feel like she was being pushed out. She felt like she was making room. It was nice. Az picked up her own mug, a pale-yellow one covered in daisies that said, "Bitch, I will put you in a trunk and help people look for you. Stop playing with me" in a lovely cursive font on the side that indicated it was for someone left-handed.

The first time Rus had seen it, she'd almost choked on her coffee. That was probably why Fernando had chosen it. A thought confirmed by the mischievous lilt to his mouth when she looked over at where he'd returned to his chair, sipping from his own plain gray mug. He was a good egg, that one. And the combination of that, the tea, and Az's side pressed warm along Rus's own did settle her. Made the panic ebb. She could do this. Because she wasn't alone.

The doorbell rang and Rus practically jumped out of

her skin, nearly spilling her tea all over herself and Az. Az tsked softly in reprimand and rose from her seat. "I'll get it. You try to compose yourself." She leaned over, pressing a kiss to Rus's temple. "Like the capable witch I know you are."

Then she left, giving Rus no room to argue, and Rus had to lift the mug of tea to her lips for another slow sip. It was good tea. The kind of tea only a Kitchen Witch could make. Infused with Fernando's calming energy and steeped to perfection.

Fernando didn't offer any empty platitudes when she looked over at him. He merely nodded. Was it in agreement with what Az had said? Was it meant to be encouragement? Was it a silent communication for Rus to drink her tea? She wasn't sure, but it settled something inside of her to see the way her closest friend was so relaxed. He was always so . . . mature for someone only a little above the legal drinking age. Seeming wise beyond his years.

"Should we move this to the office, or the kitchen maybe?" Fernando asked as Rus heard the others in the foyer removing their shoes and jackets. "Some place with more seats?"

"No," Az said when she entered the living room. "I'll stand."

Rus lifted her head to look at Hunter and his friend. He'd brought with him a witch who looked about their age, maybe a little younger, with long green hair, tanned skin, and blue eyes.

"It's okay Az, we'll head to the kitchen." Rus rose from her seat and started through the house. Fernando had a point—not one he'd said out loud, but Rus knew what he was trying to tell her. They needed to all be able to see each other's faces, to feel like they were on equal footing here.

That would be easiest done in the kitchen. The round table that had expanded to fit Az all those weeks ago was the perfect place for this discussion. Black wood gleamed beneath her hands as Rus settled into a chair and waited for the others to follow.

"I'll start with introductions," she said once everyone was seated. "I'm Icarus Ashthorne. This is my partner, Azure Elwood, and my friend Fernando Perez." Rus gestured to each in turn. Az nodded, and Fernando gave a friendly little wave before returning his hands to his mug. "In case you didn't know already, I'm a necromancer, a Crow Witch. If that's going to be a problem, I'd like to get it out of the way now."

"No problem," the woman with the green hair said. She hadn't smiled yet, but she wasn't scowling either. She'd observed everything so far with a neutral expression, and Rus took that as a good sign. "Avalyn Franklin, Stitch Witch. What designations are you two?" Avalyn nodded toward Az and Fernando.

"Kitchen witch." Fernando gave another friendly wave. He'd never much cared for being put on the spot, and Rus could tell he was uncomfortable with all of this. But he knew as well as she did that they needed him here. They needed to present a united front on this as a coven. If they couldn't stand together in this, why would anyone join them?

"I'm a Hedge Witch," Az said, her tone neutral, but Rus could tell how having to admit it grated on her. Hedge Witches were seen as lesser in most circles. They were witches who either hadn't had the power or the drive to choose a single path, a designation. Many of them hadn't found their innate gift. Many of them had not much more magic than a normie. That wasn't the case with Az, of course, Rus knew that. But it didn't change the way people saw Hedge Witches.

"No way." Hunter laughed, his smile bright. It was the first thing he'd said since he entered. Clearly he'd been holding back, letting Avalyn take point on this. Maybe because he'd already made up his mind. Or maybe because she was adept at making such serious choices. He seemed the impulsive sort. "I'm a Hedge Witch too." He leaned forward, trying to get closer to Az where she sat across the table from him. "Out of curiosity, why?"

Az shifted, uncomfortable beside Rus.

"Oh no. No. You don't have to answer that." Hunter held up his hands. "I know it's really personal. So I'll just . . . you don't have to tell me." He leaned back again, putting distance between them once more as if only now realizing he had pushed into Az's bubble to begin with. "I settled for it because my gift never manifested." Hunter shrugged, unbothered by this admission, although he had to know that in any other circumstance it would make his candidacy for a coven null. No one would want a Hedge Witch without a gift. "Probably because I moved around so much growing up."

"That's certainly possible." Rus scrubbed at the tip of her nose in thought. There were lots of reasons for some-one's gift to not manifest. Magic was a tricky mistress, and she had her own set of rules that she didn't really care to share with the rest of them. But without a place to call home? That tended to really fuck a witch up. It hadn't done so with her girls, likely because although they'd never had a *place* to call home, they'd had *people* to call home. A family. Rus could ask, but she wouldn't—that would be too much prying this early in the game. "Well, if that's the case, then joining the Coven of the Forgotten should help. You'll be tying your magic to Moondale, officially becoming one of her folk. She'll offer her power and protection in exchange."

"And what's the catch?" Avalyn asked, not giving Hunter the chance to be excited by this prospect.

Rus liked her. But then, Rus had grown up with Az, who was also a straight shooter and didn't like beating around the bush about things, so of course Rus would take to someone with a similar temperament. She also liked Hunter, but that kind of went without saying. He was the kind of person it seemed hard not to like. Smiling and cheerful. And he was whip-smart—she could tell from the last time they'd spoken.

"The catch?" Az frowned, her hands moving to rest in her lap where she could clench them into fists without being seen.

Rus reached for one, pulling it to her and carefully pulling Az's fingers apart until she could thread their hands together. "You will probably have to move to Moondale."

No *probably* about it. Rus was sure they would have to move to Moondale at least temporarily. It was a requirement of tying one's magic to the land of a place, that that place then had to become home, not just a mailing address. One could leave for periods of time, but they always had to come back home. And this early in the coven, in the transition? It would likely be necessary that they move to Moondale and not leave for a while.

"But we'll be happy to assist you in finding places to live. We have a friend who works as a real estate agent."

"So we wouldn't be able to join and stay where we are?" Hunter's face fell, his shoulders drooping. "I don't—" He looked to Avalyn as if she'd find the words for him, but she seemed to refuse. "I can't leave Eric and Tony. Not right now. Not when everything is so new."

"And I have a business in Ironport. The commute would be a pain," Avalyn said. Where Hunter had drooped, she sat up straighter. "Moving is a non-option for us, however nice the power boost from Moondale might be."

"I see." Rus deflated. Az squeezed her hand, but the grip didn't soothe the ache that started up in Rus's joints. She hadn't realized how set she was on this, how sure she was that these two would be their saving grace, until it was ripped out from under her. "I understand."

"If there was some way around that part," Hunter hedged, shifting awkwardly in his seat. Rus wondered if perhaps his gift, though unrealized, was empathy. "We'd be happy to join. Ava and I largely didn't join the coven in Ironport because we didn't agree with those in charge, or the politics. But the chance to help build one from the ground up? To decide what a coven would look like?"

"That's exactly what we'd want from a coven, if we were to join one," Avalyn agreed. "But we can't move. That's out of the question."

"I understand," Rus said again, her heart sinking into her stomach. She was going to throw up. "I'll um . . . I'll give it some thought."

"Thank you for your time." Az dipped her head in deference but didn't move to get up from her chair. Probably because of how tightly Rus was holding on to her hand.

"Of course." Avalyn pushed back from the table, clearly realizing they were being dismissed. "If something changes, please let us know."

"And um . . ." Hunter shifted, his hands gripping the back of his chair, rings tapping against the wood. "Thank you for your help with the Ghost Tracer. It was a big help."

Rus smiled, but she could feel that it didn't quite reach

her eyes. It was hard to be happy, to take the compliment, when her insides were roiling against her. "Happy to help."

"I'll walk you out," Fernando offered, already at the doorway into the main hall.

And then they were gone. And Rus realized they were well and truly fucked. She had to wonder . . . Did this mean she wasn't meant to be here at all? Was this a sign from the universe at large that she'd made the wrong choice in trying to make Moondale her home? In trying to make a home for herself? Maybe she wasn't meant to have something like that. Something . . . nice.

# Chapter 18

"There's nothing," Rus said, flopping over onto her back in the grass, rubbing the joints in her right hand as if they ached. She'd set herself up on the edge of the property to contact the spirits she sent to spy on Taryn, and Azure had come with her, waiting patiently at her side as the whispers grew near deafening. That would take some getting used to, Azure assumed—the way they hovered around Rus at almost any time of the day but grew persistent and louder when she used her magic—if Azure was to be living with Rus. Especially as the pressure of it made her ears ring slightly.

Darcy squawked from where he'd perched on a gravestone. He looked distinctly disapproving.

"Fuck off, Darcy." Rus kicked at the marker to try to dispel him but just wound up hurting her toe, if the grumble was anything to go by.

"There has to be something," Azure said reasonably. Because there *had* to be. They both knew Taryn was up to something, between the smear campaign and the changes she was pushing to be made to the centennial. How couldn't there be proof of that?

"There really isn't, Az. Not that my spies have seen. Taryn is just going about her day, normal as you please. Bitching out customer service people. Going into the office. Going home to have lunch with Vi. It's actually kind of boring." Rus turned her head to look at Azure, a bit of grass nearly poking her in the eye and tickling her nose so she scrunched it and scrubbed it away. "The only thing we can't do is see into her and Vi's house, and honestly? I don't need to know what Vi's sex life is like, thanks."

"Giving up won't solve anything." Although she didn't think Rus was giving up. Rus wasn't the type to know how to give up. But it seemed like the thing to say in this circumstance. They needed answers. They needed to know what was coming for them. And one of their best clues was Taryn.

"Sure it will." Rus's tone had pushed into forced brightness, but Azure could see the sheen of tears in her eyes. Why couldn't any part of this process be easy? Why did it seem like the Goddess was testing them at every turn? "It means I can put my focus elsewhere. Like on getting us the fuck out of here."

"You don't mean that." Azure said the words, but she wasn't sure if she believed them or if she was just willing them to be true. Her heart had stopped, stuttered, and restarted to beat so hard against her ribcage that she was sure Rus could hear it and all the soft, hollow longing that lived within it.

"I don't." Rus sighed and scooted until her head rested in Azure's lap, her gray eyes blinking up at Azure with a hushed sadness. Azure relaxed under the assurance, her fingers dipping into Rus's hair. "But honestly, Az, I'm at a loss. Maybe I'm just not meant to be in Moondale. Maybe I don't belong here."

She said it in such a way that Azure realized it had been on Rus's mind a lot lately. That it had been plaguing her. Azure needed to ease this worry now, before it got any worse, before it poisoned what they were building here more than it already had.

"I mean, we've seen it before. How Moondale can reject people. How she puts obstacle after obstacle in their path. Maybe this is just her telling me—"

"Moondale would not have accepted our blood at the Heart if she didn't mean for us to be here. For us to start this coven here. Together." Azure was certain of that much. When everything else around them was shifting and unclear, she knew that at least they had Moondale's approval for what they were doing. She had always been on their side, even when things seemed otherwise impossible. Even when Azure wasn't sure she'd ever see Rus again, Moondale had been working her magic, calling Rus home. "If she didn't want us, we wouldn't have made it up the mountain that day."

"Well, I wish she had more control over her political landscape then, because this shit is tiring."

"I know." Azure stroked her fingers through Rus's hair. The pink had grown out again, in need of a touch-up. Azure could see the beginnings of gray hairs among the dark brown at the roots. She wondered if Nesta had noticed. They likely would have demanded Rus make time for it if they had.

"Hunter seemed so promising." Rus sagged further where she rested in Azure's lap, her eyes closing a little, enjoying the closeness between them. Azure wished they could stay like this. Wished they could blot out the world and the expectations. Wished it could be easy for them how it was for some others. But nothing worth having wasn't also worth fighting for. And Azure wasn't going to lose what she'd gained in the last few months because of a few minor complications. She wouldn't be letting Rus go, not again, not without a fight, or without Azure going with her.

"I'll speak to Sunila and Indigo this evening at dinner," Azure promised, giving Rus's scalp a light scratch that seemed to lull Rus further. "Maybe they know of some young witches who haven't decided on a coven yet."

"No locals." Rus opened her eyes to fix Azure with a serious look. Where there had been softness a moment ago, now there was only the impenetrable wall of Rus's will. She had made up her mind about something, and she wasn't going to back away from it. *Stubborn*, Azure thought with fondness. "I won't have any of the other covens accusing me of poaching their initiates."

"You know," Azure said, keeping her tone light, "eventually we will have to accept local initiates. One day, witches will want to join the Coven of the Forgotten not just because it needs members, but because it offers something the others don't." She was sure of it. Even if it took time. Even if it was an uphill struggle. One day, they would reach the point where people were asking them to join, petitioning for a place among them, not vice versa. "And then we wouldn't have to worry about people needing to move here."

Rus hummed but she didn't look sold on the idea, so Azure relented.

"I'll tell them we only want to speak to out-of-state students. Happy?"

"And no one from a big-name family." Rus lifted a finger to shake at Azure. "No more Elwoods jumping ship to join my coven just because they feel bad for me. I don't need those kinds of optics."

Azure rolled her eyes and flicked Rus lightly in between her eyebrows in reprimand.

Rus gasped, her hand falling to rub at the sore spot that had turned a light pink color. "What was that for?"

"For being ridiculous. Now get up, we have work to do."

"Work? What work?" Rus yelped when Azure shifted and dumped her unceremoniously onto the ground.

"I'm going to see if we can find any other prospects and ask Sunila if maybe she knows anything about Mazarin Elwood. There might be other records outside of Moondale that I can access." Azure rose and brushed the grass and dirt from her mid-length mint-green skirt. "And you, Icarus Ashthorne, are going to get your pert ass inside, dig through your inventions, and start preparing them to be patented. Maybe you'll get lucky and you'll come across a solution to at least one of our current problems."

"You know, if you weren't so pretty, that trick wouldn't work," Rus said, scrambling to her feet, ignoring the grass stains on her faded black jean shorts.

"What trick?"

"The whole boss bitch thing." Rus gesture with her hand to Azure. The mint-green skirt, the black shirt with a white schoolgirl's collar, the sensible flats. It was a little less formal than she'd usually go, but she didn't have classes or work, and spending the day with Rus dredging up spirits required a certain amount of comfort.

"Well," Azure said, taking a step close to Rus that made her stumble back, her eyes going wide, "as Aihuan would say . . ." She was shorter than Rus, but Rus tended to slouch to try to make herself smaller, so Azure had to lean in to put their faces close enough that they were sharing breath. "Tough noogies."

Rus blinked for a moment, processing, then she threw her head back and laughed so bright and so loud, it put the sun to shame. Azure's heart kicked up in her chest, the beat unsteady, but she kept her face from turning too obviously red. At least until Rus got a hold of herself, swatted Azure's ass, and said, "All right, Maggie, let's get to work" before loping along toward the house again.

SUNILA'S APARTMENT—WHICH was really the place atop Elwood & Co. that they usually rented out to tourists—was cramped. Azure, Indigo, and Sunila were elbow to elbow around a two-person table in the galley kitchen. The third chair didn't match the other two, and Azure wondered where Sunila had conjured it from, but decided it was better not to ask.

"We could have just eaten in the living room," Sunila said around a mouthful of tofu.

"If you stain that couch, Aunt Carmine will have your head." Indigo frowned at her.

"So dramatic. This entire family. I swear." Sunila huffed, leaning back further in her chair so the front legs lifted off the floor. She was dressed in a set of bright yellow overalls, with rainbow socks, and a lime green T-shirt.

Every part of Sunila Elwood was an assault on the senses. Always had been. She was the least Elwood-like Elwood that Azure had ever met, and she'd met most of them. But in spite of that, Azure liked Sunila. Liked that she'd never once caved to the pressure to conform. Liked that she was happy to just be herself. And maybe, at some point in Azure's life, she'd been jealous of Sunila too, for all the same reasons. She wasn't jealous now. Because she'd found her own path, her own way to be herself while still being an Elwood. But still, sometimes she looked at Sunila and saw all the years she wasted trying to fit in.

"So the meeting with Dean Cochburn's hopefuls was a bust?" Indigo asked.

"Not a bust. Just—" Azure sighed. Rus was right. The politics of Moondale were a shitshow. But that didn't mean they couldn't work around them. They'd done it before, they could do it again. They just had to think. The problem was that they were running out of time. Gilroy and Brant's displeasure was a slowly tightening noose, and Azure didn't think they had much longer before she couldn't breathe, or before they convinced the town to chase Rus out with pitchforks. "They don't want to move to Moondale for personal reasons. And Rus and I don't think we can convince the board, or Moondale herself, to accept initiates who don't have any real tie to the land."

"Oh." Sunila sobered a little, the legs of her chair hitting the carpet with a dull *thunk*. "That sucks."

"It does. That's why we need more options." Azure sat up straighter, shouldering the load of this at least. She could do that. For Rus. For the girls. For their coven. She could shoulder this burden. "I'll be asking around in my own classes, but since they're in the upper levels, most of the witches have already pledged themselves to a coven."

"And Rus doesn't want to be seen poaching people." Indigo settled his fork on his plate. "Fuck, this is a mess."

"As for your other question"—Sunila scooped up her glass of water and took a sip—"I've never heard of Mazarin Elwood, but I'll ask my family. A couple of my siblings got big into Elwood history when they were younger. Maybe they found something."

"Does Aunt Carmine know anything?" Indigo brushed

his hair back from his face, a sadness to his eyes at the mention of their aunt that hadn't been there before.

"I haven't had the chance to ask her yet. And Rus is worried about this getting around Moondale. We aren't sure who knows what and who is on whose side." Not that she didn't trust Aunt Carmine—she did. But there was always the chance that Aunt Carmine might slip up and say something to Taryn, and Azure definitely did *not* trust Taryn. "How is Aunt Carmine?"

There was so much to talk about, and they only had a few short hours to do it before Azure had to head to yet another meeting to go over the vendor list for the marketplace during the centennial celebration. She didn't have time to get hung up on one thing, not when she needed help with so much. Not when the weight of all of this was slowly suffocating her. She understood why Rus had thought about just lying in the middle of the yard and not moving. It would certainly be easier. But when had Azure Elwood and Icarus Ashthorne ever taken the easy way out? Definitely not when it came to each other.

"She's better than she was. Still not great. Taryn is trying a new treatment, and it seems to be helping. But Violet thinks—" Indigo stopped, his lips pressing together hard enough to turn them white, eyes suddenly glassy. He inhaled deep through his nose, forced himself to steady and his voice to remain even as he said, "Violet thinks it might be cancer."

"But she's been to the hospital. They've run scans, and tests, and checked for that." Cancer. Not even witches could stop cancer. They could treat it. They could go into remission. But cancer was one of life's inevitabilities, the one great equalizer. It could come for any of them, normie and folk alike. Azure had never thought it would come for an Elwood. She felt suddenly ill. "Does Violet see something they don't?"

"Vi's probably getting ahead of herself," Sunila said, obviously trying to lighten the mood. "She's all doom and gloom lately. Girl needs a serious dose of therapy, if you ask me."

"I'll check in with Aunt Carmine again tomorrow," Azure promised, giving her brother's hand a squeeze. "We'll sort this out. All of it."

She didn't know how yet. But she'd find a way.

Indigo nodded and scrubbed at his eyes. "And maybe Sunila's right. Maybe Violet is just overreacting."

"Maybe."

# Chapter 19

Rus hadn't had to build the shrine on the second floor when she came to Moondale. 157 seemed to know it was what she needed and had provided a place for the tablets of Meiling and Aihuan's parents, offering herself and her girls a quiet room with soft pillows and plenty of incense to burn. A place where they could go and speak to Xueming and Eamon if they needed.

Rus hadn't been in to see them other than for a perfunctory offering since they first moved in. She knew that was wrong of her. Knew that she should have gone in and paid her respects, told Xueming and Eamon everything that was going on with her and the girls. But it felt like there was never really room to breathe, or time to think. And half the time she felt like a failure for her inability to protect the girls on her own. She was their moonmother, for Goddess's sake, she should have been able to build them a home without so much outside help.

But there she was, unable to sleep, kneeling before them, hoping to make up for lost time.

They'd forgive her. They always had in the past. Rus was known—when she was younger—for falling off the face of the earth and going completely no contact. It had been a while since she'd done that, of course, at least since before Aihuan had been born.

And really, she wasn't expecting them to answer. They

were in the After. They were resting peacefully, as they should be. Even though their deaths had been traumatic and awful, she'd made sure to lay them to rest properly. To make sure they didn't have to wander limbo like so many others.

Smoke curled up from the incense stick, drifting lazily through the air.

"They're doing well," Rus said, knowing it wasn't much, would never be enough. Nothing she said would ever make up for the fact that her two friends wouldn't get to witness their children grow up firsthand. They wouldn't get to be in the stands at graduation. They wouldn't get to walk either of their girls down the aisle. They would miss so much. They already had.

"They both like school. And they like the house here. 157 spoils them rotten. And Az . . ." She broke off her breath, squeezing in her lungs. Why was this so hard? Why couldn't they have *lived*? The girls shouldn't have lost their parents like Rus did. That stupid old superstition about mediums being orphans didn't *have* to hold true. Not with them. Her eyes burned, and she almost choked through the next bit. "Az is fucking great with them. So great. I know you always thought she might be, Xueming."

"She seemed the type to have a mothering instinct," a voice said, soft and only barely there. If Rus weren't so in tune with spirits, if the house weren't so quiet around her, she might have missed it.

"A'Xue?" Rus lifted her head, her heart slamming against her chest. It had been so long since she'd heard that voice. Over a year now. She was sure she'd never hear it again.

"You never did give her enough credit," Xueming chided gently. "Always so hung up on the image of perfection you thought Azure would be, and never able to see what she was. Putting her on a pedestal she never asked to be on. How many times did I tell you to reach out to her? How many times did you tell me you couldn't? That she'd never forgive you."

"I know." Rus ducked her head again, shame crawling along her nerves, heating her skin, like a child being put in time out. Xueming had always had the ability to make her feel so young. Even as they grew closer, even as Rus grew into herself and her power, Xueming was able to show Rus how young she still was. It was amazing for someone who was only a handful of years older. But then Rus had never had a mother, and she could only imagine this was what it must have felt like. "And you were right."

"She often is." Eamon chuckled dryly.

Rus squeezed her eyes shut, stars bursting from behind her lids as she tried to suck back the tears, to swallow them past the lump in her throat. Goddess, she had missed them. They had been her family for so many years. Raised her, in their way. Turned her from the reckless fledgling necromancer into the woman she was—a witch worthy of the designation Crow Witch. Without them, she probably would have died before she even thought to return to Moondale.

"Oh, Icarus." Xueming tutted softly, her tone kind. "You're doing a wonderful job with them. We want you to know that."

"I don't—" Rus choked, sobbed, the words seizing in her lungs, catching, and cutting. "I don't know that that's true. I feel like I'm failing them. There's something coming to Moondale, and I don't know that I can protect them from it."

"You'll be able to." Eamon had always had so much

faith in her. More than Rus ever had in herself. It was amazing. He'd never once questioned her abilities, always thinking she was more capable than she gave herself credit for. Fuck. She ached with missing them.

She had Fernando, sure, but he was a younger brother, someone who she needed to guide and help find his place in the world. All her other friends, the ones from Moondale, hadn't been there the last few years. They had talked on the phone, or texted, but they weren't *there*. They didn't pull her out of that place after Kaytee died. They didn't encourage her to find her feet with her inventions. They didn't see her grow up. To them, she was still the same old Rus, the impetuous twenty-something communing with spirits because it was scandalous. Experimenting with things she probably shouldn't have been at that age just because it got under the board's skin.

It was funny to think that when she'd left Moondale, although she'd been legally an adult by all rights, she'd still been a child. So young and foolish. A big fish in a small pond who had been suddenly dropped into the ocean. Eamon and Xueming had been the ones to show her what being a witch really meant. They taught her to swim.

"But that's not why we came." Xueming's voice was serious all the sudden, and Rus forced herself to open her eyes. To look for them in the smoke and the gloom of a room cast in shadows by early morning.

They weren't there. Stepping through from the After took more power and connection than the tablets could provide. Honestly, Rus was amazed they'd even been able to push their voices through. The veil must be thin at the moment. Which . . . didn't make any sense. With the summer solstice fast approaching, the veil should be almost at its thickest. There should be no way for a spirit to make contact from the After without extensive magic. Without someone calling for them directly by name. But there they were, reaching out to Rus to provide comfort and guidance like they always had. Goddess, Rus had gotten so lucky in finding them.

"Why did you come?" Rus frowned, scrubbing at her face.

She'd been so caught up in the emotions of hearing her friends again after so long, that she hadn't let herself wonder how the fuck she was hearing them at all when she hadn't done any sort of ritual to reach out to them. Sure, the incense and the tablets would make getting a message through to the After fairly easy, but two-way communication was unheard of from something so simple. Otherwise normies would be talking with their dead relatives every other day simply by visiting their graves. Which would throw the whole world out of balance. The dead knew far too much about things that the living had no business knowing.

"And how?" Fear crawled up along Rus's spine, replacing the sadness and the longing with cold dread. Something was wrong. Something was *deeply* wrong.

"The balance in Moondale is off," Eamon said, his tone settled and academic. He'd always been that way—able to look at a problem from a distance. Rus envied him that. She tied so much of herself up in everything she did, it was hard for her to be pragmatic about anything.

"Off how?"

"Unclear."

"The veil is thinning in that area," Xueming said. "It's either deliberate, or it's a consequence of the magic in Moondale fluctuating."

"Fluctuating?" Rus hadn't noticed that, but then she

had been a little wrapped up in everything else going on around her. It made sense that she would miss a subtle shift in the flow of magic, and that those in the After would feel it. Xueming and Eamon's tablets being inside her home gave them the connection they needed, the access to Moondale and her magic. It also gave them an in to contact Rus, but only if the veil was thin enough. Only if they were able to find the magic to do it. Only if certain conditions were met —conditions Rus didn't think would ever *be* met. Not without some major effort on her part, anyway. "Fluctuating how?"

"Unclear," Eamon said again, his tone infuriatingly calm.

"Brilliant." Rus flopped onto her back, her head thunking against the floor so she could blink up at the rafters of the round room on the second floor. They were oddly shaped to match the oddly shaped roof. And there were spiders living in them, making a home right alongside her and hers. "Just fucking great. Any theories?"

"It could be a shift in the powers that be," Xueming murmured, and if she were in the room with Rus, Rus knew she'd be pacing. That was what Xueming did. It was a habit she had picked up from Rus, ironically. Because that's what happened with friends sometimes—they rubbed off on each other. "It seems the clans of Moondale are . . . out of sync."

"Out of sync," Rus repeated. Fuck, was she going to repeat everything they told her until something made sense? Probably. There had to be a way to tap into the magic of Moondale and figure out what the fuck they were talking about. A spell or a—

She sat up so fast, her head spun. "I know how to get an answer."

Xueming and Eamon both made sounds of interest.

They'd fallen silent as she thought, letting her work her mind around the problem, knowing she needed a minute to figure it out.

"Oh, but Greer is gonna be real pissed when I ask him to help me break into the park." She laughed, manic and delighted.

"We need to go," Xueming said. She didn't sound worried at all about whatever harebrained scheme Rus had thought up. Rus was glad death hadn't changed much between them. "The hour is almost passed."

"Keep us informed," Eamon instructed.

"I will." Rus nodded, her hair falling into her face. She wondered if Greer was still up. It'd be better to do this early in the morning when no one was likely to be close to the Heart of Moondale. And they were unlikely to be caught at it. She could only guess at what the board would think she was doing up there if they found out. They'd probably assume she was trying to poison the lei lines with her necrotic magic or something stupid like that. Goddess, the shit they knew about her magic could fill a fucking acorn top.

"And Rus," Xueming said, her tone softer than it had been this entire time, "you're doing a good job with our girls. We're proud of them, and of you."

And then they were gone. Incense burned down, the room gone still, and Rus was so fucking grateful that they'd left her with a problem to solve because otherwise she'd probably be a sobbing mess in the middle of the floor. She grabbed her phone from her back pocket on her way to the door, her mind already working over everything she'd need, and dialed Greer.

"No," Greer said when he picked up. "Do you know what time it is? Whatever it is. No."

"Awww, but Greer, you haven't even let me tell you what I need yet." Rus pouted but didn't stop moving because she didn't have a lot of time. The hour was fading, like Xueming said, and it would be better to do this as close to the hour when the veil was the thinnest as possible. She checked her phone again. 3:23 a.m. A little over thirty minutes to get up the mountain, get to the Heart, and check what she needed to check.

Greer groaned. She heard shifting on the other side, like maybe he was rolling out of bed. "It's just Rus," he told someone. "No, I've got it." Then a door shut and he asked, "All right, what the fuck is it?"

"EXPLAIN TO ME," Greer said as he got out of the car, tugging his hoodie down further into place. It was chilly even for as close to summer as they were. But that was to be expected in the mountains of Moondale. "Why *I* had to help you with this particular misadventure?"

"Well, first off"—Rus held up a finger as she stomped down the path toward the Heart of Moondale—"you're the only asshole I know who has a four-wheel drive truck. Second"—she held up another—"I'm less likely to get arrested for trespassing if I'm here with the sheriff, aren't I?"

"I really hate you sometimes. Have I told you that recently?"

"Not for at least a week," Rus chirped, bouncing on her toes as she went. The forest was loud around them with chirping crickets and scuttling critters. Signs of spring. "You can stay with the car if you want. I just need to check something."

"Yeah, I'm not doing that."

Typical. Rus rolled her eyes. Greer never seemed to want to make anything easy. "Fine, but you can't tell anyone outside of our inner circle that I did this. If the board knew I came up here and fucked around with the magic at the Heart, they'd one hundred percent throw me out of Moondale."

"Like I want anyone to know I followed your dumb ass into the woods in the middle of the night."

"Actually, it's morning."

"Shut up."

Rus shrugged and kept walking. They didn't have a whole lot of time, and arguing with Greer—while fun—was definitely a waste.

The clearing where the Heart of Moondale resided looked human-made, a perfect circle of trees surrounding a large flat rock that had broken through the soil. But Rus knew that the trees had grown that way, leaving room for the Heart and its magic. She brushed her fingers over the moon face carved into a tree on the edge of the clearing—a waxing crescent—and didn't wait for Greer to join her before she pulled her athame from her pocket and pricked the end of her finger. She didn't need much blood for this, not this close, just a drop to connect directly to the Heart.

Besides, it would be easier to sketch the character needed to make this spell work that way.

It ached to press her throbbing finger against the rough stone and draw the lines necessary, but once it was done, she sank down beside the Heart, her back to it, and murmured the spell. Information came at her in a flood, assaulting her senses, overwhelming her.

It was so much. Too much.

She should have brought someone with her to help her

pick through all of this. Az was always good with statistics and historical data. But Rus hadn't wanted to wake her, not on a hunch. So instead, she took a breath and asked Moondale for what she needed, specifically.

And Moondale provided, funnily enough, with a line chart.

"Cute." Rus laughed, her eyes still closed tight as she appraised what Moondale provided. There were natural rises and falls to the energy of Moondale, following season changes. But there was more than that too. Signs that something outside of Moondale's control had affected her. Events, probably. If Rus had more time, and energy, she'd love to examine the historical significance of those dips.

But there wasn't time, and what really concerned her was how there was an unusual dip of late. Normally at this time of year, the magic would be rising, thriving right along with the spring foliage. But it wasn't. It was falling. Dipping below even the dead of winter. Low enough that Rus was surprised the wards were still functioning.

"Has this happened before?" she asked the Heart, and the Heart provided. She felt like she was tipping forward, falling into the chart as it grew in size, the line looming closer and closer until everything was just blue, like falling into the ocean.

When she surfaced again, she was standing in the middle of Main Street. Only it wasn't like the Main Street where Necromancer's sat across from Elwood & Co. and trees lined the asphalt. The road beneath her feet was dirt. The sidewalks were made of gravel instead of pavement. And none of the shops were familiar to her. None, except of course Elwood & Co., which was much smaller, only taking up the single storefront it had originally inhabited.

"You cannot!" someone shouted, her voice full of fury.

Rus whirled and came face-to-face with Mazarin Elwood. She was in a long blue dress, her hair pinned back from her face in a style that Rus could only assume was fashionable for the time period. Her eyes—wide and brown, just like Az's—looked through Rus. "Hyacinth, *please*."

"I will not have this discussion with you. Not here." Hyacinth said, her tone hard. And when Rus turned back, she found the other woman standing behind her. Tall and stately, and just as furious as her younger sister—rather similar to Violet Elwood. "Come inside."

The scene shifted. They must be inside of Elwood & Co. now, but it looked nothing like the store where Az had worked up until a few weeks ago. The shelves were not stacked with books and touristy knickknacks. They were loaded, instead, with herbs and potion bottles and every-thing a witch would need to get some serious spellwork done.

"After what you did"—Hyacinth's hand was tight around Mazarin's, her lips curled back into a snarl—"you've left me no other choice."

Mazarin stood up taller, her chin tilted back in a posture that made Rus ache at the reminder it sent through her of Az and her stubborn streak. "If you do this, if you strike my name from the record, you'll throw all of Moondale into disorder. I am the strongest of us. Think what would happen without my magic tied to one of the clans of Moon-dale. It would upset the balance."

"If you cared at all about the balance, then you would not have helped that . . . that *thing* come back from the *dead*."

"I love her," Mazarin said, as if it were the most reason-able thing in the world.

"And we all shall pay the price for it."

The world washed blue again, and Rus tipped backward, falling through time and space, dropping back into her body. "Shit." She coughed, her lungs aching from being under for too long. "This is my fault."

"What else is new?" Greer asked with all his normal pettiness from where he was leaning against one of the trees around the edge of the clearing. "What'd you do now?"

"Get me home. Now." Rus scrambled to her feet, pouring water over the character to wash away the blood and raking her hand through sweat-damp hair. "I need to see Az."

# Chapter 20

Rus was sweaty and pale when she stumbled into their bedroom and shook Azure awake. The first thing Azure saw as she blinked against the bright light of the bedside lamp was Rus's face with a thin sheen of moisture on it, her hair slicked back from her forehead, the color drained from her cheeks.

"Where have you been?" Azure asked, pushing herself up to sit. She must have fallen asleep. The book she'd been reading while she waited for Rus to return to bed was still propped up in her lap. She hadn't meant to doze off. She'd meant to wait up until Rus came back in case she needed to talk after paying her respects to Aihuan and Meiling's parents. But her eyes had grown heavier and heavier until she'd eventually lost the fight with exhaustion.

"To the Heart, but that's not important." Rus flapped her wrist, already moving toward her desk to pull out a sheet of paper.

"You look like you ran the whole way home." Azure wondered how Rus had gotten up to the Heart without setting off the wards, but she decided against asking. Sometimes it was better not to know when Rus had been up to some illegal or unethical shit.

"What?" Rus stopped and turned to look at herself in the mirror on the wardrobe. Even from a distance, it had to be clear how ragged she looked. How unkempt and almost sickly. She tilted her head for a moment and shook her head. "That's just from the piggyback."

"Piggyback?" Azure knew that term. She'd heard Rus use it before, but it had been so long she wasn't sure what it meant anymore. Even so, it set an alarm off in her head. She rose from the bed and started across the room toward Rus, intent on *making* her explain if she refused.

"Oh, you know when I like . . ." Rus wriggled her fingers as if to indicate something, but Azure wasn't sure what she was trying to say. "Piggyback on a spirit's memories and get a vision of their history. It's almost like being dropped out of time. I think the technical term is memory divining, but I always thought *piggyback* worked a little better."

Of course she did because the playful term minimized the seriousness of what she'd just done. And wasn't that Rus all over?

Rus turned back to where she was digging through her desk for something. "Super disorienting. Lots of magic," Rus continued, confirming Azure's worst fears.

Azure's stomach dropped to her feat. Memory divining. Rus had told her about that once. Told her how dangerous it was. How she could— "You can get *lost* doing that. You told me that." Azure's mouth was dry suddenly, her skin prickling with anxiety. "And never get out. You can get *stuck*."

"Yeah, but it was fine." Rus pulled out a sheet of paper and started writing. It looked like she was filling the sheet with dates.

"Did you even take Darcy with you to pull you out just in case?" Goddess, why had Azure fallen asleep? She should have been awake to go with Rus. Maybe not to stop her from doing something stupid, but to at least be there to help her if something went wrong.

"Greer was there."

*Greer was there.*

Azure grabbed Rus by the wrist to stop her frantic writing and pressed magic into the pressure point there until she could feel Rus's magic humming along beneath her skin. It was a little sluggish, tired and worn out from whatever the fuck Rus had been doing in the woods, but not depleted as it'd been in the past. She'd be fine. But Azure couldn't seem to stop the pounding of her heart. The thrumming in her blood at the thought that she could have lost Rus. That Rus could have died up there on that fucking mountain and Azure would never have known what really happened. Because Rus likely didn't tell Greer what she was doing.

"Don't do that again. Not without Darcy. Not without me," Azure pled, her eyes fixed on Rus's face. Rus softened, tilting forward to press her face into Azure's stomach, to wrap her arms around her middle. Azure sighed and stroked Rus's hair gently. It was still damp. "You scared me."

"I'm sorry," Rus murmured, the sound muffled by the fabric of Azure's pajama top. It was one of those silk button-up sets, with a cat embroidered onto the front pocket that looked like Lizzie. Indigo had done the embroidery. "That wasn't my intention when I went up there."

"What was your intention?" Her heart was settling down now, her magic calming beneath her skin, the storm passing. Rus was all right. She was safe. And it seemed she had found something that might shine some light on what the fuck was going on in Moondale. All good things. Azure could relax.

"I wanted to check on the historical flow of magic in Moondale. And you'll never guess what I found." Rus's tone was excited, but she was still pale and a little shaky. Azure wasn't sure if that was because of what she'd found or a holdover from the magic she'd used.

"No, I doubt I will. Why don't we get you into the bath and you can tell me?"

Rus leaned into the pressure of Azure's hand, a cat seeking affection, and sighed. "A bath sounds perfect. Probably need to clean off any traces of the spirit I contacted anyway. Can never be too careful."

"Exactly." Azure gave Rus's wrist a gentle tug and led her toward the bathroom.

RUS'S HAIR was up in a towel that soaked the pillow she was sharing with Azure, but Azure couldn't be bothered to even be annoyed by it. The bad habits that would normally have turned Azure off in another person were minor inconveniences with Rus. Things that hardly meant anything when compared to the fact that Azure had Rus there, in her arms, held close. That Azure had almost lost this possibility entirely.

What *did* bother her was the current discussion and the blame Rus cast upon herself.

"This isn't your fault." Azure didn't know how many times she'd said that in the last half hour, but it bore repeating. Because it was true. "I made the decision to leave Jade Waters. And there was no way we could have known that me doing that would upset the balance of Moondale so much."

"Not the balance, not really." Rus scrunched her nose, her fingers curling tighter around where she held Azure close, wrinkling the silk of her pajama top beyond smoothing. "It weakened Jade Waters specifically."

"Which in turn upset the balance." Azure rolled her eyes. It was so obvious, in hindsight, what severing her ties would do to her coven. Especially when she didn't tie herself to another coven on the board soon after. There was one solution for that, a solution Azure didn't like at all if she was being honest. "We'll just have to petition for a seat on the board sooner than we'd planned."

Rus groaned loudly, and threw a wrist over her eyes, dramatic as ever. Azure loved her so much, dramatics and all. Which was why the next thing she said, the thing that was going to be a huge pain in the ass, seemed obvious. In fact, she wondered if it had been Moondale's plan for her all along. Fate setting a path that would lead her right here, curled up around Rus, volunteering to do something for Rus that she'd never wanted to do for anyone else.

"I'll put myself up for the seat." Azure turned her head to face Rus more fully and found Rus looking back in shock, her gray eyes wide, mouth slightly agape. "There will be less fighting over it if I am the one to take it. And it's what Nixie implied I'd be doing eventually anyway." Azure shrugged, which made the pillow beneath them move, bobbing Rus's head with it. "It'll be no different than what I've been doing."

"Az." Rus sighed, reaching out to stroke Azure's cheek, her jaw, her calloused fingers warm and soothing. There was an understanding in the gesture. Rus knew, because she would always know, the deepest parts of Azure. The way she felt about things. Even if Azure tried to hide them, there would always be one person in the world she couldn't hide them from. How lucky she was that that person happened to be Icarus Ashthorne. "I know you don't want to do this.

And you don't have to. We'll find another way around it. I'll dig through my inventions. There has to be something useful there. Or I'll—I don't know, but I'll come up with another solution. You never wanted to be an elder, and you shouldn't have to do something you don't want to."

She *didn't* want to do this, but she *did* have to. Azure recognized that now. Everything in her life—every lesson, every moment—had been for this. So she'd be prepared for this. And really, why shouldn't it be her? She was the best qualified of the three of them. The most in tune with the politics of the board and the magic of the land.

Goddess, Moondale could be a real bitch sometimes, couldn't she?

What was Azure for if not this? She didn't have the inventive spirit Rus did. She couldn't bring innovation to their coven the way Rus could. And Fernando wasn't born in Moondale, hadn't been a part of her network of magic long enough, making him ineligible. That just left Azure, and maybe one of the girls, once they were old enough.

"I'm already doing the work of an elder. What's the difference?"

"You know the difference," Rus said patiently, her fingers curling into Azure's jaw, leading her in closer.

Azure let out a slow breath and pressed her lips to Rus's for a soft kiss. "It'll be fine."

IT WASN'T FINE. But Azure was going to keep under wraps how very not fine it was as best she could. She'd foolishly thought she'd have more time. That she'd be able to find some way around becoming the elder. That she could rail against her destiny. Moondale wouldn't let that happen, it seemed. Moondale would have it her way, and there was nothing Azure or anyone else could do to fight against it.

Which was why she was almost relieved the following morning when she received a text from Cagney that simply said:

CAGNEY

Lunch at Talbot's. Don't be late.

As if Azure had ever been late in her life. And it was as good an excuse as any to get out of the house where Rus had holed herself up in her office to go through her files of past inventions and start the process of patenting everything she had. The floor was littered in notebooks and looseleaf sheets of paper that must have been at least five years old. It looked like a tornado had rolled through the place, and Rus had probably been muttering to herself all night, not even bothering to sleep, if the dark rings around her eyes were anything to go by.

Azure needed to get out, to breathe away from the obligation for a minute.

"I'm going to lunch. I'll bring you back something," Azure said from the door, not daring to step across the papers for a goodbye kiss, lest she crumple something important. "Please don't forget to drink some water."

Rus looked up from where she'd been poring over a piece of lined paper that looked like it'd been torn from one of those tightly spiraled notebooks she used in high school. Azure wasn't sure how anything Rus had thought up in high school would help them now, but she wasn't going to argue. With her pink hair tied back in a short ponytail at the crown of her head, Rus grumbled at Azure from the floor. "I'm an adult, you know."

"And yet, here we are," Azure teased in a deadpan tone, hoping to lighten the mood. "Consistently dehydrated and having to be reminded to eat by your children."

"Aaaaz." Rus rolled her eyes and dropped the bit of paper she'd been inspecting to pick her way across the room and press herself against Azure. "You don't need to babysit me all the time."

"Of course not," Azure agreed, brushing a kiss to Rus's temple. "I shouldn't be long, and when I get back, I'll help you organize all of this. I want those patents in before I go before the board."

"What are you talking about? This *is* organized?"

Azure leveled Rus with a look, brows raised just a hair, and Rus laughed, eyes bright.

"All right, fine. But hurry back, yeah? We won't get many more days that the girls are in school, and everything is just . . . quiet."

"Yes." Azure pressed another soft kiss to Rus's temple, then her nose, then her lips, where she lingered for a moment before pulling back.

It was hard to pull herself away from Rus when Rus was looking so soft and small. When their world was caving in around them. But she needed the time to breathe away from the house, away from the expectation. She needed to come to terms with what was coming.

ONLY IT SEEMED THAT CAGNEY, Nesta, and Evander weren't going to give Azure the room to breathe she needed.

"Brenton is worried about Vi," Nesta said before Azure

had even sat down. They looked worried too. There was a napkin twisted almost beyond recognition in front of them, as well as many empty cups of what had either been tea or coffee.

"I see," Azure said, sliding down into the chair on the other side of where Cagney, Nesta, and Evander had squeezed into one booth seat. Nesta sat in the center, as if Evander and Cagney were trying to box them in. To keep them from running maybe? Or maybe to keep them from slumping down so far, they disappeared under the table. "And how do you know this?"

"Phyre told us," Cagney volunteered.

That explained how they knew, but it didn't explain why Nesta looked like they were about to shake apart at the seams. As far as Azure knew, Brenton Ironwood—Brant Ironwood's nephew, Phyre Ironwood's adopted brother— wasn't particularly close to any of them. He was a few years older, had been in Violet's graduating class, and had never really hung around the others. Unless something had changed without Azure knowing.

"Why is Brenton worried about Violet? And why does Nesta look as if they want to disappear into the bench?" Azure was aware she could be terribly blunt sometimes, but she didn't exactly have the time or the mental bandwidth to fuck around with this. She wanted to go for a run before she went home to Rus to dig into the problem of adding to their ranks.

"Because I made the match that brought all this about." Nesta swallowed, their throat clicking with how dry it was. "I set up Taryn and Violet."

"Wait." Azure stilled entirely, her hands clasping at the table as if it might hold her up. None of this made sense. She felt like she was coming in halfway through a conversation, and she didn't like it. There was too much going on for those around her to be talking in fucking riddles. "What *exactly* is going on with Taryn and Violet?"

"Azure . . ." Cagney reached for her, regret layered in her tone as she settled her hand on top of Azure's. Which was strange, because they'd never been on touching terms. Cagney only ever seemed to tolerate Azure because Rus loved her. No other reason. If anything, their friendship was begrudging.

"We think Taryn is abusing Violet," Greer said when neither of his companions seemed able to find the words. Azure appreciated that he could be just as blunt as she could. He didn't beat around the bush and try to soften the blow. But . . . For the second time in twenty-four hours, Azure's stomach dropped to her feet. "Not hitting her. But there's something going on there. Something not right."

Why had no one come to her with this? Why had no one said anything? Why hadn't Indigo brought this up? Or Sunila? Or Maureen? Why hadn't Azure *noticed* something wasn't right with her sister? They were fighting, yes, but that didn't mean she wouldn't notice, did it? That didn't mean she wouldn't see when Violet was hurting. Azure had been in her house, for fuck's sake, not much more than a few days ago. If there was abuse going on, she would have seen it, wouldn't she? Why hadn't she? Was someone trying to keep her from noticing? Was all this shit with Taryn and the board just a distraction for something else? How . . . how hadn't she noticed?

But that wasn't true, was it? The mark on Violet's arm that she'd rushed to hide. The way she'd hardly touched her meal, and instead drank more than usual. The words "a wife to keep happy." They were all nothing in the moment, but now . . .

Why hadn't Violet *come to her?*

"And we can't get her out," Nesta whispered softly, the words sounding like they were coming through glass, muffled and indistinct. Azure was going to be sick. "She won't leave. We thought maybe you could—"

Azure's phone vibrated in her pocket and she pulled it out, only half paying attention as she hit the answer button and held it up to her ear.

"I'm on my way to the hospital," Rus said in a rush, not waiting for Azure to acknowledge that she'd picked up. "An ambulance just pulled up outside your aunts'. I think they're taking Carmine in."

Azure lost track of everything else because her ears started to ring and the world darkened around the edges. She barely registered as someone leaned forward and took the phone from her hand to speak into it words she couldn't hear, much less understand.

Taryn was hurting Violet.

Carmine was going to the hospital.

They might lose their bid for the Coven of the Forgotten.

Her family . . . her family was falling *apart.*

# Chapter 21

Rus had never seen Az like this before. She was almost catatonic—unblinking, unmoving, unspeaking. Her grief so palpable that Rus was practically choking on it by just sitting next to her. But Rus wouldn't be anywhere else, *couldn't* be anywhere else. Because Az needed her.

The fingers in between her own were sweaty—Az's hands never sweated, she was too dignified for all that—and trembling even as they didn't really hold Rus's hand back. Too loose, as if Az didn't have the strength to grip her fingers. But that was all right. That was fine. Because Rus would have the strength for both of them. Just as Az had the strength for her weeks ago when she'd needed it most. Now Rus would be the one shouldering everything, keeping them both upright. That's what their relationship was—a partnership, the ability to share any burden.

"She's gonna be all right," Rus promised, although she didn't really know if that was true, and there was no way for her to guarantee it. Not with what Maureen had said: Carmine had taken a nap after breakfast, and Maureen couldn't wake her for lunch. Not with how they still hadn't heard anything an hour later. But she'd find a way to fix this if she had to. To make it right. For Az, Indigo, and Maureen. Even for Violet, who—

Who wasn't there. Where the fuck *was* Violet?

"Hey, did no one call Vi?" Rus whispered to Indigo, who was on her other side. He seemed to be fairing a bit better. Maybe because he'd seen this coming more than Az had. Or maybe there was some other reason. Rus wasn't sure, and she wasn't exactly about to ask. For one, it would be rude. For two, it would just make him feel bad, probably, about the way his own grief didn't look like Az's. Which was silly because grief looked different for everyone. And it looked different at different times.

Some people stopped altogether, unable to move through the panic, like Az had. Others refused to sit still, needing something to do, needing to keep themselves in motion to keep from breaking down. Maureen hadn't sat down the entire hour Rus had been in the waiting room with her. Making calls and filling water cups. Rus admired her. She didn't think she'd have the strength for that if she were in Maureen's shoes, if it were Az in the hospital. Indigo, while quiet, seemed almost entirely himself. Well, maybe not entirely himself. He hadn't looked at his phone once. He just kept following Maureen's movements about the room, a little frown on his face as if he thought he should tell her to sit down and rest.

"She said her car isn't working," Indigo said, his eyes shifting to follow Maureen as she made another trek across the room to the desk to ask the nurses if they'd heard anything yet. "That she's gonna wait for Taryn to get off work and bring her."

Rus frowned. There was something to that. Something that didn't sit right with her. Violet should be there. Even if she wasn't getting along with her siblings at the moment, she should *be* there. "When will Taryn be off work?"

Indigo shrugged, his head turning to follow Maureen's progress back to the vending machine where she looked to be trying to buy snacks for everyone. "She's got an event this evening, might not be till late."

"She's got an event," Rus repeated, the information feeling strangely abstract. "What the fuck does that have to do with anything? Why can't she take off and come get Vi and bring her to the hospital? Vi's aunt is in intensive care, for fuck's sake."

"Icarus," Maureen hissed, glaring at Rus.

Rus shrank down in her seat. She hadn't realized she was close to shouting, and people were staring at her. But it seemed to shake Az a bit, and she squeezed Rus's hand and said, "Can you—can you go get her?"

"I—" Rus turned to look back at Az. She'd slouched down into the chair beside Rus, her head tilted against Rus's shoulder. But she was looking up at Rus now. Those big brown eyes soft and pleading. It was an objectively terrible idea. Rus and Violet were in no way on good terms. And Rus felt she needed to be here, to look after Az, but— "I don't know, Az. Don't you want me here, with you?"

Az closed her eyes for a moment, giving Rus the smallest break from the expression in them, the sadness. Rus tried to catch her breath in the space provided to her. She'd never seen Az look like that before. Like she was breaking apart into a million little pieces that Rus might never be able to collect, might never be able to fit back together. Yes, Az had hurt before, experienced heartbreak before. But those events were always met with a stony resolve, a righteous fury. Even when Rus left Az behind, even when she tried to break up with her. Az hadn't fallen to pieces, she'd gotten pissed. Rus found she preferred that to this. But then . . .

How often did a person have to come to the realization that one day they would lose their mom? Which was exactly what Carmine was to Az: her mom. Rus knew that Az hardly remembered her parents. Most of her memories growing up were Carmine and Maureen looking after her, teaching her everything she needed to know to be a good little Elwood. And now, here Az was, maybe about to lose Carmine. Honestly, it was a miracle she was upright at all.

"I think Taryn is keeping her from us," Az said so lowly that Rus could have missed it with the quiet chatter of the waiting room, the buzzing of the lights overhead, the beeping of machines down the hall. But she didn't. And the pain in that tone almost stopped her cold.

"Why would she do that?" Rus leaned in closer, pressing her face so close to Az's that their eyes met. She'd say the accusation was ridiculous, but there was real fear in Az's gaze. And suddenly, a lot of things slotted into place.

*She's a nasty one, she is.*

"Okay," Rus said, straightening, not needing any more explanation. "I'll go pick her up. You two just sit tight." She patted Az's hand, pressing a kiss to her forehead and giving Indigo's shoulder a squeeze, then rose and went to Maureen. "I'm going to pick up Vi. Do you guys need anything while I'm out? Decent coffee? Dinner?"

"No. We're fine. Don't worry about us, Rus." Maureen smiled, but it looked stretched thin even in its kindness. "Thank you for going to get Violet. I'll let her know you're coming."

Rus nodded and turned for the door.

It took her all of five minutes to get across town to where Violet and Taryn lived in a cute little place on the water. It had a dock and everything. Room for a boat, if they had one. And a great view of the bay. It was exactly the kind of place where Rus would have pictured Violet living. A one bedroom with a thriving vegetable garden and a wrought iron arbor arch right at the end of the sidewalk leading up to the house covered in vines that looked like they might flower soon.

*Tranquil*, Rus would have said normally.

But there was nothing normal about the house on Turtle Lane where Violet and Taryn Elwood had made their home. Nothing tranquil at all.

"What the fuck?" Rus said, putting Blue in park and peeking through the passenger side window at where a row of spirits stood in the front garden like fucking boxwoods. "Are you seeing this shit, Blue?"

Blue revved her engine to confirm that yes, she was seeing this shit.

Good, so it wasn't just Rus then. Delightful. Perfect.

Fuck.

Rus could feel the chill the spirits were putting off through the air in the vents.

Why hadn't her spies noticed *this*? What kind of heavy-duty glamour was this house behind that even ghosts couldn't see what was going on?

In addition to the spirits in the front garden, there were several in the yard as well. Each one standing eerily still like a statue. Which wasn't—look, that's not how spirits behaved, all right? Not in Rus's experience, anyway. The ones she'd interacted with in the wild were ever moving. As if remaining in one place for too long would make them forget that they weren't gone, and they'd disappear entirely. Which was actually possible, so it made sense that their natural patterns were . . . not static.

There was only one reason why a spirit would be still like this, and it was never good news for the spirit or the living in the area.

It was honestly a wonder no one else in Moondale knew

they were there, but then, Rus supposed, she was one of the few mediums. And the only one who'd taken the time to hone their skills the way she had. Turning them into the blade of a knife instead of the blunt object she'd been born with.

"All right, super. So what the fuck is she powering?" Rus asked, tapping her fingers on the steering wheel. There were all sorts of things a witch could use spirits for, but the big one—the one that would take *that* many—was powerful spellcraft. Rus wasn't entirely against using the dead like batteries, particularly not when they were shitty people while they'd been alive, or shitty people when they were spirits. A ghost terrorizing a child was definitely an asshole, and she'd have absolutely no qualms strapping it to a grounding item and using its latent energy for something actually, you know, useful.

There was no way that was the case with all of these. And some of them—Rus hated to even think it—gave her the distinct impression that they'd been ripped out of the After for this very purpose. She couldn't explain exactly how she could tell, there was a vague put-togetherness of a spirit in the After that one stuck in limbo or on the plane of the living wouldn't have. Their essence was less ragged and torn apart. Like the difference between someone who had the money to buy a new pair of socks every other month versus someone who wore them until there were holes.

These spirits didn't have holes in their socks.

"So that's not shady at all," Rus murmured, taking a deep breath. This was going to fucking suck. But she'd made a promise to Az, and she was going to get Violet to that hospital.

"Keep the engine running, girl, I'll be right back." She patted Blue's dash and flung the door open.

The spirits moaned at her approach, the air thickening, like walking through the bay, the muddy bottom giving beneath her feet, threatening to suck her under. She was out of breath before she'd even reached the middle of the path, but that wasn't going to stop her. Even if they grabbed at her, pawed at her, tried to weigh her down with them the way the spirits in the river of Styx might. Fuck. She wasn't recovered enough from her piggybacking the night before for this. It didn't matter.

By the time she reached the door, a thin layer of sweat coated her face and trickled down her spine. The dead around her hadn't moved, but she could feel the way their awareness followed her, mouths open and hungry, sucking down any stray bit of magic they could from her. That was going to hurt in the morning. It would ache right down to her bones like her joints on a cold and rainy day. She'd have to use her cane tomorrow.

Raising her hand to knock took an embarrassing amount of energy, but she did it, then stepped back to wait for the door to open.

The air was getting thinner and colder around her. But Rus didn't look away from the door. She refused to acknowledge the way the spirits had directed their focus entirely to her. If they knew she could see them they might latch on, try to use her energy to power their existence and by extension the spell at work here. And while she felt bad for them, there was nothing she could do for them at the moment. First, she'd need to free them, then she'd need to send them over. With this many spirits, she'd need more than the magic living under her skin. She'd need supplies.

She began compiling the list of everything that would make the project as painless as possible for all parties when the door opened on Taryn Elwood, and Rus *saw* her for perhaps the first time. Here, in her home, there was no reason for Taryn to hide behind a glamour.

Or rather, there was no reason for the thing wearing Taryn's skin to hide behind a glamour.

A spirit.

An old one.

"Icarus," Taryn said pleasantly, but there was an edge to the smile, a sharpness. She knew that Rus knew. Fuck. That could be dangerous.

"Taryn." Rus smiled back and reached out with her magic, subtle and quiet, trying to find the place where the spirit had attached itself to Taryn's essence. To pick at the seal. But . . . but there was none. There was no seam to tear. It was as if the two had fused entirely, become one. That was . . . That was *bad*. "I came to pick up Vi to take her to the hospital. I heard there was some car trouble going on, so I figured I'd offer my services."

"How kind of you," she said, but it sounded as if she meant that Rus was sticking her nose in where it didn't belong, making a nuisance of herself. Yeah, Rus had heard that tone enough times in her life to recognize it pretty easily. "Won't you come in?"

"Oh no, I don't think that's necessary." Rus shook her head. Standing outside was uncomfortable enough with the spirits at her back, the ones Taryn had to know Rus could see and feel. Going in would be worse. Putting herself behind Taryn's wards would be putting herself at the other witch's mercy, and that wasn't something she could afford to do. Not right now anyway. Fuck. She should have brought Darcy along. "Just let Vi know I'm here, and I'll wait out in my car, yeah?"

"It could be a minute." Taryn tilted her head, but the act had slipped a little, the face losing its sheen of humanity now that Rus saw it for what it was. "You should come in."

"No. Thank you." Rus took a step back, putting space between herself and Taryn. Nausea had crawled into her belly and made a home for itself there. When she got back to the hospital, Az was going to think she was sick. She'd probably be pissed thinking Rus had run off and performed a spell without help, again. Taryn stepped closer, and Rus nearly fell on her ass on the sidewalk when she came down on her ankle too hard off the front step. "I need to make some calls anyway," she lied. "Check in with the girls. It's almost bedtime."

Taryn's eyes cut to something over Rus's shoulder, and she slunk back into the shadow of the house. "I'll let Violet know you're waiting outside. Thank you for volunteering to take her."

"Of course." Rus gave a hasty dip that was almost a bow and scurried backward down the path toward her car, unwilling to turn her back on the thing wearing Taryn's skin.

Once she was outside of the bubble of spirit magic feeding Taryn's spell, she found Darcy perched on the fence, watching the door shut slowly behind Taryn. He squawked, embittered and disapproving.

"Well, I didn't fucking *know* I was walking into the den of a fucking jumper, now did I?" Which begged the question, why hadn't the Ghost Tracer picked this up? This was a lot of negative energy in one place. It should have been a huge dot on the map, shining brightly, but she'd seen nothing of it when she'd checked the app to make sure it was functioning correctly the night before. Taryn must be cloaking the energy somehow.

Rus rubbed her hands together, trying to get feeling

back into her frozen fingertips. She wondered if there were any snacks for the girls that she could munch on tucked into the glove compartment to get her energy stores back up.

Darcy gurgled, annoyed, but came to rest on her shoulder, his talons pressing into the thin long-sleeved T-shirt she had on. It took a moment, but as he nipped at her ear she felt his energy seep into her, regulating her own stores at least enough that her legs stopped trembling.

"Thanks."

Darcy grunted.

"Yeah, Az is gonna freak the fuck out about this. And honestly . . . same. How did we not know there was a soul jumper in Moondale? Just making itself at home here? And how long has it fucking been here?"

Darcy grumbled.

"Well, that's not good." Rus rubbed at her face with her still tingling fingertips. At least a lifetime. Probably longer. To be that powerful? Definitely longer. But how long had it been in Taryn?

Darcy nipped her ear, this time less affectionately, and she hissed at him, swatting him away.

"Asshole," she muttered and headed back to Blue to wait for Violet.

# Chapter 22

Maybe it was sheer dumb luck. Maybe it was the act of some vengeful god. Maybe Azure had wronged someone in a past life and this was her karma. But at the exact moment the doctor came out to the waiting room, he focused on her and the family huddled around her and said, "We've gotten her stabilized. She's up and talking finally. You can see her if you'd like."

Azure's phone vibrated in her pocket.

She was going to ignore it because relief flooded through her so heavy and all-consuming that she sagged in her chair. Only to be replaced a second later by the buzzing desire to see her aunt, to make sure she was all right with her own eyes. But Rus still wasn't back yet with Violet, and after what Azure had heard at lunch, she wasn't about to take for granted that both Rus and Violet were safe.

"I'll be right behind you," she promised Indigo and Aunt Maureen as they rose to follow the doctor to Aunt Carmine's room. She waited until they were out of sight, turning around the corner to head down the hall, then she pulled out her phone to check and be sure it wasn't Rus texting her with bad news.

Nothing could have prepared her for the text from Nixie Virnan.

NIXIE VIRNAN

Herne and Ironwood have called an emergency closed-door meeting. They're making their move, and it looks like your sister-in-law is helping.

Get here. Now.

Why was it that when one thing went wrong, it felt like everything else had to go to shit at the exact same time? Like a domino effect. Like someone had lined them all up nice and neat and flicked them so everything would hit her at once. Except it wasn't some vague someone now, was it? It was Taryn. It had to be Taryn.

Well. That was one mystery solved. It had been Taryn pulling the strings with Brant all along. Paying her way until she could get what she wanted. Which was obviously Azure and Rus covenless and cast adrift by Moondale's magic.

The question was: *Why?*

Rus hustled Violet into the waiting room, both of them looking drawn. There was a pale sheen to Violet's face, the color washed away like an old photograph, that Azure had never seen, and it made her hands twitch to reach for her sister. To pull Violet in close and shield her from the world in a way Azure had never done before. There wasn't time for that. Taryn had seen to that.

"You'll never believe what I just—"

"Fill me in on the way," Azure said, cutting Rus off and grabbing her purse.

"On the way where?" Violet blinked, the motion slow and a little hazy. Like she was in a fog, or just waking up.

"I'll tell you when I get back." Azure pulled her sister into a tight hug and wished that she had the time or the strength to press her magic into Violet's skin, to rejuvenate her. She didn't, so she'd have to settle for this. "Aunt Carmine is in room 303, on the right. Indigo and Aunt Maureen are with her. Let them know I'll be back as soon as I can."

She didn't know when that would be. An hour? Two? Would she have time to come back tomorrow? There was no way to be sure. But she couldn't be here, sitting by Aunt Carmine's bedside as Taryn tried to topple everything she'd worked so hard for. Aunt Carmine would understand. Especially because the toppling of the Forgotten would likely take Jade Waters down with it.

"But—"

Azure pressed a kiss to her sister's cheek, silencing her. They were still fighting. They still hadn't apologized to one another. But Azure loved her sister, always would, and at times like these, Violet needed to be reminded of that. "Go on back."

When she pulled back again, Violet's eyes were blurred with tears, and she gave a shaky nod. "Okay." Her tone came out distinctly watery, then she followed Azure's directions and disappeared around the corner.

"You still haven't told me where we're going," Rus said, but she moved to hold the door for Azure so they could step out into the late evening air. The glaring lights of the parking lot reminded Azure that she'd been sitting in the waiting room for hours already. She'd lost track of time at some point under the fluorescent bulbs, but that was normal. That happened in hospitals.

She remembered spending what felt like years in the hospital waiting for news about her parents when she was little. Violet's hand holding hers. They'd both been so small then. Their feet hadn't even reached the floor when they sat in the waiting room chairs. The memory sent an ache through Azure's chest that she couldn't really explain. Because she remembered that. She remembered the smell of the waiting room, and the way the too-bright lights gave her a headache—or maybe that had been the crying—but she couldn't remember what her mother's laugh sounded like. She couldn't remember the shape of her father's smile.

The years had worn them away, and all she had left now was Aunt Carmine and Aunt Maureen. And she was not going to lose them too. She was not going to let Taryn take them, and the rest of the family Azure had built, away from her.

"To the Board of Magic building. It would seem Brant and Gilroy have decided to finally make their move."

"You've got to be fucking kidding me." Rus's face twisted in fury, her magic hopping around her arms like static jumping from one point of contact to the next. Lightning preparing to strike. "While your aunt is in the fucking *hospital?*"

"I have little doubt this is precisely *because* my aunt is in the fucking hospital." Azure couldn't help the warm feeling that spread through her at Rus's anger on her behalf. "They thought it would keep me from finding out."

Rus snorted, throwing the door to Blue open and dropping into the seat. "They'll have warded the doors."

"Oh, I'm sure." Azure settled on the passenger side, flipping down the visor to see how bad she looked, but it was hard to tell in the dark, and it didn't really matter anyway. She was going to the meeting. "Good thing I'm bringing someone who knows how to get past them."

Rus turned to her, her smile sharp. Azure's stomach did a little flip. "Good thing."

RUS DIDN'T CUT QUITE the same figure in a pair of baggy joggers and a hoodie as she had the first night she'd broken the wards of the Board of Magic building, but she was no less imposing for it. At least, not in Azure's opinion.

The whispers that always seemed to trail behind Rus—the dead wanting a moment of her time, waiting in the wings to serve their mistress—kicked up into screams. Green magic, so bright it could rival the moon, rose from seemingly nowhere, forming a mist at Rus's feet, her ankles, her calves, casting her face into sharp, eerie relief. Making her look half-dead herself.

She was powerful.

She was terrifying.

She was making it very hard to focus on anything but how much of a competency kink Azure apparently had. *Good to know.*

The doors to the Board of Magic building flung open wide, Rus's magic acting as a battering ram for the wards, leaving them to fizzle and hiss uselessly at Azure's and Rus's feet as they entered.

Someone shouted from the table at the center of the room where the elders sat, but Rus paid them no mind. She merely bent at the waist, bowing to Azure, and said, "After you, love."

Azure couldn't help the smirk that ticked up the corners of her mouth. The proud lilt to her chin as she tipped it back. As a furious hush settled over the room, she said, "I've come to petition for an elder seat on behalf of my coven."

More shouting. Everyone yelling over one another,

trying to have their objections heard. Azure saw Rus join her, just a step behind, her magic curling along the floor to rest beneath Azure as well, as if lending it to her should she need it. She wouldn't, not for this. But it was a sweet gesture all the same.

Nixie rapped her fist against the table and the room quieted once more. "If you wish to petition for a seat"—Nixie's tone was neutral, but a sharp light in her eyes said she approved—"state your case." She gestured to the floor just before the table, and several members shifted so their backs wouldn't be turned to Azure and Rus as they approached.

Azure dipped her head in deference to Nixie, then lifted it again. The air was charged with fury, disbelief, and indignation, and Taryn's gaze burned like a brand on the side of Azure's face from where she sat. In the place that belonged to the Elwoods. The place where Aunt Carmine would have sat were she not in the hospital.

Watching. Waiting. Expecting Azure to fail.

She wouldn't.

"If the board wishes to continue benefiting from our efforts to blend technology with magic, we require a seat at the table." Azure resisted the urge to fidget, to pull at her clothes and try to make sure she was presentable. She folded her arms behind her back, making herself remain still, holding tightly to the file folder Rus had grabbed from 157 on their way over. Standing tall in the face of all this. A wisp of Rus's magic wrapped around her wrist, unseen by those watching but sending a zing of electricity up Azure's arm, raising the hairs in its wake. Silent support. "Many of you are utilizing the Ghost Tracer app. I've even heard that some have begun converting your grimoires to digital using our technology. Our coven has a host of inventions already in the process of being patented through the Moondale system that all our clans would benefit from."

She stepped forward to flop the thick folder onto the table with a loud *thwap*. It wasn't even half of what Rus had in her office, she knew that. That folder was only the beginning.

"But without representation—" Azure shrugged as if this was of little bother to her, little value. "Perhaps it would be best we take such advancements elsewhere, and the clans of Moondale can pay for access to them once they're out of the beta stages."

It went without saying that that could take years. It went without saying that it could be prohibitively expensive. The magic around her wrist almost purred with delight at the implications, Rus's approval evident.

"I suppose Ashthorne will want to be your representative?" Brant snorted, his eyes rolling as if that were the most ridiculous thing he'd ever heard. Goddess, he was lucky Azure had never been a particularly violent woman, or she might come across the table and smack him.

"No." Azure's smirk widened, curling up her face, cartoonish in its size. She glanced at Taryn and saw the way Taryn was watching her. As if Azure was a vicious ghost about to rip them all to shreds. "My partner"—the word tasted like *wife* on her tongue—"has decided to bestow that particular *honor* on me."

It wasn't an honor. It was a burden. But Azure was too polite to say so.

"And you expect to do this with only three witches to your roster?" Gilroy leaned his head back and laughed, loud and full bellied. Like a cynical bastardization of the normies' Santa Claus.

"We'll have five in time for the full moon," Azure volunteered before she'd even thought it through. It was only a few days away, just before Rus was meant to start her guest lectures at Moondale University. "I believe that ought to be sufficient time for us to finalize the paperwork and get the ritual in order that would induct me as an elder. Am I correct, Elder Virnan?"

"You are," Nixie said. She wasn't smiling, but she looked like maybe she wanted to. A good sign.

"You have until the end of the week," Clianthe Greer said, superseding everyone else, but no one argued. "It'll take us at least the weekend to get everything in order, and we won't start preparations until we're sure you have the numbers."

"Of course," Azure said, the image of calm. All the while wondering how the fuck they were going to pull that off. They would. Of course they would. Because they had no other choice, and Azure had faith in Rus's abilities. She just wasn't sure exactly *how* yet. "We'll have our full coven list to you by Friday."

"We will?" Rus asked out of the corner of her mouth, low enough that no one else would hear.

"Ah! Congratulations, Azure." Taryn rose from her seat to clap softly. Azure had never much cared for Taryn, but now that Rus had told her everything she'd seen at their house on Turtle Lane, it was hard to mistake the way Taryn's gaze fixated on her. The cold whisper of something no longer alive lingering in her step. It had always been there, Azure supposed, she just hadn't seen it through the glamour Taryn wore when people were looking. Azure wondered how long. Maybe Rus would be able to tell her when they had a moment to discuss it more in-depth.

"While we're on the topic of elder seats," Taryn said, as if what she was about to say was the logical next step, as if she'd been planning this all along. There was a glint in her eyes of malice and hate. As if she knew that what she was doing would hurt Azure, especially now that Azure saw her for what she was, and it made a cold shiver crawl across Azure's skin. Rus stepped forward, pressing herself into Azure's side, lending support for whatever was coming. She probably felt the shift in the air as much as Azure did. "Perhaps we should consider my candidacy for the position of Elder of the Circle of Jade Waters."

"You—" Azure started forward, fury racing through her veins, an accusation on her lips. An accusation that she couldn't prove. Not yet, anyway. Not so long as the glamour held true. Not so long as Taryn had the others under her spell. Not until they knew what Taryn had done to Aunt Carmine and Violet, and how to break it without hurting them.

"I second this motion," Brant said, not giving Azure a chance to argue. "With the centennial coming, we need someone more capable in the seat."

"Third," Gilroy agreed.

"Fourth." Dhiren, the elder from the Circle of the Emerald Forge, the clan of wish granters, raised his hand a little.

"Well," Nixie said, stopping it before it could get out of hand—or at least, Azure hoped so—"we will certainly take that into consideration." She sat straighter, her expression suddenly pinched. She hadn't anticipated that. She didn't know that Taryn was the one pulling the strings. How many of them had Taryn gotten on her side? And how? "If everyone who is not yet a member of the board will please excuse us, we'd like to begin deliberation now."

"Of course." Azure turned on her heel, not really wanting to turn her back on Taryn, but knowing she needed to if she didn't want to look too suspicious. Although Taryn had to know that Rus had seen her, that Rus had filled Azure in on what was going on. Rus moved in behind her, putting herself bodily between Azure and Taryn, close enough that Azure could feel her heat. And she stayed there all the way to the car.

With the doors shut, Blue's wards, and the darkness hemming them in, Azure slumped back into the seat, her head tilted to look at the ceiling. "Is there anything that can be done?"

"Honestly?" Rus asked. She sounded tired, like the last few hours had aged her decades. Azure felt that down to her bones. "I'm not sure. From what I saw, they're melded together pretty good. If I were a betting woman—"

"Which you are."

"Which I am." Rus sounded like she was smiling, Azure tilted her head so she could see it and let it soothe her. Not much. But enough that her shoulders no longer ached with the tension of being held up around her ears. "I'd say Taryn made a deal with it. Probably years ago. Maybe before I even left, in fact. And once that's done . . ."

Rus didn't need to finish that sentence. Azure understood. Once that was done, there wasn't much anyone could do. Taryn had let it into her body voluntarily, given it power in exchange for something else.

"I'll dig into my notes from the last soul jumper I encountered," Rus promised, and Blue kicked to life with a sputter. "But I'm not making any promises that I can get that thing out of Taryn and leave her alive."

What had Rus said a few days ago when they'd found out about the prophecy? Oh. Right. "Add it to the fucking list."

Rus chuckled darkly and pulled out of the parking spot. "Should I take you back to the hospital?"

"No. I'm no good to anyone there. I'll come home with you and help you dig through your notes." She knew without a single doubt that if she sat beside Aunt Carmine's bedside now . . . If she walked into that room and saw the woman who'd raised her attached to machines, so small in a bed, she'd give up. She'd crumple under the weight of everything. They couldn't afford that. "Maybe a fresh set of eyes will help. We should call in Hunter and Ava too. I know they haven't agreed to join the coven yet, but maybe someone outside of this will see something we miss."

Rus didn't look like she agreed, but she said, "Maybe" and took them home anyway.

# Chapter 23

Rus had too many balls in the air.

And she'd never been particularly adept at juggling.

She was drowning, falling under the weight of expectation. Failing. Everyone was counting on her to find answers, to solve all their problems. And she just . . . she wasn't sure if she was up to the task.

They helped—or tried to anyway.

Az helped. Fernando helped. Everyone helped.

They packed themselves into the rooms of her house, papers and notebooks and books and file folders spread all around them. Searching for answers. Trying to come up with something that would make this easy.

Nothing good in life was easy, Rus had found.

But at the end of the day, when all was said and done, so much of what lay ahead of them would come down to her and her abilities. She would have to find a way for two witches to join her ragtag coven without having to move. She had to finish checking over the house at 155 Mourning Moore to see if it would facilitate her needs as a witch. The house seemed to think so, but that didn't mean it was correct. Her abilities as a necromancer would come into question when they sought to separate Taryn from the soul jumper. Then there was the matter of organizing all her inventions so they could patent them, find something useful, and maybe solve the mystery of Az's ancestor.

Okay. Maybe those last two were more of a group project, hence the people packed into her house. But it still stood to reason that Rus was overwhelmed.

Overwhelmed and overcome by the realization that she could so easily fuck this up. One wrong move, and every ball currently suspended in the air would plummet to the ground and shatter.

Maybe they weren't balls after all. Maybe they were orbs, or eggs. Or . . .

Fuck. She'd taken this analogy too far, and all it was doing was distracting her when she needed to focus.

"And a simple cleansing won't work?" Phyre asked from where she was curled up in the corner of the couch, one of Rus's more beat-up travel notebooks resting against her knees. Rus had never been more grateful for the compulsive urge to journal that she'd picked up from Cagney when she was in high school. She just hoped her friends didn't find anything embarrassing in those pages. She couldn't remember what half of them had in them, or what time period of her life they were from. At least there wouldn't be anything about Kaytee in them. Those were lost years, as Rus liked to think of them. They had been some of the lowest in her life, and Kaytee had thought journaling was stupid. Told Rus that no one would read them so why bother? "Rus."

"Huh?" Rus lifted her head to focus on Phyre. She'd gotten lost in her head again, hadn't she? Damn it. She couldn't afford to be doing that shit. There wasn't time.

"No, a cleansing won't work at all," she said, her brain finally processing what she'd heard. "Because this thing isn't just inhabiting Taryn's body. It's literally fused with her spirit to some degree. I need to untangle them and sever the connection. I'd need to—" She broke off, jaw clenching and unclenching as she thought about what she was about to say. This was going to fucking suck, and she knew it. "I'd need to either let it latch on to me, and deal with it that way, or jump myself."

"Jump . . . *yourself?*" Ava frowned in confusion.

"Push my own spirit into Taryn and fight it there." Rus didn't like the sound of that, even as she said it. It would give the soul jumper home court advantage, and she had no idea how strong it was. Darcy said it was old, but neither of them could tell *how* old. And the longer it had been jumping? The more folk it connected to and leeched off? She was looking at something maybe not more powerful than Kaytee had been as a soul eater, but certainly trickier, more wily. It had had Goddess knew how long to learn.

"Okay, well we're not doing that," Greer said as if it wasn't even a question.

A murmur of agreement went through the room, and Rus supposed she was outnumbered. Which was kind of nice, actually. Made something warm and soft settle into her chest like contentment. Like home. Like family. Goddess, she didn't even fucking like Greer. She was a bitch to him 90 percent of the time. And yet here he was, curled over a folder from the year 2018 stuffed full of the shit she'd thought up that year. It was mostly trash, probably. Most of her ideas weren't viable. But she kept them, just in case. Sometimes they inspired new ideas. Sometimes she found ways to build off them. Sometimes they weren't viable at the time but with more experience, they became so.

Az shifted beside her, reaching for another notebook in the stack in front of them on the coffee table. They were from the early years, when she'd first started keeping track of herself and wasn't anywhere near as consistent as she was these days. Also, before she'd switched to Moleskine notebooks, which seemed to hold up a bit better and definitely looked more professional. Maybe she should set about transferring everything over to those. That'd certainly be less messy than the pile of mismatched spiral notebooks with pages half sticking out of them.

The purple one in Az's hand was one of the first. Rus had been fifteen—sixteen maybe?—when she'd started it. It was probably chock full of drivel. Her mooning over Az. Her complaining about their teachers and how the other students were such stuck-up little gits half the time. But Az held it delicately, as if it were a treasure.

Not delicately enough.

A page fluttered from it, landing on the floor between them where they sat.

Rus blinked down at it.

Az blinked down at it. Then up at Rus, eyes suddenly wide.

"Is that—" Az asked, her fingers almost trembling as she reached for it, and Rus's heart hammered against her ribcage.

The early years. The years with Az in them. When Rus had spent her time following Az like a puppy. Wagging her tail and yipping for attention the entire time. The years when Rus had worshipped the very ground Az walked on. Arguably that hadn't changed, but you know, she didn't exactly want the proof of that all over their living room floor.

And there it was. Proof.

A crumpled bit of notebook paper stapled to another sheet that had obviously broken free of the spiral.

Rus's heart moved into her throat.

IT WAS A TALISMAN, the paper wrinkled almost to the point where Azure couldn't tell what it had been for at all. But there was no mistaking the neat strokes, the way the lines moved across the paper, the unique style of character distribution.

It was one of hers. Maybe one of her first.

From the year when she dedicated some serious time to the study. When she actually thought it could be something. Before the world had told her otherwise. Before she'd given up on that to focus on more "serious" pursuits. Before.

She reached for it, fingers trembling, not understanding exactly what she was seeing.

"Oh, I'll look through that one, Az. You don't have to—" Rus reached for the notebook.

Azure shifted, pulling it closer to her chest, not giving Rus the time to hide it away before she saw what was inside. The notebook fell open in her lap, and there was another of her crumpled talismans taped to the paper. Underneath it, in a messy scrawl, Rus had written notes about how it could be used, improved upon even. They'd never discussed Azure's talisman work before Rus came back to Moondale. Azure didn't think Rus had even noticed it was something she was interested in back then. Rus had always seemed so wrapped up in other things. In her necromancy. In her own genius. There wasn't room to pay attention to the things Azure hyper-fixated on.

She'd been wrong. All this time, she'd been so wrong.

About Rus. About herself. About her own abilities . . . maybe.

"Az, don't—" but Rus hadn't moved to stop her again. Instead she waited, her freckled cheeks turning red, hardly blinking. Maybe afraid she'd break whatever spell was between them.

Azure's throat ran dry, but she could hardly stop herself from flipping through to the next page and the next. Page upon page of crinkled, discarded talismans. Not just from that first year, but from the years that followed. She watched as the lines became more sure, as her understanding of form and negative space took shape. They also felt fewer, further between. But the whole book, the entire thing, was full of her work. Her creativity.

The thing Azure had never thought she had. The dream she'd given up and was only now finding her footing in again. And all this time, Rus had held on to it for her. Documented it.

"Why did you keep these?" Azure felt stupid asking, but there was no clear reason why Rus would bother. They were scrap. Half of them wouldn't do anything, and the other half likely wouldn't do the thing they were designed to. They were rudimentary. Crude. Like a child drawing a horse without first seeing one. She'd understood, even before her teachers and the elders of her coven had steered her away from pursuing talisman craft as a serious avenue of study, that she wasn't skilled in it. Not yet. It would take time, patience, practice. And then Azure had given up on it, put it behind her. She never even kept any of her early attempts.

Rus, it would seem, had never given up. Not on Azure. Not on her dream.

"Because they were awesome," Rus said, leaning in

closer, her breath slightly quickened. "Don't you see how great they were? Yeah, they needed some work, but they were amazing first drafts. And like . . . Az." Rus took the notebook and flipped through it herself. "I've used some of these."

"You have?"

"Az, come on." Rus chuckled in disbelief. "You have to know how great these are. I mean yeah, they were a little rough, but they were a start. And there was so much potential here. So much room to grow. I couldn't—I wasn't going to let them go to waste.

"And like this one," she said, pointing to a warming talisman. "Great for keeping meals warm on the go. Or . . . Oh, this one saved my a—" She stopped, glancing at where the girls were curled up on the couch near Phyre. Aihuan asleep with her head in Meiling's lap. Meiling watched them with keen brown eyes. "Ass," Rus finished, and stuck her tongue out at Meiling when she looked like she might say something, "when I had to deal with a particularly nasty spirit in Melbourne."

"Did you dig them out of the trash can?" Cagney asked, her tone judging, suddenly leaning over Rus's shoulder. "You little scavenger. What have we talked about pulling things out of the bin?"

"Shut up, Cags." Rus spun around to swat her best friend away. "If you were smart, you wouldn't throw away half the shit you did."

The two settled into bickering, and Azure pulled the notebook from Rus's lap to inspect again. The page she'd indicated as having used in Melbourne held a bonding talisman that Azure had been toying with. She didn't remember what exactly had prompted it, but . . .

Bonding. It gave her an idea.

"What if we could infuse a tattoo with a bit of Moondale's essence?" Azure lifted her head and found Rus and Cagney sitting frozen in place, their eyes fixed on her.

"A tattoo?" Hunter asked, scooting closer, leaving a mark from his jeans on the rug beneath the couch. "What kind of tattoo? What would it do?"

"It'd allow a person to carry a piece of Moondale with them." Azure wasn't sure how, but there was something there. Definitely. Potential, like Rus said.

"What would we need to do that for?" Avalyn frowned, her nose wrinkled in distaste.

But Rus had already caught on, and Azure could see the way her eyes danced with an idea. "We'd have to be careful about it, and not overwhelm it. The power boost from Moondale wouldn't be as great as living on the land every day. And it'd need to be charged, at least monthly to start. But yes. Yes. This could work!"

"I'd need to make some changes, alter the nature of the binding."

"Right. And the strength behind it."

"You'd need to make it more flexible. This one is very rigid, it's more of a cage. We don't want a cage, we want more of a wire?" Hunter chimed in. He'd gotten so close now, he was practically curled around the bit of paper.

"A line. Like a mooring line." Azure was dizzy with the back and forth. With the push and pull of her mind and Rus's. When was the last time they had done this? Had they ever? She couldn't remember. And it didn't matter. It didn't matter at all. Because if they ever had, it had been over Rus's ideas. It had been Azure augmenting and helping Rus understand her own genius better. But this wasn't Rus's, this was her own. This was . . . this was something she was bringing to the coven.

"Exactly!" Rus grinned more broadly. "Goddess, Az, you're so smart!"

Azure's face grew hot, but she couldn't look away from Rus. Could only squirm under her attention.

"You can do that, right? What am I talking about. Of course you can! You're Azure Elwood!" Rus grabbed the pad she'd been taking notes on, and a pen, and thrust them at Azure. "You get to work on that. And you've given me another idea, a way to maybe explain what's going on with Carmine and Vi. But I'm going to need some supplies." Then she was on her feet, scurrying from the room. "And your keys to the Jade Waters coven house."

The room was weirdly silent after she left and Azure gripped the pen in her hand tighter, her heart still hammering against her chest. They could do this. They could make this work. And then Azure . . . Azure could have everything she'd ever wanted.

Maybe it was time she get that ring cleaned.

"Uh . . ." Nesta said, their eyes flicking from where Rus had just disappeared to the rest of the room. "Does anyone know what in the name of the Goddess just happened?"

Greer shifted in his seat. He looked distinctly uncomfortable, but his tone was fond when he said, "I'd say Azure and Ashthorne just found a way to add witches to their coven without them having to move to Moondale."

"Hell yeah," Hunter laughed, delighted.

# Chapter 24

"What do we do if cutting the soul jumper off from the source of magic kills Taryn?" Az asked, her head tilted back to look up at the manor that Jade Waters liked to call a coven house. It made the house that would soon be their own look like a one-room apartment. But that was fair, Rus supposed, seeing as how Jade Waters had been with Moondale since the beginning, and the Forgotten was just getting started.

Rus shrugged, pushing her hair back from her face and hitching the duffle further up her shoulder. "I suppose we could always bury her under your aunt's roses. You don't think she'd make them bloom off season, do you?"

Az turned to look at her, fixing her with a blank expression.

"Oh come on, you have to remember *Practical Magic.*" Rus huffed. "We watched it—"

"I remember *Practical Magic.*" Az shook her head, a fond lilt to her mouth. "But I hardly think now is the time for jokes."

The witching hour loomed ahead of them. A short window where they would do what Rus could only pray to the Goddess was possible: sever the soul jumper's connection to Jade Waters, and by extension to Violet and Carmine Elwood, and to Moondale. It wouldn't kill the soul jumper, but it might weaken it and make it easier to separate from Taryn. If the process didn't kill her, of course.

There were a lot of ifs in there, Rus recognized that. But soul jumpers weren't exactly common, and she'd never tried to force one out of someone's body before.

Rus's stomach churned, turning sour and acidic at the bottom in her anxiety. She was playing games with someone else's life, and she didn't like it. It was okay when it was *her* existence on the line. When it was her soul that might be obliterated by the task ahead. But this was Taryn. Someone she didn't really like, granted, but still another soul, another witch, another *person*.

"We have about ten minutes to get set up," Az pressed, checking the time on her phone. She was calm and sure in all of this. Rus didn't know how she did that. Stared down the face of what might go wrong and was still so certain of what lay ahead. The possibility for harm had Rus shying away, but . . .

If it was Taryn or Carmine and Violet, Rus knew her answer, and she knew Az's too. One life. For the lives of two people Az loved dearly. Her family. One life for possibly the lives of all of Moondale. They still didn't know what the fuck the soul jumper was after in all of this, aside from the obvious power grab. And Rus didn't think she wanted to find out.

One breath in, sucking down humid air and ignoring the way a cold sweat trickled down her spine.

One breath out.

"Let's get this over with." She hitched the bag up further on her shoulder and stepped to the door of the Jade Waters coven house. It didn't creak as they entered—hinges too meticulously kept to ever make a sound—and silence lay beyond. Not the quiet of a dead place, Rus had been to enough of those over the years to note the difference, but the quiet of a place holding its breath. Waiting. As if to see what she and Az would do inside its walls. Rus had always felt this place didn't care for her much. That it found her distasteful. She shook that thought aside.

"Where did they hold the hand-fasting ceremony?"

"In the banquet hall." Az led the way.

Rus had only been inside of the Jade Waters banquet hall once. It was during Yule, when she and Az were dating. Elwoods from all over the place had made the trip, and Az wanted Rus there with her, or so she said. It hadn't ended well. Rus wound up getting into a fight with one of the Elwood elders over politics. Rus didn't even remember exactly over what, she just remembered the devastated look on Az's face when Rus excused herself and skulked away to hide in the library.

It looked different now, and yet the same. The big table that had stood at the center that night, made of some kind of light-colored wood Rus couldn't name—birch or maple or something—and carved with a map of Moondale, was gone. In storage maybe. And in its place were rows upon rows of chairs. All facing a small arbor made of birch trees with the bark still on them. What the fuck?

Az stopped at the top of the aisle, her face unreadable for a moment. And then it clicked into place what Rus was seeing, what the coven house had done. This was what a hand-fasting ceremony in the Jade Waters coven house must look like. What it had looked like on the day Violet and Taryn were married. What it would have looked like if Az were to marry someone respectable, someone worthy of her. It would be held here, in this room, under this arbor. With all the Elwoods watching on in approval. Just as every other Elwood hand-fasting ceremony had been held.

Az would never have that now. She wasn't a member of Jade Waters anymore.

"We're going to need to clear a space near the front," Rus said, not wanting to give either of them too long to think about Az's sacrifices. Because if they did, Rus was pretty sure she'd walk right out that door and beg for Carmine to take Az back. Beg for Az to go home. Then she'd be alone again. And she was too selfish for that.

Az's fingers twitched at her side between her and Rus, as if she meant to reach out and stop Rus from ruining the setup. But in the end, she didn't reach, and instead she lifted that same hand to sweep it through the air. The chairs scraped against the floor as they parted for her and Rus, clattering against each other, against the walls. It was overkill. They didn't need that much space. An emotional response.

Rus cleared her throat to keep from saying something stupid and forced out a single strangled "great" as she made her way to the front. She tried to ignore the way her boots wrinkled the pale blue silk fabric that made up the aisle.

They pulled away the piece of silk used for where she assumed the brides and bridal party would stand, leaving the wood floor bare enough that Rus could create a small circle around what she estimated as the spot where Violet and Taryn had said their vows.

She hoped this worked. It was just guesswork. And in a place where so many others had bound themselves to each other, it was risky trying to use the mark left behind to unbind a single couple. If she fucked up, several Jade Waters couples might have to get married again. That wasn't the worst that could happen, of course, but it was a far funnier consequence than the others. So she allowed herself to focus on it instead. Imagine . . . *so* many weddings.

Az stepped into the middle of the circle and started on the character work they'd need to do the unbinding, while Rus went to the door to lay down a thin salt line. It was a modification on the binding talisman she'd created all those years ago. Reversed to be a mirror image of itself. Expanded to specify who she wanted to target. Rus could hardly look away as Az worked, her brow pinched in the middle, her mouth set into a grim line. The sidewalk chalk was staining her fingers blue. But she looked . . .

Goddess, she was *breathtaking*.

"How much blood will we need?" Az asked, breaking Rus from her trance, and Rus shook herself. Right. Blood. Candles. Salt. Other things she needed to set up while Az focused on this.

"Just enough to trace the Elwood symbols into the talisman, I'd say." She wasn't really sure. They should have done more research. They should have taken their time. This kind of magic was not something to be fucked with. But they couldn't risk Carmine getting sicker. They couldn't risk Violet being drained completely. They couldn't risk Taryn making a move that would keep them from doing what they had to. There were too many consequences to waiting. So they were rushing the magic a bit here. Rus hoped Moondale would understand and would bless them for trying to do the right thing. But she was a fickle bitch sometimes, so there was no way to tell.

Rus forced herself to stand and went back to the duffle bag to begin setting up the rest of the unbinding ritual.

The clock in the hall chimed 3 a.m. just as Rus put the finishing touches on everything they needed. Lighting the last candle with the lighter she'd pulled from the kitchen drawer. The flames that surrounded them flickered as if someone had opened a door and let the wind in, but they held strong. Good.

"The talisman?" Rus asked, turning back to where she'd left Az in the middle of the circle, and her breath lodged in her chest.

How hadn't she heard Taryn and Violet come in?

Violet's face was ashen, glistening with sweat in the candlelight. Her brown eyes were wild, wide, eating up every other feature. And where Taryn pressed a thin athame to her neck, a trail of blood trickled into the collar of her T-shirt.

"Did someone summon me?" Taryn asked, mouth twisted into something cruel and unyielding. An expression Rus had never seen on her face before, not in all the years she'd known her. But then, this wasn't Taryn, was it? This was the soul jumper. The person who had decided they didn't want to die, and so had found a way to live indefinitely by taking over the body of another. No better than a parasite.

"Azure," Violet choked out, and was silenced by the press of the blade.

Rus heard Az stand more than saw it in her periphery, because it was hard to focus on anything outside of the writhing spirits twisting and swirling dark and deadly around Taryn. It wasn't the blade they needed to worry about. It was the magic. The souls that had attached themselves to Taryn and grown ravenous.

"You're a little early," Rus shot back, forcing a smile onto her face that felt shaky even to her. "We didn't need you for at least another ten minutes or so."

If she could get close enough to pull the athame to herself with magic, would that be enough to end the threat? No. Taryn could do worse than cut Violet open. The shades around her could rend Violet's soul to pieces, leaving nothing behind for the After. A hollow shell.

Az stepped forward, and Rus moved to step in front of her, putting herself bodily between the danger Az might not be able to see and Az.

"Why don't you let Vi go? And we can talk about this necromancer to necromancer, huh?" Rus held up her hands, showing Taryn that she had nothing in them, not even magic at the moment. Not that it would stop her from doing what they needed to to save Az's family. If she had to throw herself at the shades and let them rip her apart instead of Violet, she would.

Now, there was an idea.

A smile, sharp and cruel, curled up Rus's face, and she felt Az shift beside her as if Az knew exactly what she was about to do.

"Once I get Vi clear of the shades," Rus said, her voice soft in the space between them, "get both of your asses in that circle and finish the ritual."

Az's head jerked around to look at her, panic lining her face. Rus could see it out of the corners of her eyes. But it wasn't going to stop her. Nothing was.

"Who said I'm a necromancer?" Taryn tilted her head, birdlike and terrifying. Well. That was a development Rus hadn't considered. That the soul jumper hadn't been the one to do the ritual themselves. That someone else had done it, or taught it to them, or helped them. Az's ancestor maybe. That was something they'd have to consider later.

"You could let Taryn go, then," Rus said, trying to sound reasonable. The athame in the front of her hoodie pocket was heavy, calling to her, and it was easy to slip her hand inside and slice her palm open.

And wait.

# Chapter 25

The spirits rushed Rus a moment later. Fresh blood from the source of someone who straddles the line between the living and the dead too tempting to ignore. Her back slammed into the ground hard enough to shake the floor beneath Azure's feet.

It didn't give Azure much time to get to her sister, to grab Violet by the wrist and yank her away from where Taryn had lost her grip on the dagger in her distraction, but it gave her enough. Just enough. They raced back across the room toward the circle of protection Rus created for her, the talisman she'd drawn so meticulously. Safety.

Taryn screamed, the sound heartrending and violent, and the ground shook beneath them again. Azure felt something grapple at her ankle, insubstantial, and when she looked down, she saw a hand broken through the splintered floorboards. Dismembered from the body it'd been attached to, but bearing a mark she would recognize anywhere. The Elwood family crest, carved into the pinky finger, tattooed there for all to see. Meant to be their ticket to the After.

The dead. Taryn was raising the dead.

No, this wasn't the same as what Rus did. These dead weren't *raised*, they were *puppeted*. Ripped from the ground and stuffed full of hate like marionettes. They had no will of their own.

Not a necromancer, her fucking ass.

Azure wasn't even sure how this was *possible*. The Elwoods weren't buried beneath the coven house. They would have to dig from the graveyard behind.

Azure and Violet ran, stumbled, tripped over hands, feet, legs, and more, the dead ripped from their resting place. Struggled to get to the circle while pieces of their ancestors did everything in their power to stop them.

Azure glanced over her shoulder once and found Taryn not following. The warding magic of the salt line at the door held fast, for the moment. It wouldn't last long. An ill wind was picking up. Like someone had opened a window during a storm. It would carve away at their protections. And there was still Rus to think of.

Rus.

Azure tripped into the circle with Violet and grabbed the athame she'd left behind, cutting into her palm, getting the blood where she needed it and slamming her hand into the edge of the circle. It wasn't much. But it would keep Violet safe for the moment. Long enough for Azure to do something reckless.

"Stay," she said, not giving Violet a chance to argue, to pull her back, and spun to find Rus among the wreckage.

A thick black smoke coated the floor, making it almost impossible to see the pale wood below. It moved in waves over where Rus was still struggling against something Azure couldn't see. The shades. How many had there been? How had Taryn controlled them when clearly they were feral? Maybe she hadn't. Maybe that was the point. Maybe she'd simply tied them to herself to suck dry like some kind of spiritual vampire. Only she hadn't counted on their hunger, their thirst for power being stronger than her own magic. Hadn't counted on Rus being just stupid and self-sacrificing enough to open a vein and invite them in.

Foolish, really. Anyone who knew anything about Rus knew she'd do something like that in a heartbeat if it meant saving someone else.

Azure dug around in her mental arsenal to think of a spell that would push them back, at the very least, to give Rus a moment to breathe. But there was nothing. Her lack of battle magic made her weak. Useless. *Again.* When this was done, Rus was going to train her, teach her to protect them both and their little family, their coven. Even if she never needed the skill again, and the rest of their lives was calm, at least she would have it in case.

She struggled across the room, stumbling over another dismembered hand.

What she settled on, when she could think of nothing offensive, was an old calming spell she'd used when Indigo was a baby. The tune that went with it was soothing and soft, meant to inspire tranquility, drowsiness. It might do nothing, but at least it wouldn't stir them up more, and it gave her something to do while she moved across the battle-field toward Rus.

The hand around her ankle was missing fingernails and showing bone in places, but it loosened its grip as if sleepy. With a boost of confidence, Azure sang louder, picking her way toward Rus. She kept an eye on Taryn and another on Violet, praying that she'd have at least a moment to pull her partner out of the fray, to get her to safety.

Violet had slumped into the circle, hand gripping her neck as if it'd been cut, but there was no blood. It was just a body's natural response to a threat.

Taryn was banging her fists against the salt barrier like a mime, still unable to cross it because she'd not been the one to set it. Icarus Ashthorne, for all she tended to be unable to settle, flitting from thought to thought like a bee, was good with intention. She'd laid the salt line and so long as it was in place, no one she'd intended to keep out would be able to cross it. Azure would be proud of her, brag about it a little to Taryn, if they had the time.

The wind picked up further. It whipped at her, ripping her hair from its tight braid. But Taryn hadn't moved yet. She seemed to be biding her time, waiting for something. That was never a good sign.

Still, it gave Azure the moment she needed to reach into the smoke—which had grown slower, sluggish from her singing—and pull up a gasping Rus. A scratch down the length of Rus's cheek dripped lazily, and it was hard to tell if Rus had done it herself or if one of the spirits caught her. It didn't matter.

"Thanks," Rus said, swallowing with a dry click, her eyes bloodshot. She didn't wait for Azure to respond, just pinched at her palm, drawing more blood to the surface, and with it came the leaping green magic. It snapped in fury on behalf of its mistress. Then Rus murmured, "Peace" so softly it seemed a prayer, and the green slid from her skin to join the black smoke on the floor. Spreading through it like gas and eating it up until there was almost nothing left. Until Rus had freed every spirit trapped in Taryn's orbit.

Rus stumbled, her knees seemingly going weak, and Azure caught her before she fell to the ground. Azure's hands tight around her waist.

Taryn screamed, and the wind hit Azure with a force so hard it sent her and Rus reeling.

The salt was gone.

A spell barreled across the room, violent red, picking up speed as it came. The smell of burned silk and charred flesh replaced the smell of candles and blood so quickly, Azure was almost dizzy.

She didn't think, she just stepped in front of the spell. Putting herself between it and Rus as Rus continued to talk to the spirits, trying to ease them into the After. Into peace. A protective barrier while Rus was at her most vulnerable.

It hit her like a truck. Azure stumbled back under the force of it, gasping at the burn as it caught fire along her skin. There were no actual flames, of course, just magic, just the heat searing her flesh. But it gave Rus the moment she needed to dispel the last of the spirits.

It also gave Taryn the time to stalk across the room until she was right before Azure. Practically nose to nose. Her eyes were black, lacking the whites and any color. And the smile on her face had morphed into something chilled to the core.

"Az, the—" Rus yelped and grabbed for Azure's wrist to try to pull her away, to put distance between them and their attacker, but Azure would not back down. Would not run away.

"Get in the circle with Violet," Azure said, not taking her eyes off Taryn. Who hadn't moved yet. Hadn't reached for the magic that lingered under her skin or lifted the athame still resting at her side. Azure wondered what she was waiting for. What was keeping her in place. But she didn't want to ask either. Maybe the soul jumper thought it could make a deal with Azure. Maybe it thought it could take hold of her the way it had Taryn. "Finish it."

"It really should be—"

"Violet is there. She'll be enough."

Rus didn't move. Azure could still feel her heat at her back.

"Rus."

"Okay." Rus stepped away.

Taryn tilted her head but didn't watch Rus walk away.

She kept her eyes on Azure the entire time. "She wanted to be like you, do you know that?" the soul jumper asked. "This little witch. She wanted to be just like *you*."

"She can get in line." Azure smiled, cold and cutting. How many people had said that throughout her life? How many had sought her power, her prestige, without fully understanding the price she paid for those things? How many had revered her, thought her untouchable? But had never thought to befriend her. Never thought to love her. Rus had been the first to do that. The only one to do it so wholly. To see Azure, not just another perfect Elwood.

Taryn threw her head back and laughed. Then she tried to sidestep Azure, her magic lashing out toward the circle where Rus's back was turned while she worked. Azure threw up a wall of magic, a shield. The spell fizzled out, settled on the ground like discarded glitter.

"Do you know who I *am*?" Taryn asked, trying to side-step her again. Azure followed. Stayed between Taryn and her family, her magic answering the call under her skin. A torrent, a rising tide. She would wash Taryn away in it if that's what it took to protect them.

"No." Azure didn't care either. Another spell lashed against her body. There would be wounds, real ones, bloody and ragged. Scars would form to match Rus's. But that was fine. They would finally be a matched set on the outside the way they were two halves of a whole on the inside.

"I'm the most powerful witch Moondale has ever *seen*," Taryn said, the red of her magic sizzling against her skin like heat. She was so sure of herself. So certain that Azure would fear her. Azure found she wasn't afraid of anything so much as she was afraid of Rus walking away from Moon-dale. That had already happened once, and she'd survived. So what was left to be scared of? "I've lived for five hundred years. You should bow at my feet. You should worship me for what I've done. I am a god."

"No," Azure repeated, a creeping satisfaction settling into her as the words she'd say next sat on her tongue. She would go down, she was sure of it now. Because she wasn't as strong as whatever was wearing Taryn's skin like a cheap suit. So yes, she'd go down. She'd falter. But not before she was sure Rus had disconnected this bitch from her family. "You're just an asshole too afraid to die."

Taryn screamed, her magic lashing out at Azure, snapping against her skin, drawing blood. Maybe this is why Rus liked riling people the way she did—it was deeply gratifying to see the way they lost their hold on themselves. A wave crested inside of her, the magic building enough to throw into a spell that wrapped around Taryn's limbs, yanking her back, her heels skidding against the floor. It gave Azure more room to fight. Put more distance between Taryn and where Rus was working.

She needed to keep her busy. Just a bit longer. Then Rus would have severed Taryn's ties, and the magic she was privileged to as a spouse of Jade Waters would evaporate. The house would turn against her. It would swallow her whole.

Just a bit longer.

The spell didn't keep Taryn away for long. She raced back toward Azure, her magic whipping out now rapid fire. Death by a thousand cuts. But Azure gave back as good as she got. Her magic flowed over Taryn, drowning her, threatening to suck her under into a riptide. She didn't want to kill the host, didn't want to hurt the body. She needed to hold back, just a little, just enough. But there was only so much she could do while protecting herself and the people she loved. While keeping her footing.

She panted, sucked in deep gasping breaths of air still acrid with the stench of the dead. But at least she faced only one opponent now. At least there were no more spirits near enough for Taryn to call to her to use.

They moved around the room, trading blows in an ugly mimicry of when Azure had danced with Rus in this room all those years ago. Out the corner of her eyes, Azure kept track of Rus and Violet. They were working together. Violet was fumbling, her hands unsteady, her magic weak. But Rus was patient with her, guiding her through the ritual that Azure herself was meant to help with.

"NO!" Taryn screamed, drawing Azure's attention back to her. Taryn wasn't looking at her. She'd stopped in the middle of whatever spell she'd been working up, her gaze fixed on Rus over Azure's shoulder.

Blood trickled down Azure's skin under her shirt, and her chest heaved. She turned, just her head, to find Rus's hands twisted in a long strand of pale-blue silk. A hand-fasting rope. Azure recognized it immediately. Rus's magic burned along it, turning the silk from pale to black, making the room stink of it.

"You bitch!" Taryn flew across the floor, her feet hardly touching it.

Azure had a moment, just one blink, to put herself between the sharp blade of Taryn's athame and Rus. It glanced off her side, leaving a deep gash along her ribs. Her magic flared around her, angry and hurt, and she bound Taryn with a murmured spell, a spoken talisman in its way, augmented from her original work to cage, to bind, to hold in place. Her knees buckled under her, her magic near spent, even as Moondale tried to pump her full of more. Her body could take only so much.

Taryn thrashed and screamed.

It was too late.

The binding broke like a shockwave, making the ground shudder beneath them, the walls around them rumbling in warning. Azure turned back to Rus to find Rus's face pale, drawn. She wobbled on her feet, teetering on the edge of consciousness. Violet looked a little steadier, but only just.

"I'm sorry. I didn't—I didn't want this," someone whispered, their voice broken and choked. It took Azure a moment to realize that it was Taryn. That the eyes that lifted from her feet to meet Azure's were a different color, a softer shade of gray than she'd ever seen in Taryn's face. "I was . . . I was only twenty. So young. So stupid."

"Weren't we all," Rus mumbled from behind Azure.

"She promised me everything I'd ever wanted. Prestige. Worth. I didn't mean—I only wanted—Help me."

"Yeah," Rus said, her own voice shaking as she pushed off her knees, climbing to her feet. "Well. What's the first rule of necromancy, Az?"

"Spirits lie," Azure responded dutifully.

"Exactly." Rus stepped closer to the edge of the circle, reaching for Azure. "You made a deal with it."

Taryn nodded, although that hadn't been a question, and ducked her head again.

"I couldn't get you free now, even if I wanted to." Rus sniffed, scrubbing the tip of her nose along her torn and bloodied sleeve, and Azure wondered if she was about to cry. Maybe she was.

"So you don't"—Taryn's voice changed, grew hard—"want to help her."

Azure's heart leaped into her throat. A cold sweat broke out over her body. There was a breath, a single inhale where Azure wasn't quite sure what she was seeing. It clicked into place right before Taryn broke free of her binding, her magic bursting out of her like an explosion. Azure threw up a shield spell, grabbed Rus and Violet, and ran.

The room collapsed. Debris fell from the second floor, the third, around them like rain. Bouncing off her weakening magic like droplets on a tin roof. She had to get them out of the house. She had to make it to the door. The world rocked under them, threatening to take her from her feet. But she pushed on, forced herself to run faster, her heart slamming against her chest, her legs burning so badly she thought they might stop.

Rus and Violet followed as best they could. Half stumbled. Half allowed her to drag them.

Until they were outside in the humid late spring air.

Rus fell to her knees beside Azure, almost bringing Azure down with her. But the rumbling sound of a collapsing building had her turning instead.

Turning and watching as half the Jade Waters coven house fell in on itself. Became rubble and broken beams.

She stood there, her legs shaking beneath her for a long moment while the dust settled. The silence of their disbelief, their pain, was only broken by Rus saying, "Okay, someone's gonna have to tell Carmine that wasn't my fault."

Azure dropped to her knees beside Rus and laughed, harsh and brittle, pushing her face into Rus's shoulder. Letting Rus hold her up where she couldn't anymore.

"I'll speak to the elders," Violet volunteered. "I'll tell them . . . everything."

Azure looked over her shoulder at her sister and thought for the first time since she was a child how small she looked. How lost. Violet had always been sure of herself, steady in her knowledge that what she was doing was the right thing. Now, she was bereft, a ship unmoored.

"We'll help explain," Rus said, without even having to

be asked. As if she understood what Violet was feeling, as if she couldn't stand to see someone drift away like that. "You won't have to do it alone."

Violet turned to look at them, her eyes wide and uncertain. "Thank you."

"Hey, that's what family is for." Rus grinned and pulled Azure in closer, pressing a kiss to the top of her head. And that was the end of that.

# Chapter 26

The gavel came down hard. The sound a whip crack that echoed through the room.

Rus had never heard the Board of Magic so silent before. But there they sat, stunned by all they'd learned, disbelief coloring every blink. As if they'd never thought for a single second that one of their own could do such a thing. Which was ironic if you asked Rus, because the system they created was a breeding ground for this kind of thing. They made it almost easy for someone to say the right words, flatter the right people, and infiltrate their ranks in a bid to grab power. Shame she and Az had never been the flattering kind.

"And we're just supposed to"—Brant shifted, the metal chair creaking beneath him—"to believe that all this time, Taryn Elwood—"

"Taryn Addington," Az corrected, and Rus reached over to thread her fingers with Az's, she heard the chairs behind them creak—where Hunter, Ava, and Nando sat. She couldn't offer much comfort to the Elwoods during all of this. Especially to Violet, who had only grown thinner in the weeks that passed. She wasn't as pale though, and she seemed to be regaining her strength and magic. Rus counted that as a win, but it was a small one. Tiny in comparison to the pain Violet was going through, and Rus's inability to help. Az's inability to make this better. Rus could see how that weighed on Az, made this harder. Az had always been the fixer of their family. The one to make things okay again when they'd gone to shit. But there was no making this okay.

"Taryn Addington," Brant amended, "was a five-hundred-year-old witch. And that five-hundred-year-old witch has been inhabiting witches' bodies in Moondale for . . . what purpose?"

"We don't know," Rus supplied. Which didn't really help their case, and she recognized that. "It's not like they did an evil monologue or something."

Brant shot her an annoyed look and opened his mouth to say something snide—Rus could tell by the tilt of his mouth—but Clianthe cut him off. "Either way, it is clear that the Coven of the Forgotten has done us a favor in resolving this problem before it could become more of an issue."

Resolving. Meaning Taryn Addington was dead.

Or so they thought, anyway. They hadn't found a body while clearing the rubble leftover from that night a couple weeks ago, and Rus wasn't stupid enough to think that it would have just disappeared, or that the thing inside of Taryn would have allowed itself to be ripped apart by the spirits it had been controlling. No. Taryn Addington and whatever she'd made a deal with had escaped. And they were not done with Moondale, not by a long shot. Still, if it made the board feel better to think that Rus and Az had dealt with them, Rus supposed it would be all right for them to relax.

For a little while, anyway. There were other things to handle while they waited for Taryn and the soul jumper to strike again. The centennial to look toward. Carmine's and Violet's recovery. Their work on the coven tattoos.

But Rus was keeping an eye on the Ghost Tracer, checking it regularly to try to find Taryn. She wasn't inside the Moondale wards, but she likely hadn't gone far.

"Here, here," Nixie agreed, buoyant in what Rus was sure she perceived to be her victory. Goddess, Rus hoped Nixie wasn't stupid enough to think this was over too. She'd always thought the head of the Ladies of Nimue was smarter than that. "That being said," she continued, her eyes turning sharp and knowing, "we cannot think this is the last we've seen of the spirit inhabiting Taryn Addington. Even if Taryn lost her life in the collapse—"

Violet flinched beside Rus. Rus resisted the urge to pull her into a tight hug, to remind her that she wasn't alone. She didn't think Violet would much appreciate that. There was a carefully curated distance between Violet and Az these days—much less Rus. As if maybe she blamed them for what happened to Taryn to some degree, even if she knew it wasn't logical. Rus couldn't fault her for feeling that way. She'd be furious if she lost Az and would likely skin alive whoever had anything to do with it. And even if Taryn had been abusive, even if the soul jumper was by all accounts evil, that had still been Violet's wife.

"—we have no way of knowing that the soul jumper is gone. Correct?" Nixie's eyes fixed on Rus, and anxiety prickled along Rus's skin. Fuck, she hated being put on the spot like this.

"Right." Rus nodded. "The ritual we did was just to unbind Taryn, and by extension the soul jumper, from the Elwood family. To dissipate a spirit of that kind, I'd have to try something else." What else, she wasn't sure yet. She'd dealt with a soul jumper only once before, and that one had destroyed itself. Ripped to shreds by its own lack of a grip on reality after so many years hopping from one body to the next. This one was different. This one was still very much in control of its faculties. Likely because it hadn't done so much jumping around. It had made a deal with one witch at a time and stayed there until the body inevitably failed it. Which could have taken decades, maybe a century or two if the witch was particularly powerful.

And while she was at it, she wasn't sure she *wanted* to do it. Whatever that thing was, Violet had fallen in love with it. How would Violet feel about Rus if she were to destroy it entirely?

"More reason to keep the Coven of the Forgotten close." Nixie smiled as if this had been her intention all along. Maybe it had been. Maybe she'd known the soul jumper was there the entire time and had been waiting for Rus to find it.

Rus narrowed her eyes, watching the other woman more closely. Had she had her suspicions? If so, for how long? Since Rus had been pushed from Moondale when she came of age? Honestly, it would make sense that Taryn had something to do with that. Rus was the only one within the wards of Moondale likely to find Taryn out and expose her. Why not get rid of Rus then? Have her exile herself? The surest way to do that would have been to have Az matched with someone else. It made so much sense, now that she was thinking about it through this lens.

Only it hadn't stuck, had it? Rus had returned years later, her children in tow, and had to be dealt with another way. Thus, the smear campaign. She wondered what Taryn had been gearing herself up for. What she would have framed Rus for if given a bit more time. Good thing Rus had found her out.

"Which is why," Nixie said, drawing Rus back to the present, "we have decided to approve the Forgotten's petition for an elder seat. The ceremony will be held the month prior to the centennial, as requested by Miss Elwood, right alongside the binding ceremony for your new coven members."

The room erupted into cheers and whoops of excitement.

"I told you we could do it," Hunter said, giving Rus's shoulder a shove, and when Rus looked back at the rest of her coven, him, Avalyn, and Fernando were grinning back at her so wide, it looked like it might hurt.

The gavel slammed against the table again—where the fuck had Nixie even gotten that damn thing?—and she grinned wider. "I hereby dismiss this meeting of the Board of Magic."

"DO you think having a soul jumper in town will cover the whole 'the shadows of our past walk amongst us' thing in the prophecy?" Rus asked hopefully once they were both loaded up in Azure's car and on their way home. It was late, but Azure knew they wouldn't be sleeping once they returned to the house.

There was still too much to do, to prepare, too much to clean up. Thankfully, she'd had a little time since the fight with Taryn to finalize the binding talisman that would need to be tattooed into the skin of their new coven members. But that wasn't to say there was nothing left to do.

Even with Aunt Carmine on the mend and released from the hospital, there wasn't time to relax.

Azure turned to look at Rus, her face blank.

"No. You're right." Rus sighed, leaning back in her seat more. "We wouldn't get that lucky."

Rus reached over and took her hand, threading their fingers together.

They wouldn't get that lucky. But . . . at least they would be doing this together now. At least they wouldn't have to face what was coming alone.

"Let's go home," Rus said, lifting Azure's hand to her mouth and pressing a kiss into the back of it.

"Home?" Az asked. "Do you want me to move in now?"

Rus laughed, the warmth of her breath against Azure's skin. "We've broken at minimum thirty witchy laws since I came back to Moondale. We'll probably break another thirty more before the centennial. Yeah . . . I think it's probably about time you put your socks in my drawers."

"All right. Home," Azure agreed. Everything else, they could deal with tomorrow.

# GLOSSARY

Pronunciation Guide

- **Aihuan:** Aye-hoo-wahn
- **Meiling:** May-lee-ng
- **Jiejie:** Gee-ay-gee-ay

Terms Guide

## <u>Witch Terms</u>

- **Athame:** A ceremonial blade used in ritual magic.
- **Aura:** An emanation surrounding the body of a living creature , regarded as an essential part of the individual.

- **Covenless:** A witch who does not belong to a formal coven.
- **Familiars:** A living creature (traditionally a cat) attending and obeying a witch.
- **Folk:** A word used to reference any person of magical lineage.
- **Moonmother:** A witch assigned by a child's parents to take responsibility for the child in the event the parents are unable.
- **Poppet:** A small figure or doll used in sorcery or witchcraft.
- **Possession:** The act of having one's body inhabited by a spirit.
- **Reanimated:** A being that has been brought back to life through magical means.
- **Soul Eater:** A spirit that has consumed another spirit as a means to gain power.
- **Spellcraft:** The act of creating new or using existing spells.
- **Talismans:** An item, or paper, inscribed with magical characters or runes to perform a specific spell.
- **Wards**: A magical barrier set using either spellwork, talismans, or runes to protect a specific place.

## Chinese Terms Guide

- **Jiejie:** A familiar way to refer to an older sister or older female friend, used by someone substantially younger.
- **Niang:** Mama

- **Baba:** Papa
- **A-:** Familiar diminutive
- **-Er:** A word for "child", added to a name to express affection.

## **<u>Circle of Jade Waters</u>**
### **WITCHES**
*best known for scholarly pursuits*

Elder: Carmine Elwood

Members:

- Carmine Elwood
- Maureen Beecher
- Violet Elwood
- ~~Taryn Elwood~~
- ~~Azure Elwood~~
- Indigo Elwood
- Sunila Elwood

## **<u>Circle of the Silver Flame</u>**
### **WITCHES**
*best known for weapons & wand makers*

Elder: Brant Ironwood

Members:

- Brant Ironwood
- Brenton Ironwood
- Phyre Ironwood

<u>**Circle of the Crimson Tide**</u>
**WITCHES**
*best known for security & ward work*

Elder: Cliantha Greer

Members:

- Cliantha Greer
- Evander Greer

<u>**Clan of Crescentia**</u>
**FAIRIES - Cupids**
*best known for their skills in matchmaking*

Elder: Enfys Snowthorn

Members:

- Nesta Holyore
- Dillan Holyore

## <u>Grove of Elderwood</u>
### DRUIDS

*best known for their agricultural skills*

Elder: Gilroy Herne

Members:

- Gilroy Herne
- Cagney Cashel

## <u>Chesapeake Pack</u>
### SHIFTERS

*best known for their efforts forest preservation*

Elder: Chelsea Horst

Members:

## <u>Circle of the Emerald Forge</u>
### WISH GRANTERS

*best known for preservation of the Moondale lei lines*

Elder: Dhiren

Members:

## <u>Ladies of Nimue</u>
### WATER FOLK

*best known for their efforts in bay preservation*

Elder: Nixie Virnan

Members:

## **<u>Clan of the Unseen Moon</u>**
## **UNSEELIE FAE**
*best known for*

Elder: Yaereene

Members:

## **<u>Sisters of the Meadow</u>**
## **SEELIE FAE**
*best known for*

Elder:

Members:

## **<u>Coven of the Forgotten</u>**
## **WITCHES**
*best known for their advancements in magical technology*

Elder:

Members:

- Icarus Ashthorne
- Azure Elwood
- Fernando

**Sneak Peek!**

continue reading for a sneak peek of Witches of Moondale
book #4: A Hex To Remember

Please note: This is an unedited sneak peek.

Order your copy!

# Chapter 1

"*Y*ou *bring him back to us!*"

The words echoed in Azure's head over and over again. It wasn't the words *themselves* that made them stick there, but the fire in Tony McMahon's eyes as he said them, as he hunched over the body of the man he loved and demanded Rus bring Eric Marcelino back from the dead. Not just for himself but for Hunter as well. Azure understood it, perhaps better than she'd ever be able to express in words. After all, she would do the same were she in his shoes, clutching the body of Rus in her arms and demanding the universe bend to her will, give her just one more day with the woman she loved.

Especially now that Rus was back in her life after so long. Azure would not give her up so easily. Even if it were a consequence of the job, as it was for a vampire hunter like Eric.

"I know you don't approve," Rus said, dragging Azure out of her own head. She was on her tiptoes, trying to reach something on the top shelf at the back of their wardrobe. Her fingers scraped against the wood in the silence of their home—like nails on a chalkboard.

"Hm?" Azure asked, her steps soft and careful on the dark-stained floorboards as she joined Rus in front of the oversized piece of furniture. Peering through the darkness, she found a worn duffle stuffed onto the back of the shelf, far out of reach of little hands. Maybe even out of sight and out of mind.

"You don't approve of what I'm about to do," Rus repeated. Finally, her fingers caught on the long strap of the bag, and she was able to yank it from its hiding place down into waiting arms. It landed with a muted *thump* before Rus dropped into a squat to dig through it, pulling items from the dark recesses. A switchblade, looking as unceremonial as a kitchen knife. A few vials of dark, congealed blood that Rus uncorked, sniffed, and curled her nose up at. A notebook with pages falling from it. Some chalk pencils that were sharpened down to nubs.

Azure had to shake herself and return her mind again to what Rus was saying instead of the capable, sure way Rus handled this kit of items Azure had never seen before. "I don't believe I said that."

"Yeah, but you didn't have to, did you? It's necromancy. I know how you feel about that, Az." Rus exhaled a short breath, her shoulders hunching as if readying for a blow that would never land. "You don't have to be there when we do this. I'd understand if you weren't."

"I'm coming with you. You are not doing this alone." Which seemed obvious to Azure. She couldn't let Rus face this by herself. They were coven. They were a team. They would stare down the reaper together and bring their friends' friend back. Azure may not know Eric at all, but she knew Hunter and Ava. They were coven, too, and anyone who meant enough to them to demand a necromancer bring him back must be the best kind of person. And even if he weren't? Azure could hardly deny that she would do anything to mitigate the reminder of that pain in Tony's eyes for fear she'd find it mirrored in her own one day.

"Well, not alone, obviously. Ava and Hunter will be

there. And Tony, I'm sure. I don't think he'll leave Eric alone for a—"

"Icarus," Azure said her name on a sigh as she reached for Rus's trembling hands. It took her a moment, but when Rus finally lifted her gray eyes to meet Azure's, there was an uncertainty there that would not stand. "I was wrong, before, when I parroted the things the elders said about your magic," Azure assured her softly. It was something she had wanted to say to Rus for months now but hadn't yet found the opportunity. "There is nothing dark or evil about what you do. There is nothing wrong with giving life to those whose time has been cut short. Nothing wrong with helping the dead when so many of us ignore them. I understand you and what you do better now, and I would like to continue to learn more. I apologize if I ever made you feel otherwise."

Rus blinked, mouth falling open in a stunned silence that was so beautiful, Azure wanted to lean forward and taste it on her lips. She'd done that. She'd said something so deep, so wonderful—at least, she hoped that's why Rus was shocked—that it had stilled Rus's tongue for perhaps the first time in her entire life.

"Az, I—" Rus inhaled sharply, leaning in to where Azure lifted her hand to brush her thumb against Rus's cheek like a cat seeking warmth. Ravishing and pliant. Azure could close the distance between them, swallow her whole. She could—

The back door creaked open, and Nando's soft voice carried up the steps of 157 Mourning Moore. "Rus. Azure. We've got everything together."

"Shit." Rus hissed. Then she spun to shove things back into the bag, and Azure noticed that her hands no longer trembled. "What time is it?"

Azure checked her watch. "Quarter to three."

"We need to hurry. It'll take time to set up the array and the sheeting and stuff." With that, she pushed to her feet and slung the bag over her shoulder before heading for the door.

"Do you need me to grab anything from the pantry downstairs?"

There was a helpless feeling settling into Azure's chest she didn't care for. She didn't know enough about what Rus was going to do to be of any real use. Her magic wasn't geared toward this sort of thing. And even if she accepted Rus and all that she was, there was still a nagging discomfort that went along with the idea of dragging a soul back to the plane of the living. A feeling that she was sure would linger, perhaps for years, because it was so engrained in her from a lifetime of listening to the elders speak of mediums and necromancy as if it were taboo, forbidden, dirty. She knew better now, of course, but that gut reaction stuck with her.

"No. I have everything I need in here." Rus patted the bag hanging at her hip. Then she held her hand out to Azure, and Azure was helpless but to take it, to let Rus lead her down through their sleeping home, out to the quiet of the yard, and across the crisp grass toward the house next door—155 Mourning Moore, their coven house.

When they arrived, someone had already covered the worn floorboards and the minimal furnishings they'd managed to move into the living room with plastic sheeting. Standing in the center of the big open front room, right next to the fireplace, was a calf. Azure didn't want to think about how Ava and Vanessa had gotten the animal inside without being seen, nor where it'd come from at this time of night. Darcy—Rus's crow familiar—sat on its shoulder, chittering softly and soothingly to the creature.

Explaining to it why it was there, asking it if it would go willingly.

"Does Darcy always do that?" Azure asked in a whisper, hoping not to draw the attention of the others in the room as they entered. Not that it mattered. The moment Rus stepped over the threshold, all eyes turned to them. Ava and Vanessa, where they huddled in one corner, Ava's eyes red rimmed and puffy. Hunter and Tony, where they were crouched on the floor, unwilling to leave the still form of Eric for a single moment. Even the calf next to the hearth. All attention shifted.

Rus shrugged. "The last time I sacrificed an animal to bring someone back, it was *for* Darcy."

Evasive as ever, but Azure would let it go, at least for now. Rus had once said that she'd only brought two beings back from the After that mattered: Darcy and Aihuan. But that didn't for one second mean those were the only two times she'd performed this ritual. And considering the state of her kit for it...

"You're going to have to step away from him," Rus said, dropping Azure's hand and crossing the room to where Hunter and Tony cradled Eric's lifeless body. Her hands lifted to brush their shoulders in a gesture that was likely meant to be comforting, but both men flinched away. "I'm sorry."

"Come on, sweetheart, let's let the lady work," Tony murmured. He settled Eric gently onto the floor and reached for Hunter instead, his hands shaking much the same as Rus's had been not but a few minutes ago as he peeled Hunter's fingers away from the material of Eric's shirt. "Let's let Ashthorne do her thing."

Hunter nodded but didn't speak. There was a quiet to him unlike Azure had seen before. When he looked up at

Tony, it was as if he weren't really seeing at all. Grief had stolen so much from him, Azure hardly recognized the quick-witted, tattooed Black man who helped them overcome a soul jumper.

"He'll be back," Rus promised with a conviction Azure admired. Icarus Ashthorne might be unsure about other things—about their relationship and her place in the world—but she knew her capability. She knew her magic. And she knew she could bring Eric Marcelino, vampire hunter, back from the dead. It was super sexy. Azure would have to address that later.

Hunter nodded again and let Tony lead him to one of the plastic-covered couches pushed against the curtained windows.

"Az, can you put up a security ward to make sure no one does any peeking?" Rus dropped down beside Eric. She pulled out a notebook and pen from the bag to hold out to Azure before getting everything she needed together while Azure turned to the windows without a word.

The setup took much less time than Azure would have thought. Between Rus and Nando, they moved like a well-oiled machine, which again, made Azure wonder how frequently Rus had done this.

Three intersecting protection circles were drawn in dry-erase marker around Eric, the calf, and Rus. Candles were lit around the room, and the house took the initiative to lower the lights. Rus settled into her circle, hands resting on her knees, Darcy on her shoulder, eyes closed. Green magic twisted around her, whispers growing louder and louder as Rus plunged herself into the After with only Darcy to tether her to this plane.

Azure's hands itched to reach for her, to pull her back from the brink. She knew what she'd have to do if Rus got lost in there, if she couldn't find her way back. She'd done it before.

It seemed like it was taking too long. Seconds ticking by into minutes.

The shine of the pendant around Rus's throat—the one Azure forged for her—would ensure Rus couldn't get trapped there easily, not the way she was once in danger of doing. Things would struggle to cling to her. But would it be enough? It never seemed like enough. Nothing Azure could do would mitigate all the dangers of this kind of magic. But she also wouldn't keep Rus from doing it. Not anymore. She wouldn't push Rus away like that. Not again.

It took several minutes. The only sounds were the soft breathing of the people around her and the calf shifting slightly against the plastic sheeting, before Rus finally came up for air. When she opened her eyes, they glowed the way a glow stick would, and a thin sheen of sweat glittered against her skin.

"He's here," she said in a voice that echoed with those of the dead, her magic swirling more quickly around her. Not violent and volatile the way it did when it was ready to go on the offensive. But not slow and lazy either, as it did some-times when Rus was just checking in with the spirits that surrounded them on the daily.

Hunter lifted his head and looked around, like he could see the spirit of the deceased vampire hunter floating right there in the middle of the room. But there was nothing. Just the glow of candles and Rus's magic glinting off the sharp edge of the athame as she rose and moved toward the calf.

Darcy cawed softly, a question.

The calf answered, bowing its head and lying down.

Rus rested her hand on its shoulder, murmuring softly

to it, her magic swirling around it, lazy and comforting. Lulling the creature into a state of twilight.

A spell lingered in the air that Azure recognized. One of sleep, of rest. Something to send the creature into the After without the trauma usually associated with ritual sacrifices. A kindness that made Azure's heart leap into her throat.

Then in a movement so swift Azure couldn't track it, Rus cut the main artery in the calf's neck, and blood dripped steadily onto the plastic beneath it. Rus did something with the blood Azure couldn't see over her shoulder, her finger swiping through the viscous liquid. It took a few moments, but once all breath stopped in the creature, she turned back to Eric.

Blood dripped from Rus's hands, her eyes glowing still, her magic making her hair float around her face. Azure's breath caught in her throat. She'd never seen something so beautiful in her entire life. That was *her* Rus. Her partner. Her girlfriend. And one day, her wife. Azure wouldn't rest until Rus agreed to that.

With her clean hand, Rus tipped Eric's chin, opening his mouth, then dripped some of the blood inside. The whispers hit a fever pitch, so loud the entire room covered their ears. And Azure might have been imagining it, but she would swear she saw a pale-blue wisp break off from Rus's magic and settle onto Eric's tongue just before Rus slammed his jaw closed and held it shut.

Eric started struggling.

Arms flailed, smacking Rus. Nearly knocked her hand away, but she held him firmly even as his breaths came in ragged sips. Even as tears streamed down to his temples.

Hunter let out a soft squawk of upset and leapt forward as if to stop her, but Tony held him fast, and Azure took a step in between them, protecting Rus from whatever Hunter thought he might do to put an end to this.

Sweat gathered in thick drops on Rus's hairline. Her cheeks flushed. Her chest heaved in hard pants.

The silent battle between Eric's body, his spirit, and the necromancer forcing them back together went on for an agonizingly long time. Every second that ticked by, Rus looked paler and paler, her magic growing more violent around her, the whispers and the wind picking up. The candles guttered. The room grew so cold, Azure could see her breath. A shiver raked its fingers down her spine.

And then everything stopped.

The candles went out.

Rus's magic died away.

Plastic no longer crinkled.

Someone gasped. Eric, probably. The sound wet and guttural as he reached for the newly stitched wound on his throat, his movements just visible in the dim light coming through the curtains from the streetlights outside.

"Where am I?" a man asked into the silence, a voice Azure didn't recognize, so it could only be Eric. It was wreaked, and choked either by the wound he'd suffered, or by something else.

"Take it easy," Rus said gently as she helped him sit up. "Slow, shallow breaths. That's it."

Azure snapped her fingers, and the candles relit, their flames rising so high and so bright, they were near blinding, her magic overreacting in her panic. But once she could see clearly again, she found Rus sitting next to Eric, both looking drawn and tired but upright, nonetheless.

"Where am I?" Eric asked again, his voice raspy.

Rus gave his hand a squeeze and met his gaze. There was something twisted and lost in Eric's expression, something Azure didn't think she was equipped to identify, much less understand, but Rus gave a subtle nod as if she did.

"Oh," Eric said. His eyes flicked to meet Hunter's and Tony's over Rus's shoulder. The smile that lifted his mouth was slow, strained, but it was honest. "Can I get a hug?"

"You're home," Tony whispered, a little disbelieving. Then, "You're home!" He, Hunter, and Ava rushed from their respective corners to tackle Eric. To pull him in close. To check him over to make sure he was all right.

Rus pushed herself out of the way, skidding across the plastic on her ass until she could press her back into Azure's knees and look up at her with a tired, lopsided smile, blood smeared across her cheeks and in her hair. "Hey, Magpie, you ready to head home?"

And Azure... Well. Her heart was in her throat, her cheeks on fire, her blood pumping so loud and so quick she could hear it. And she was so, *so* in love with Icarus Ashthorne. What else could she say but "Marry me?"

# ACKNOWLEDGMENTS

I always start these things but thanking the reader, and this one is no different. I want to thank you—whether you're a returning reader or Lou is new to you—for picking up my little indie published book, supporting my dream, and following along with Rus and Az on their journey. Without readers, I can't do what I do, so I greatly appreciate the support.

If you loved every moment of Rus and Az's story (as I hope you did) please leave a review, follow me on social media, or give me a shout out. I love hearing from you guys, it's really the best part of writing.

Next I'd like to thank my family who supports me in this weird journey I'm on to become an established author. They show up to my signings, they listen to my rants about my characters, they look at my covers and tell me when they're complete shit (I design my covers FYI), and they're the best people to have in my corner, no joke.

Then there is the small hoard of beta readers I had look at this bugger to tell me if any of it actually made sense, and if I'm as funny as I think I am (turns out I am). Thanks Meg, Val, and Nancy! You guys provided so much helpful feedback, and I'm super grateful.

And of course my editor, Brenna. Who continues to give The Bay of the Dead 'verse her love, and enjoys these books as much as I do.

And last but certainly not least, thank you to my small writing support group. Tiss, Elle, Whitney, Nancy, Jasmine, and the rest of my MTP family—without you there would be no Lou.

# ABOUT LOU WILHAM

 Born and raised in a small town near the Chesapeake Bay, Lou Wilham grew up on a steady diet of fiction, arts and crafts, and Old Bay. After years of absorbing everything, there was to absorb of fiction, fantasy, and sci-fi she's left with a serious writing/drawing habit that just won't quit. These days, she spends much of her time writing, drawing, and chasing a very short Basset Hound named Sherlock.

When not, daydreaming up new characters to write and draw she can be found crocheting, making cute bookmarks, and binge-watching whatever happens to catch her eye.

Learn more about Lou and her future projects on her website: http://louinprogress.com/ or join her mailing list at: http://subscribepage.com/mailermailer

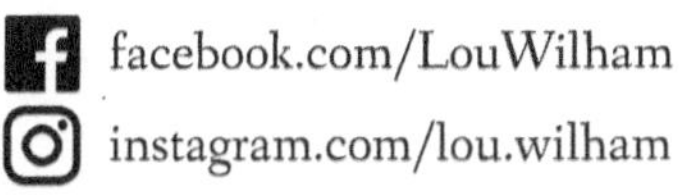

facebook.com/LouWilham

instagram.com/lou.wilham

Also By Lou Wilham

The Witches of Moondale
    The Hex Next Door
    The Ghost of Hexes Past
    Home is Where the Hex Is
    A Hex To Remember

The Hunters of Ironport
    Overkill
    Fresh Kill
    Kill Your Darlings

The Fae of Eventide
    An Offer Fae Can't Refuse

Sanctuary of the Lost
    Of Loyalties and Wreckage
    Of Love and Ruin
    Of Hope & Blight
    Of Blight & Ruin

**Completed Series**
    The Heir to Moondust
    The Tales of the Sea Trilogy
    Villainous Heroics
    The Clockwork Chronicles
    The Curse Collection
    Benvolio & Mercutio Turn Back Time

**Beneath the Willow by Elle Beaumont**

Love deserves a second chance.
Something lurks deep within the mysterious inn, and when a paranormal expert arrives, so does an unexpected visitor.

A woman pores over letters she discovered in an old bookstore, and every time she reads them, she can feel the presence of the man who wrote them, making her uncertain of her sanity.

A spirit plagues the owner of an inn, but when a paranormal investigator arrives, he requires the aid of the anomaly, or the owner risks losing everything.

After a tragic loss, a man leaves his old life behind. Beginning a new adventure should be easy, but when a friendly ghost appears, he realizes nothing ever is. But with memories of his past haunting him, will he ever be truly ready?

BENEATH THE WILLOW *is a romantic collection of ghost stories that will haunt you long after reading. From newfound love to rekindled flames, and even healing after loss, these contents are dark, beautiful, and tragic, surely inspiring heart-pounding moments and tears.*

*Available Now*

**Those We Couldn't Burn by Whitney L.
Spradling**

Worlds collide when an ancient vision brings a witch and witch hunter together.

Prince Tyberius Berkshire, witch hunter extraordinaire, has been set with an impossible task—discover the truth of an ancient vision to keep his family on the throne. His world crashes down around him, when an intricate piece of the vision's puzzle falls into place in the form of a purple-haired witch.

Neave Paker has spent the past ten years quietly taking revenge against the witch hunters. Until the prince of the hunters captures her. Taken to the palace, she's given the choice to either work for the enemy or burn at the stake.

Together, they set out to discover the truth. But difficulties lie ahead as they fight attraction and animosity. When they uncover more than they bargained for, the unlikely duo must determine what is more important to them: their beliefs or their hearts.

*Available Now*

**_Dead Rockstar by Lillah Lawson_**

Stormy Spooner is at her wits' end. Careening towards bitter after a nasty divorce, she sometimes wonders what her life is becoming.

After unearthing a cryptic set of lines from a dusty album cover, Stormy tries the impossible: to resurrect Phillip Deville, enigmatic former frontman of the Bloomer Demons. Stormy's love for her favorite dead rockstar knows no bounds...but it was all supposed to be a joke.

When she answers a knock on her door the next day and finds herself face to face with the dark-haired rock god of her every teenage fantasy, her entire world is turned upside down.

Turns out, she's awakened more than just Philip, and Stormy will have to do battle against a cast of strange characters to keep herself and her new undead boyfriend safe.

_Available May 15, 2024_